# THE RISE OF THE FORGOTTEN

## JESSICA GOLLUB

First Printing, 2015

ISBN: 978-1-926479-04-0

*To Leonida, Ralph, Cameron and Shalisa.*
*Taken too soon, but never forgotten.*

# ONE

"I AM THE PRESIDENT of the United States. I am the President of the United States"

I was muttering under my breath and trying to convince myself of something I no longer fully believed. I hadn't really been in control for many years, and now as it seemed like the truth was slipping farther and farther away, I felt the need for a mantra. This one was as good as any other. I had used it many times before, and no matter the circumstances, it had always gotten me through. Not many people could say they were the Commander in Chief of what had once been one of the most powerful countries in the world.

Were. I didn't miss my own use of the past tense.

Was I still?

I trudged along, unwilling to answer my own question.

We had been walking for two days. Blisters had formed and popped and I was sure they had started forming again, but we rarely stopped. There was no time to stop. I would suffer through the pain behind everyone else. Angela walked in front of me, while Jude and Dutch followed behind, with Finn and Rebekkah bringing up the rear of our party. They had rigged up a sled for

Rebekkah and a harness to pull her. Finn typically wore it, though Jude and Dutch spelled him off now and then to give him a rest. Jonah ran with Renny and the other younger boys, weaving through the line, laughing and shouting as we hiked. Rayne was the only one who seemed to know where we were going. He walked at the front with Olly. In between us was every boy he had taken in over the years. There was no way they would be left behind. Rayne had originally suggested just that, but no one consented. They all needed to come. However much longer it would take us to travel with more than thirty people, there was no other option. The boys seemed almost giddy as they walked. They were the forgotten, the children robbed of history and future—yet they were given a purpose, and not one of them was going to reject it.

I was glad they had come. Extra strong backs meant I didn't need to carry much of my own. I had a small pack full of extra clothes for myself and a few personal items. It was unlikely I'd come back to the hospital again, so I took my few meager possessions. Under my thick down coat I could feel the chafing of my leather holster and handgun. I had carried that from the estate, though at the time I had been far too weak to use it. I hadn't even told Jude about it. I had a full clip in the gun and a spare. There wasn't much ammunition, but it was enough to get me out of a bind.

Food, water, and some rudimentary survival supplies were carried by the young men. We had camped in the forest the night before, and as the sun began to set it was looking more and more like we would be doing the same. It wasn't as cold as it had been; the weather had begun to steadily warm up again, bringing with it the first hints of spring. While the warming air bore a welcome freshness, it made for more difficult walking. The warmer temperatures meant that snow that had once been packed down melted in the sun and turned to ice overnight. We slipped and plodded along, earning each mile with blisters, sweat, and tears.

The scouts could travel this distance in a day, their giant beasts of horses galloping over the packed snow. Our large party would take much longer, three or four days perhaps. We followed their beaten trail through the trees, moving as quickly as we could.

"We need to stop soon," said Rebekkah. "I'm exhausted."

Finn burst out laughing.

"Poor thing!" he said to his wife as he pulled the sled over a mound in the snow.

Rebekkah's eyes sparkled with personal amusement. I admired their relationship. I had a special place in my heart for Rebekkah, and in the short time since they arrived, nothing made me happier than seeing them together. Nadia's lust for power had taken something from each of us, and because of that, I felt a certain kinship toward Rebekkah. She had lost the use of her legs, and I had lost years of my life, stuck in a medically induced coma to keep myself safe from my half-sister.

"Would it also be wrong to shout 'mush'?" she asked, barely able to contain her laughter.

Finn exhaled loudly in mock outrage as the rest of us laughed.

It felt good to laugh.

I didn't laugh enough.

Jonah ran with the other boys his age. He and Renny—the child Jude and I had rescued from the basket hanging in the woods—were inseparable and never far from Ricker and Landon, other children that Rayne and Angela had saved from the same fate. It was entirely possible Renny, Ricker and Landon were brothers, and at times I found it hard to tell them apart, but that might have been because they all moved so fast and never sat still long enough. Jonah was easy to spot. His dark curls and pale eyes were striking. Jude told me he looked exactly like his mother, Kenzie. I felt a pang of guilt for never really knowing her or what was going on in my own government, not to mention being powerless to stop it.

The pace was slowing and I could tell, even from the back of the procession, that we were getting ready to stop for the night. Rayne would be looking for an adequate spot to set up camp, and already the mood had shifted. There was nothing comfortable about sleeping in the woods, but somehow it was better than walking in the woods any longer. I followed the group into a small clearing, just off the main path. It was surrounded by trees and shrubs that would help block the wind that tore through the cleared corridor we travelled on. It was probably an old road from before the freeze, but with the thick layer of snow, it was impossible to tell. I tried to keep my eyes open for clues, like old street signs, but I knew that almost any material of value had likely been scavenged by now. There was a lot that could be done with a straight metal pole, or a large flat metal disc. I had seen the creativity of survival first-hand living at the hospital. Every so often, when I grew frustrated at how much I had lost; I could hear the words, as if whispered directly into my ear. They were words my grandfather would say, and I could hear it in his deep rasp of a voice: "Use it up, wear it out, make it do, or do without."

This wasn't new.

We weren't the first people to struggle; the only ones to have the rug pulled out from under us just as we had gotten comfortable and complacent.

But it was new to us. My generation had not felt the sting of forced self-reliance, the pain of having everything you had needed or wanted ripped from your grasp. It was sudden and complete, and not everyone survived. In fact, most didn't. I had spent my life working with my mind, my smile, my handshake. Now those soft hands were rough and hard, and muscles that I had worked to sculpt to look good on television were strong and powerful, wiry and lean. We were a privileged generation until the cold enveloped us.

I looked around at our scraggly caravan. Such a difference more than eighteen years had made. Many of these men likely wouldn't remember the days before, other than a few snippets of green grass or bicycle rides. Some of them hadn't even been born, yet here they were, men—their whole lives spent in this perpetual cold.

"Gather up," shouted Rayne across the nattering voices of road-weary boys and men. He was standing with his hands up. Everyone moved closer to him until we were a tight group, shorter people naturally navigating to the front, and many of them dropping to their knees in the polite habit Rayne had drilled into them. Once Rayne was satisfied everyone could see and hear him, he cleared his throat.

"We're only a few hours out, but we're going to stay here tonight. I don't want to come upon their sentinels in the dark."

There was nodding and a few groans. I understood. I didn't want to stay out here for another night, but being pierced through by a nervous watchman wasn't my idea of a good time either.

"Let's get some fires going, and make them big. We have no need to hide and if they see us first, we don't need to worry about surprising them."

All around me young men were dropping their packs and stretching, finding places to call their own for the night and heading off into the bush for some firewood. A nice hot fire sounded like just the thing to relax my aching muscles. The previous night we had been too close to Amazon territory to build a decent fire. We built a small one to boil water to cook some meager stew and spent the night huddled together, shivering.

"Sore?" asked Jude.

I nodded, my breath halted by the deep shoulder stretch. I exhaled slowly.

"I'm not as young as I used to be," I said. "And even when I was that young, I don't think I would have found this hike an easy feat."

"There's nothing about this hike that's easy," he said.

"Young or old."

I didn't need to ask him what he meant. I knew he wasn't talking about aching muscles and blistered feet. Jude hiked with another purpose. He carried the added burden of worry and pain and guilt. For so long he had considered Rhea dead, and now finding out that she lived—if being held as a breeder in suspended animation could truly be called living—had lined his face and set his jaw. I knew we walked too slowly for him, that given the opportunity he would rather run back to the estate.

"There's nothing you can do on your own, Jude," I said, my voice low amid the shouts and laughter of those around us.

"I know."

"This truly is your best bet."

He nodded and slipped off into the crowd to help set up camp.

I too found something to do. Sitting idle did nothing good for me. I found Angela in the thick of things, right where she always was--shouting directions as she dug through the food packs to see what she could make for us to eat. We didn't bring much meat, so if there was any chance of having any in our stew today, it was up to some of the boys to find it. More than likely we would sit down today to a meal of rice and beans. My stomach growled at the thought. I had grown accustomed to the simple fare, such a difference from what I had been fed in my years at the White House. Gone were the rich sauces and almost airy morsels that tickled the tongue and flirted with the senses. I didn't mind though. I found nearly as much pleasure in the hearty weight of a

7

solid meal. It meant we were still alive, and if I couldn't be grateful for that...

"Could you make me a fire?" asked Angela.

I didn't answer, since I knew it wasn't really a question.

The boys had begun to pile their armloads of dry branches in a tangled heap, so I set to work snapping twigs and constructing a pile of tinder that could be used to start one of the massive fires Rayne had suggested. There were bigger logs, as thick as my leg and as tall as I was. Those we would use later, once the fires were tall and the cooking was done. For now, we needed something small and manageable, with enough heat to cook our supper.

"Do we still have any starter?" I asked.

Angela nodded and tilted her head toward one of the packs as she silently counted out scoops of rice into the large, dented metal prep bowl.

I followed her gesture to a heavy canvas sack. In one of the outside pockets was a small leather bag, as waterproof as possible. Inside was a matted mass of shredded cotton, mostly from clothes that had grown too thin to patch or use for other things, bits of birch bark and small woodchips collected from the chopping pile. Angela had even sacrificed the end of one of our precious beeswax candles that had come in one of the packs from the scouts, and melted the wax all over the bits and shreds to make the most reliable fire-starter possible. It was rare that we needed to start a fire at the hospital, since there were always fires burning somewhere. After Rayne instituted the watch, whoever was stationed would keep a fire going through the night. Even if the cooking fires went out, it was a simple thing to start them again. Out here, we had no constant fire to rely on, so Angela's fire-starter was protected.

We had enough to start two fires, so I gently pulled it, breaking the mass into two smaller lumps. I rolled one together with my hands and slid it back into the pouch, just in case. The second one I pulled apart slightly with my mittened hands and dug into the pack for flint. We hadn't had matches or lighters or any other such conveniences for a very long time, though we did have a chunk of flint that was even more protected than the fire-starter. In fact, we had two pieces of flint. One of them was worn on a chain around Rayne's neck at all times for fear that it would be lost otherwise. Without fire there was no hope of survival in the snow.

Within minutes I had a blazing fire. The flames devoured the dry wood as I added twigs and then larger sticks and branches. The fire grew hot and began to warm my stiff fingers through my mittens, sending painful tingles through my hands. I closed my eyes and relished the dry heat on my face. Any warmth that the sun had brought—or the heat I had generated from the exertion of hiking all day—was gone. As the sun set the chill descended on us.

The boys began to circle the fire. Much of the camp was ready for the night and they too were feeling the chill of the darkness. I had the ends of a number of branches wedged into the hottest parts of the fire, and one by one they were pulled from the flames to start the other fires that had been being built nearby. As the darkness settled I could see an orange glow flickering around camp, filtering through the shadows that milled between them. The other fires were built big from the start, and I could hear the roar and pop as they devoured the piles of wood.

A peaceful stillness descended over the camp as the boys warmed themselves in the mesmerizing dance of the flames.

It wouldn't last—quiet never did with this bunch—but even Rayne and Angela, who never stopped moving, seemed tranquil in this moment. Every movement seemed slower, every sound hushed.

The silence broke almost as quickly as it came, as if everyone had thawed at once and boisterous laughter and teasing lifted through the dark trees that arched above, silhouetted against the darkening sky.

"How's the fire?" Angela asked.

"Ready for snow."

We'd need to melt enough to cook the dry beans, which took a while all on its own. As I arranged the charred logs to make a flat place above the embers, Angela hoisted a large metal pot that was packed to the top and mounded with snow. It was the biggest pot we had brought. I was sure Angela wished for the giant commercial ones that she had used at the hospital, but they were heavy and impractical to carry. Instead we relied on this much smaller one. It would need to be refilled a few times before everyone was fed, but we'd all have full bellies by the time we slept.

"Gibs and Fernie," called Angela across the fire to the two

boys, "Go find out if anyone has any meat."

"I think Dutch snagged a rabbit while we were hiking," said Fernie, as Gibs nodded beside him. "I don't know if he has anything else."

"Go find out, and ask around to any of the others. I want it skinned and in my hands."

They nodded and hurried off. My mouth watered at the thought of meat—even something as small as a rabbit would add flavor and richness to our supper. I hoped a few of the boys had been able to find something. Anyone who hunted had a standing order for any meat they could bring. Knowing my own hunger, I knew that a full stomach was reward enough for all of these growing men.

It had been a good day. Dutch's rabbit was in fine company with a large squirrel and a decent-sized bird of some kind. Perhaps a grouse or a pheasant, but lacking a head and feathers, it was difficult for me to tell.

Angela deftly hacked the meat into equal portions so she would have enough for each of the three full stew-pots she would be preparing. She untied a low pan from one of the packs, and began to sear the meat, sending the smell of rending fat through the camp. The boys knew better than to start gathering when she fried the meat, it would be a while before anything would be ready to eat, but it was fun to watch as the aromas met each nose. One by one they would pause, smile and inhale deeply, relishing the scent.

I picked up the long wooden spoon that lay on the snow

beside the fire and pushed it into the pot where snow was melting. I wasn't sure stirring it would help it melt faster, but it gave me something to do as Angela dropped some of our dried foraged herbs into the pan with the meat. Once there was enough water in the pot she would throw it all in with some properly measured rice and beans and stir it into a rich stew.

"Do you know where the kettle is?" I asked Jude as he plopped down next to me.

He groaned.

"Are you seriously going to make me get up again?"

I swatted him with the spoon.

"Yeah, yeah," he said chuckling as he pushed himself back up.

"And fill it with snow too, would ya?"

He grunted in reply.

The kettle, a stretch to call it that, since it was really more like a pot with a spout, needed to get on the fire too. It was difficult to keep everyone hydrated properly when canteens and water jugs froze so easily. The few people who had metal canteens had already packed them full of snow and they stood in a neat line beside the fire, everyone else needed hot water. It served a dual purpose. Filling jugs and bottles with hot water kept everyone warm in their blankets overnight. Combined with the shared body heat of so many people sleeping together, the water would stay liquid all night. It also made for one less thing to do when we broke camp in the morning. We made tea for everyone before bed with dried nettles and chamomile that we had foraged when the weather warmed. It gave everyone some much needed vitamins, plus the chamomile ensured a restful sleep.

"Here you go," said Jude, sliding the kettle over the hot embers beside the stew pot that was now bubbling with the heated water, herbs and meat. He also carried a large plastic pail filled to the brim with snow. I would need to keep refilling the kettle, so I was thankful for his foresight.

"Thank you Jude," I said.

We sat beside each other in silence. I barely knew his name when we began this journey, when my body, weak from years in a medically-induced coma, struggled to hold onto him as he drove the snowmobile down from the mountain, away from our shared captivity. For a long time neither of us knew if we were "running from" or "running to", but we ran all the same. It wasn't until Finn arrived with Rebekkah and Jonah, only days ago, that we understood the full reality of the situation. Those in the estate hadn't perished in the avalanche like we'd thought. Instead, the virus that was my half-sister had spread, affecting nearly everyone in the posh property. We had grieved together, healed together, and now those old, scarred wounds were torn open again, with a searing poultice of guilt liberally applied.

Neither of us needed to speak to know that we felt the same thing. Jude was my son. We shared no DNA, but we shared more than enough of everything else.

# Two

THE SUN SEEMED TO rise too early. Our exhaustion aside, there was an air of excitement in the camp. Today we would arrive. We didn't have far to go to find Rayne's brother Amos, or "The Shepherd", the name we were reminded to use when referring to him. It seemed rather melodramatic to me, but at the same time I had been referred to as a position rather than as a person for long enough to understand.

Jude seemed anxious to get going.

"Do you remember Amos?" I asked him. Delta had raised them both, making them something like brothers. Jude had some memories of Rayne, who was only five or six years older than he was, but even that was minimal. By the time Jude was old enough to have more than scattered bits of memory, Rayne had decided to live full-time with Amos and Elias in the apartment they grew up in. Delta supported them financially, as she had found a job in the government and was given housing there. Simeon had found his own path resulting in his son Jude, and then marrying Tess McAllister, a woman who went on to become one of my senators.

He shook his head. "I'm not sure we ever really met, and if we did, I don't remember. I suppose he's my uncle."

I nodded, they were both raised by the same woman, but Simeon and Amos were raised as brothers, so it made sense for Jude to think of him more as an uncle.

Rayne also milled about camp with a restless energy. He was going to see his brother, yet there seemed to be more apprehension than excitement.

"Is he going to be ok?" I asked Angela, who was packing up the last of the cooking utensils beside the dying embers of the fire.

She chuckled. "There's a lot of history between Rayne and Amos."

I noted that she didn't bother to call him "The Shepherd".

"For one, Amos doesn't like me," Angela said, shrugging, "and he never really approved of our little orphanage here. Amos has always been a bit nuts about disaster preparation, and he figured that having this many mouths to feed was... not the smartest decision."

"But how could you have abandoned them?"

"That's what I thought," said Angela. "Amos is different. He makes decisions with his head instead of his heart, at least, that's how he was for a few years before the frozen days began. He really went a bit on the loony side then."

"He wasn't always like that?"

"Oh no, not really, He and Simeon were the ones who brought Rayne's older brother Elias home, and took him in. Rayne kind of fell out with Amos when I started coming around. He had a weird thing about women in general I think. After that, who knows? He kind of spiralled there for a bit, though, I have to say, all his crazy preparations are really the reason we've survived too. While Rayne always said that Amos didn't have room for all of us, he sure shared enough of their supplies."

"So why is Rayne so antsy? His brother must care for him."

"Sure, he cares, but with Amos, you just never know what he's gotten into his head. He calls himself 'The Shepherd' for crying out loud."

I chuckled.

Angela grew serious. "I don't really know for sure, but I think part of the reason Rayne avoided his brother was because of me."

"Because Amos didn't like you?"

She shook her head.

"No," she said, "More like Rayne was intentionally keeping me away from him, protecting me or something."

That seemed like something Rayne would do, though it was rare that he overreacted to even a perceived threat.

"Are we ready?" asked Rayne, coming up from behind me.

"Just about," said Angela, tying up the laces on the last pack. "Douse the fire."

Rayne picked up the plastic bucket, scooped up a pail full of snow from one of the drifts nearby and dumped it onto the fire, causing steam and sizzles as the red embers were smothered.

"Everyone, packs on. Let's get this show on the road," Rayne shouted.

He held a hand down to Angela who took it and let him pull her to her feet.

"Ready?" she asked him.

"No."

She nodded. "Me neither. Meredith over here is the President of the United States though. She'll protect us from your brother."

Rayne hooted with laughter that exploded out of his mouth with such an unexpected fervor, I couldn't help but laugh myself.

Angela winked at me.

All around me, I saw packs being slung onto backs. Rebekkah and Finn were ready with their improvised sled, Jude standing beside Finn, laden with his heavy pack. Shi and Fernie were dousing fires and Dutch was leaning on a tree looking menacing with his longbow. Jonah, Renny, Ricker and Landon were running around with a kind of energy known only to young boys and everyone else was chatting and waiting for the go ahead. Angela slung her bag over her shoulders and took Rayne's hand. Together they walked to the edge of the clearing and disappeared as men and boys fell in step behind them.

RAYNE WAS RIGHT. WE weren't far at all.

I heard someone swear loudly about the same time I heard the sound of an arrow embedding itself into a tree.

"Get down!" shouted Jude, who was closest to the arrow, still quivering from its flight.

We dropped to our knees and waited, listening carefully for

any sound of attack.

"AHOY!" shouted Rayne through the trees, his voice echoing. "Please stand down, we come in peace!"

Through the cold, still air we heard another swear and a burst of male laughter.

"Come on in!" the male shouted. "I'll tell the infantry to hold their fire!"

He was perilously close to uncontrollable laughter, I could tell, even from this distance.

We moved forward until we came to the edge of the trees. There stood a tall young man, and beside him, a very embarrassed looking teenage girl in a long green cloak trimmed with fox fur, holding a bow. Behind them was a fenced compound, with four towers stationed around it, at the corners of the fence. A small square building sat on one side of the yard, with what looked like a large metal machine shop behind it. On the other side of the yard there seemed to be a low bank of windows, flush with the ground, almost camouflaged in the snow. It didn't look nearly big enough for more than twenty people, but perhaps this was just a small part of their community.

"Pardon us," the man said with mock formality, still obviously trying to control his laughter. "Leona here didn't mean to fire on you, she's just having a bit of trouble hitting the target."

She glared at him.

"Maybe I'll cut off a few of your fingers and see how well you do." She muttered under her breath.

I looked more closely and noticed that the hand holding

the bow was indeed missing a few fingers, though someone had carefully tailored her leather gloves to fit properly.

"Next time put up a sign that you have a girl shooting," called Dutch from where he stood, leaning back against a tree, "We'll cut a wide berth."

He turned his head and laughed to Olly, who was standing next to him.

I barely saw the girl move, yet in a breath I saw the glint of a knife in the sunlight. The next thing I knew Rayne was laughing and Dutch was shouting in indignation. The knife had cut through part of his long ponytail and was embedded in the tree at the base of his neck.

"Leona, honestly?" said the man, who, while trying to be serious, was still smirking.

"My knife skills are still top-notch," she said.

"We can see that," said Rayne, who was also trying not to laugh as Olly pulled the knife from the tree and Dutch fumed over the chunk of hair that floated down onto the snow.

"You still missed," he muttered, barely loud enough for Leona to hear.

"I wasn't planning on killing you," she said. "If I had, you wouldn't be whining so much."

The man with her laughed again.

"My name is Orion", he said, "And you've met Leona."

"Leona?" said Rayne, finally catching her name. "Elias' girl?"

Her eye bore into him and she nodded, but with a

strange stiffness.

"Who are you?" she asked.

"My name is Rayne, I am Elias' brother."

"You look nothing like him," she said giving Rayne the once over.

"And I'd assume you know why."

She nodded, satisfied with his response.

"Where can I find my brother?" asked Rayne, walking toward them.

"Elias is dead," Leona said, her voice wavering almost imperceptibly.

Rayne stopped short.

"No," he said.

Orion nodded. "It's true."

"When?" asked Rayne, struggling to hold himself together.

"A few months ago," said Leona. "He was killed by my father."

I didn't try to understand what she was talking about, though Rayne seemed much less confused.

"Then could you take me to our brother?"

"Elias didn't have any brothers here," said Orion.

I watched the girl, she seemed to expect the question.

"He did, as I do. You know him as 'The Shepherd'."

Orion bristled, but Leona laid a hand on his arm.

"He's not lying," she said.

"Elias and The Shepherd are brothers?" he said. "And you knew?"

"I suspected."

"But they look nothing alike."

Leona rolled her eyes and nodded her head in Rayne's direction, as if he was proof of her statement.

Orion shrugged.

"Wouldn't be the first time they didn't tell me the whole story," he said.

The door of the small building opened and another woman in a hooded cloak called out. Long black hair framed her face, and flew in the breeze.

"Leona! Arys needs you."

"Can you handle these ruffians on your own?" she asked Orion.

He shrugged. "I've handled worse."

She turned and hurried toward the compound as Orion faced us.

"I assume you're telling the truth when you say you mean us no harm, but in case you were thinking of trying anything, there are sentinels in the towers, and they are all armed with enough weapons to put you all flat on your face in seconds. If you manage to get past them, Leona will take out the rest of you."

He winked at Dutch, who flushed.

"We respect that," said Rayne.

We had barely made it through the gate before the door of the building opened again. This time a man came through the doorway.

"Hello Rayne," he said.

"Archer."

"What brings you here, with... everyone?" He let his eyes drift from person to person as he spoke. I pulled my cap down low and stayed tucked behind Jude's broad shoulders. I didn't know who these people were, and until I could gauge their loyalties, it was best that I not be too obvious.

"There have been some developments since we last spoke," Rayne said. "I need to speak with The Shepherd."

"I'm not sure if he will want the same."

"Archer," said Rayne, his voice low. "This is serious. He needs to know."

Archer nodded. "Come with me."

I helped Finn out of his harness and together with Jude we helped Rebekkah onto his back.

We filed through the door, down a flight of stairs, and then another, and another. When we reached the bottom, another door opened into a long hallway that stretched out in front of us. There were people walking back and forth, but many of them slipped through doorways to get out of the way as we passed.

Archer led us through the maze of underground hallways. I peeked into as many of the rooms as I could, though I needed to walk fairly quickly to keep up. I saw women sewing and men working. We passed what looked like a large school room, where children of all ages peered at us over their books.

All the women I saw were dressed similarly, in the same dark wool skirts and lighter muslin tunics. Many of them wore thick wool sweaters, which made sense, since it wasn't all that warm. The men were dressed similarly, though in pants and heavier shirts. Orion walked at the front with Archer. He was the only man I had seen who wasn't wearing heavy brown wool trousers. Instead, he wore a pair of well-worn buckskins, tailored perfectly for his long, muscular legs.

The dark haired girl stood in one of the doorways as we passed, a baby cradled in her arms. Leona was inside the room, also holding an infant—perhaps that was Arys.

Finally Archer stepped aside at a large set of double doors and motioned us inside. No one had said anything in a while, so we just silently went in. The room was large, and filled with rows of tables. There was a kitchen nearby; I could hear the sounds of food preparation and people washing dishes.

"Find a seat... rest. I will see to it that you are given lunch, and I will go speak with The Shepherd.

"Thank you, Archer," said Rayne.

"Orion, stay here with them and make sure they are comfortable."

The tall man nodded as he began to peel off his layers of outdoor clothing.

We did the same, stacking our packs in a pile on the floor and laying our jackets and outdoor wear on the tables around us. Then we waited.

True to his word, a group of women brought us lunch. It was nothing fancy, but it was warm and filling, not unlike the food Angela fed us, though the stew here was flanked with warm rolls. It had been a long time since I'd had proper bread—it was one thing that was next to impossible to make at the hospital no matter how hard Angela tried. I ate my roll slowly, letting it melt in my mouth. It was some sort of sourdough I guessed, which made sense since yeast would be hard to come by at this point, and sourdough cultures can last for decades.

"This bun is amazing," said Jude as he pushed it into his mouth. He apparently favored the stuff method, rather than the savoring one I had employed.

"I know."

"I miss bread," said Angela.

Some of the younger boys watched us with raised eyebrows. They hadn't even touched theirs, which made no sense, until I realized they had probably never eaten fresh bread. I laughed as they picked up their rolls, examined them, smelled them, and then finally tried a nibble.

"Watch them," I said, nudging Jude. "Maybe if you convince them that they don't like bread, you can score us a few more."

Jude laughed.

I did too, but that didn't mean I wasn't going to watch for any discarded bread.

# Three

"NO?"

"YOU NEED TO understand, there is no benefit to us to get involved."

"No benefit?" asked Rayne, "Other than being a good person, right? Taking care of people who can't care for themselves."

The Shepherd's eyes narrowed at his brother.

"If I did everything out of charity, it's unlikely we would have survived, and therefore unlikely you would have either."

"You mean we weren't a charity case?" asked Rayne.

"That's different."

"In what way? You could have left us to die."

Rayne's brother shook his head.

The Shepherd had finally agreed to see us, just as the other members of "the caves" as they called it had started to arrive for supper. There wasn't enough room in his office for all of us, so only Rayne, Angela, Finn, and Rebekkah had been ushered in. The rest of us waited silently in the hallway, sitting on the floor and straining to hear as they spoke. Orion was still with us, and he and Leona sat together, listening and whispering to each other.

"How could we possibly help you?" The Shepherd asked, "This is a community with women and children. If all the men leave to fight some unwinnable battle, who would be here protecting them?"

"You have a contained compound, Amos," said Rayne, ignoring his brother's reaction to the use of his given name. "If they aren't safe here, they're not safe anywhere."

The Shepherd set his jaw. "I'm sorry Rayne, my answer is no. You are welcome to stay here for a few days to rest and regroup, and then I wish you the best."

"There's nothing I could say to convince you?"

He shook his head and sat down at the large wood desk in the centre of the room.

"I am afraid not."

"What are we going to do?" Jude asked me in a whisper. "Rhea..."

"We'll get her back Jude, whatever it takes, even if no one goes but you and me, we'll figure it out."

I heard Rayne mutter a string of obscenities and then I heard the scrape of his chair on the concrete floor.

"Thanks for nothing, Amos."

"Excuse me, before we go..."

Finn's voice was clear and strong.

"Delta gave this to me. She told me that you probably weren't going to be of much help. She is a wise woman apparently. She said if that was the case, I was supposed to give this to you and perhaps it would convince you."

I peeked around the door frame just in time to see Finn hand The Shepherd a folded envelope. He unfolded it and stared at it. His hands began to shake.

"Out." He said. "Everyone leave now."

"Amos?" said Rayne.

"I said leave!" The Shepherd roared, slamming his hands on the desk.

No one questioned him again. Those of us who were in the hallway stood as Rayne, Angela, Finn and Rebekkah filed out of the office. Orion had risen to his feet and pushed his way through the people to lead us to wherever it was that we were supposed to go.

"What was that?" asked Jude as Finn and Rebekkah came up behind us.

"A letter."

"From who?"

"I don't know," said Finn. "I didn't ask, and Delta didn't tell me, but I do know that it didn't seem to work the way Delta planned it."

"YOU'LL BE STAYING HERE for the night," said Archer. "I'm sorry it's not more comfortable, but there aren't many places we can host a group of your size without getting in the way."

We stood in the middle of a giant garden. Angela was looking around with her eyes wide, probably imagining everything that she could cook with this bounty. There were tomatoes, cucumbers, greens, herbs and a dozen other vegetables.

"Strawberries," I said, noticing the wall of hydroponic tubes.

She nodded beside me, unable to speak.

"We'd prefer it if you didn't snack from the garden," said Archer. "Unauthorized eating is against the rules here. What is grown for the community is shared by the community."

We nodded, still unable to keep our eyes off the varied plants. Most of the boys had never eaten a tomato, much less had any idea how they grew, or what they looked like.

"Thank you Archer," said Rayne. "We will do our best to not be a bother, and be on our way as soon as possible."

I could hear the heaviness in Rayne's words, the disappointment and anguish over his brother's refusal.

Archer nodded with a quick, curt movement and left, leaving us alone in the beautiful and plentiful garden.

Everyone was quieter than normal. Gone was the impetuous laughter and play that I was used to from this group. As a whole they mirrored their leader: sullen, somber and silent.

They brought us more soup, the women who dished it out held the same expressions everyone here did. They smiled, but beneath the veneer of friendliness and hospitality there was an undercurrent of wariness and distrust.

What had The Shepherd told them about us? Did they even know we existed? That they had sustained us for years? The scouts knew, of course, but did the community at large?

I bit into the roll they offered us again, but this time it tasted like sawdust in my mouth. Hope was gone and with it went any pleasure derived from the simple things.

*I am the President of the United States. I am the President of the United States.*

I ran the mantra through my head, more out of habit than anything. There wasn't much good it would do me.

One by one, men and boys stretched out on the floor between the vegetable beds. They rolled up their jackets as pillows and fell asleep in clumps, just as we did when we slept outdoors. There was no need to sleep so close, even tender plants were safe in this climate, but I understood. They were disheartened, and any comfort that could be derived from their brothers was welcomed.

I wasn't tired nor was I fully awake. My body was worn and sore and numb all at the same time. My mind raced. My mind once ran a country, once made decisions for hundreds of millions of people, once controlled the most powerful army in the world...

I controlled the most powerful army in the world.

I control the most powerful army in the world.

How had I not thought of this before?

Jude was lying nearby, his arm folded over his eyes and his long legs stretched out and crossed at the ankles.

"Jude," I said, my voice a whisper. I knew he wouldn't be asleep yet. He and I tended to be plagued with the same worries, and those worries always manifested themselves when everyone else was sleeping.

He slid his elbow from his eyes and peeked at me.

"I need to talk to you," I said, and motioned with my head to the hallway.

He nodded, sat up and followed me into the dim light of the hall. It was quiet, though I noticed right away that we weren't alone.

Orion sat, with his back to the wall a few feet from the door. I glanced at Jude who shrugged.

"Hey, don't look at me," he said. "I don't want to be here anymore than you want me here, but I drew the short straw."

Jude and I found a place to sit against the opposite wall.

"Are you supposed to spy on us?" Jude asked.

"If by 'spy' you mean, make sure you don't make off with the women, children, and strawberries, I guess that's what I'm doing. It's unlikely that I give two licks about whatever it is you two are out here to talk about." He yawned. "I'd much rather be in bed with my wife if I had any say in the matter."

"You look familiar to me," said Jude, after a long pause. "I thought that when I saw you when we first arrived, but I haven't been able to place you."

He didn't look familiar to me at all.

"It's my stunning good looks," he said, laughing. "They're incredibly memorable."

"Wait a minute, I know," said Jude. "I saw you in the woods once, years ago. You shot my deer."

"If your 'dear' got shot with one of my love arrows, that's just not my fault. It happens all the time. Sorry man, it's my curse." Orion said, chuckling at his own joke.

"Not that kind of deer, you idiot, the kind with hooves and antlers. My friend Dutch was about to take it down and you swooped in and took it away on your horse."

"That does sound like something I'd do."

"You said you were on your way to the Amazons."

He laughed, though I could see the lines around his eyes deepen.

"Amazons, huh? Sounds about right, but that's not what I call them."

"What do you call them?" I asked.

"Psycho chicks, mostly," he said. "Though now that Asari is dead, they're not so bad. Still a bit on the high-strung side for my liking. Around here we just call them 'the tribe'."

"Did they like your deer?" asked Jude.

He shrugged. "I don't know actually. The whole thing didn't really end up going like I had planned."

We didn't press further, nor did he offer any additional explanation.

"Well, I'm going to have a snooze if it's all the same to you," he said, pushing himself away from the wall and making himself comfortable on the floor. "If you guys are planning to steal all our stuff, could you wake me up and let me know first?"

"Of course," I said.

We sat in silence for a few minutes. I didn't know whether Orion was really asleep, but at this point I didn't care.

"I have an idea," I said, choosing my words carefully in case Orion was listening. "Before the freeze, it had been suggested to me that I might need a bit of extra help. I didn't trust my half-sister even then, and some of my most trusted advisors thought that I might need an 'out' one day."

Jude nodded, not entirely sure where I was going.

"There's a military bunker somewhere in the area, though I'm not exactly sure where we are, so finding it might be tricky, but she," I said, hoping Jude understood that I was talking about Nadia, "doesn't know about it. It's been twenty years and a lot has happened since then, so I don't even know if anyone is still there, but it's possible that at least some of them survived and are still holed up there. It's full of emergency supplies, so it makes sense that at least some of them chose to ride out the freeze there."

Jude was nodding along. It was a long-shot, I knew, but at this point a long-shot was all we had.

"I don't care about how we do this; I just need to get Rhea out of there. If I had known she was alive this whole time..."

"I know."

"Hang on a second."

Jude and I both looked up to see a very awake Orion sitting cross-legged with both of his index fingers pointing in different directions.

"Ignoring all the whole 'knowing about a secret military bunker' deal," he said, forming his words carefully. "What was that name you just said?"

"Rhea," I said.

"That's not a common name."

Jude and I both shook our heads.

"Sit tight," Orion said, springing to his feet. "I'll be right back."

We watched as he stalked down the hallway and disappeared around a corner.

"What was that?" Jude asked.

I just shrugged and shook my head.

"Do you think there's any chance he knows who Rhea is?"

"I'd say that would be surprising, but given the circumstances, not much is surprising me anymore," I said.

Orion was back in moments, behind him trailing Leona and the dark-haired girl we had seen when we arrived. He stopped directly in front of us, dropping to the floor and leaning in so he and Jude were almost nose to nose.

"Ok, start that bit again," he said, motioning for Leona and the other girl to sit.

"Which bit?" asked Jude

"Not the army part. The other part."

"The part about Rhea?"

As soon as the name slipped from his mouth I heard both girls gasp.

"You've seen Rhea?" the dark-haired girl asked. She had the most beautiful dark eyes. Her mouth was open and I could tell she was trying her hardest to control her excitement.

"Yes," said Jude, "but not for a long time."

His voice wavered as he spoke.

"How old is she?" asked Leona, "This Rhea person that you know."

"I'm not sure, exactly," said Jude. "I think she was a few years younger than me, and I'm, what, thirty-five now?"

"What did she look like?" asked Orion.

It seemed as though both Leona and Orion were asking the questions for the dark-haired girl, who looked like she was having trouble forming words.

"Um, brown hair," said Jude.

"Her eyes." The dark haired girl blurted, cutting him off as she rose to her knees in front of us. "What color are her eyes?"

"Violet."

She crumpled to the floor, both Orion and Leona reached for her.

"It has to be her," said Leona to Orion.

"You know Rhea?" I asked.

The dark-haired girl nodded, tears forming in her eyes.

"She's my sister."

# FOUR

## *Shayna*

THE KNOCK WAS SHORT and soft.

It was rare that anyone knocked before coming into my office. The only person that visited me by choice was Delta. Everyone else barged in with their version of an emergency. I was the only doctor left on site after Dr. Earickson died that specialized in something other than the science of fertility and obstetrics-gynecology. As a result, every splinter and cough and rash came to me. True emergencies were rare. I'd had a few after the avalanche, Dr. Earickson included, but the heart-attack of a dumpy, unhealthy, over-the-hill, pain-in-the-ass, didn't really rate on my list of exciting cases. Considering the suspicion that arose when Nadia found out Meredith was missing, his death had come with impeccable timing. My position was secure, since the estate needed someone with medical and surgical training. I hated to think what Nadia would have done with me if I had been expendable.

"Come in, Delta."

She came through the door with the deliberate movements of a woman her age. She had to be in her sixties, though I had never really asked her age. It just reminded me of my own age.

I had crossed the threshold into my fifties a few years ago, and didn't really enjoy being reminded of it. Delta was as spry as anyone in this estate, though I had noticed she had been getting slower in the past few years.

She lowered herself into the chair across the desk from me. She came every day. She usually had some reason, a medical question to ask or a problem to discuss, but I knew the real reason she came. It was the same one that made me look forward to her daily visits. She was lonely, like me. In this vast estate, full of people, there were so few we could trust. I spent most of my days dealing with people and discussing their problems all whilst burying my own. Delta shared that with me. We had worked together to keep Nadia from seeing Meredith as a threat. We had orchestrated her escape, and though neither of us knew if she and Jude had made it far enough from the building to avoid the avalanche, we also shared that hope.

"How are the girls today?" asked Delta.

It was the same way she started every conversation.

I shrugged. My answer was always the same too.

"They need to be awake."

She nodded slowly.

Their bodies were wasting away, and there was very little I could do to stop it. As much as I wanted to wake them up, I wasn't sure how many of them—if any—were strong enough to recover. For years their bodies had been factories for Nadia's plan, and between the five of those that still remained in their drug-induced coma, they had borne seventeen live children and forty-six miscarriages. Of the children who had lived, twelve were girls, and still lived. The numbers were staggering. Kenzie alone had given birth to eight children, her tiny body barely given enough time to recover before being impregnated again. Even Shalisa had begun to overcome the effects of her childhood cellutation, and had carried three living children. Rhea was the only one who had yet to give birth.

"Rhea?" asked Delta, as if she could read my mind.

"Still nothing," I said. "Nadia has been putting pressure on Dr. Harris. If she doesn't conceive during this next round of drug testing, they're going to discontinue."

Delta's brow furrowed. I wasn't telling her something she didn't already know.

"Discontinue," she said. "That's a rather sterile word."

I nodded. It wasn't the word I would have chosen, but I wasn't allowed to say things like "murder" and "execute".

"Aster is nearly thirteen." I said. Willow had been the first to give birth to a girl, so many years ago. They named them all alphabetically using flowers. After her came Bellis and Calla. All three of them were nearing puberty.

"Have the medications been working?"

I nodded. Nadia had ordered the young girls to undergo hormone treatment to ensure that they start puberty as soon as possible. Rhea, Willow, Kenzie, Hazel and Shalisa were getting to the age where consistent conception was becoming less likely. Nadia was looking to replace them as soon as possible.

I had been charged with the daily care of the younger

girls to allow the other doctors to focus on a way of standardizing conception rates as well as gender selection. They had given me the hormones, but I had replaced them with drugs that were known to delay the onset of puberty.

"I don't have much left, though. I can only keep them on the drugs for another month if I'm lucky. After that, I can't stop puberty."

"I guess it's not like they stocked the place with emergency puberty-delaying drugs," said Delta.

"No," I said. "The drugs I'm using were all here for other purposes, but they all have a similar side effect. As it is, they're taking medications for conditions they don't have in hopes that the side effect will keep them infertile a little bit longer. It's a tricky balance at best."

Delta nodded, letting her breath out slowly.

"If I keep them on these medications any longer, we run the risk of more permanent side-effects," I said. "There are better medications for this, but we just don't have them."

We sat in silence for a while, letting the impossibility of the situation sink in. My head was starting to throb, so I rubbed my temples with my index fingers.

"Do you think Finn found them?" I asked.

Delta shrugged. "I don't know anymore," she said. "I used to feel like I could tell if my boys were safe, if they were gone from me. But these days, everything is so muddled. I can't tell if it's just blind hope anymore, not that I'm sure I have much of that left."

"Do you think Amos is still alive?" I asked.

"You know as well as I do—maybe even better—that Amos was prepared for a situation like this," Delta said. "And Elias was with him, if they couldn't survive in that bunker of theirs, there isn't much hope for anyone else out there."

I nodded. I did know.

"I think he's alive," I said.

"Me too."

He had to be alive, they all did: Rayne, Amos and Elias. I didn't know what we were going to do if Finn didn't find them, and bring them here. I felt that desperation from the moment I put pen to paper to write to Amos. I had tried to write to him so many times, but every time the words failed me. I had been stubborn, hard-headed, and self-absorbed. I wanted him to give me what I wanted without asking for anything in return.

As I wrote to him I realized that I was asking for something again, begging and promising nothing in return.

"It's been too long, Delta," I said.

She watched me with her soft, sympathetic eyes as a tear spilled from my eye and slid quickly down the side of my nose to the edge of my lip.

She shook her head.

"He will come," she said. "If they find him, he will come."

# FIVE

## *Shayna – Eighteen years earlier*

"I DON'T. WANT. TO WORK. At MedTech," I said, enunciating my words with a clear, crisp staccato. I had said them all so many times that I couldn't for the life of me understand how he wasn't hearing me.

"It's the perfect solution," said Amos, coming close to pleading with me.

His eyes peeked out from underneath dark, straight, shaggy hair, surrounded by the mass of freckles that scattered themselves across his cheeks and nose. It was hard to say no to Amos, but this time I wasn't backing down.

"For whom?" I asked, doing my best to ensure my eyes held the same intensity as my fiery mane.

"For us."

"No, for you," I said, "I went into medicine because I want to help people."

"You will be helping them," he said. "MedTech does a lot of good work."

"Of course they do," I said, exasperated that we were having this conversation again. "But I want to interact with people, not sit in a lab staring into microscopes and genome scans all day."

"You could make a new discovery," he said, obviously hoping to garner a foothold by digging his toes into my ambitious side.

This time it wasn't going to work. My ambition had already gotten me what I wanted.

"No, Amos. You need to hear me," I said. "I was offered an internship and I'm taking it. The President asked for me herself. You don't say no to that."

I was at a tipping point, I could feel it. If he pushed me any farther, I wouldn't be able to control my rage. I paced the small kitchen like a lion in the zoo, struggling to keep my breath even.

Amos looked dejected as he settled himself on a stool at the island, and leaned forward on my pristine marble countertops.

"Shay," he said, his voice deep and soothing. He knew me well enough to back down and play passive, but I knew him well enough to know that he wasn't giving in. "I just want what's best for you."

"And I don't?"

"I talked to Mitchell last week..."

"Mitchell? Are you seriously bringing Mitchell into this?"

He was walking a very fine line and he knew it. I had no patience for Mitchell and his doomsday prophecies. I tolerated Amos' mild obsession with disaster preparation, and in a small way it was nice that he seemed to have a plan for those "just in case" scenarios, but Mitchell was a bad influence.

"What is it this time? Flood? Solar flares? Or have we made

it all the way to zombie apocalypse already?"

Amos rolled his eyes.

"You're going to thank me one day," he said. "And if Mitchell is right, that day might be very soon."

"Mitchell has never been right!" I shouted at him.

He stood and slammed his hands on the counter, knocking his stool over and sending it clattering to the tile floor. I resisted the urge to check for cracked tiles or scratched cabinets, holding my eyes in our locked stare.

"He will be. You'll see."

"You know what? I'm going to take my chances." Amos broke the stare and in that moment I knew I had won.

"I'm taking the internship with the White House Medical Team. I start on Monday."

Amos said nothing. He was angry, I could tell, but the emotion winning right now was disappointment. I didn't share his vision and he knew it.

I knew it.

But that was ok, we didn't have to have the same vision. We were different people. Being in a relationship didn't mean that we were clones of each other, alike in every way. We had different strengths and different ideas and at this moment, mine was right.

"Goodbye Shayna," he said, righting the stool and heading for the door.

It might take him a while, but he would understand. It always took Amos a while to come around.

I watched as he opened the door and headed out into the

hallway of my apartment complex.

I couldn't resist having the last word.

"Give my regards to Mitchell," I said, the venomous tone of my voice as sarcastic and cutting as I could manage.

He gave me one last sorrowful look and turned his back on me.

I bit my lip as he exited my apartment, wishing I could suck the last ten minutes back into my head. Wishing that I could find a way to make him understand without resorting to petty arguments.

But I couldn't.

I wouldn't.

Instead I silently watched the love of my life walk through the door.


"ARE YOU READY, SWEETHEART?"

The voice came from behind me as I stood watching the lit up numbers of the elevator move from floor to floor. I tensed slightly until I realized I knew that voice. It was soft, and calming.

"Delta," I said as I turned around. "How did I not notice you when I got into the elevator."

"It's your first day working for the President," she said, laughing. "I'll give you a week before you get your head down out of the clouds."

I knew she worked here, managing the pages and taking care of some of the day-to-day administration, but I hadn't even thought to watch for her.

The elevator glided to a stop almost imperceptibly, the door sliding open behind me as a soft chime sounded its arrival.

"This is me," I said.

"Me too," said Delta, walking out of the elevator behind me. "You want me to take you?"

I nodded. I had no idea where I was going, so a friendly face to guide me was too good to pass up, even for someone as stubbornly self-sufficient as me.

"A week, huh?" I said.

"I was being generous because I know you. It takes most people a month."

I laughed. I hadn't realized how much tension I was carrying in my shoulders until a little bit of it slipped away.

"Have you talked to Amos recently?" I asked. I should have been paying attention to where we were going so I'd be able to find the elevators again, but I couldn't resist asking Delta the question that had been on my lips the moment I saw her. Delta had taken Amos in when he was a child, and though she had never been able to afford a legal adoption, he considered her his mother.

She shook her head.

"I know about your fight," she said, "And for the record, I think he's wrong, but I honestly haven't talked to him much about it."

It made me feel a bit better to know that Delta sided with me. Amos had been unreasonable, that much was true, but there had been times while I agonized over our last conversation that I wasn't so sure being right was the same as doing what was right.

"Do you think he'll call me?"

Delta smiled. "Probably. Eventually."

She stopped in the hallway and reached for my hand. I gave it to her and she held it with both of hers.

"Shayna, Amos is the second most stubborn person I know," she said. "I love that he's stubborn because it means that if he points himself in the right direction, he's going to get wherever it is he's going, rest assured. The problem is that sometimes there's a very short leap from stubbornness to full-out pigheadedness, and once it gets to that point, there's very little anyone can do. Only he can let that go, and he needs to make that choice."

I nodded.

"We're here," she said, letting go of my hand. I let it drop to my side and turned in the direction she was pointing. The clinic doors were open and I could already smell the familiar scent of my chosen career.

"Good luck," said Delta, patting me on the back and starting off down the hall.

"Delta?"

She turned back.

"Who is the most stubborn person?"

She laughed.

"You, Darling. You."

# SIX

## *Meredith*

"OK, LET'S SEE IF I have all this right," said Leona, pointing at me. "You are the President of the United States and you were trapped in a coma until Jude there rescued you, and you've both been hanging out with the brother my father never told me he had, until you guys showed up."

She pointed at Finn and Rebekkah. We had gathered in a small dark room that was lit only with a candle. Orion had brought us here because he knew we were less likely to be overheard. The light played off our faces and as my eyes adjusted to the room, I had noticed that the walls were covered in writing. It was well after midnight, and though my body was tired, my mind was moving racing.

Finn and Rebekkah nodded.

"And Ember's sister Rhea is where all of you came from, and she's in a coma too, so she can be used as a breeding machine for the government, which is now under the control of the Vice-President, aka, your half-sister Nadia."

She pointed at me again, and I nodded.

Leona, Ember and Orion glanced at each other, mouths agape and eyes wide.

"When you put it all like that, it does sound kind of insane," said Finn.

"And The Shepherd is my uncle." added Leona, sounding more like a statement confirming something she already knew than an actual question.

"That's what Delta told us," said Jude.

"Delta," said Leona quietly as she stood, picking up the candle.

She stepped over Orion's long legs and walked to the wall.

"I grew up thinking Delta was my mother," she said, her three fingers tracing the words on the wall. "My father thought she was dead, and wrote her name here to remember her. When he died, I wrote his name beside hers, because it felt like that's where he would have wanted to be."

No one spoke.

"Is my grandmother alive?" she asked, turning to us.

"She was when we left her," said Finn.

Leona moved down the wall, looking for something else. Ember stood and joined her, placing her hand over Leona's as she found the name she was looking for.

"And Rhea is alive too?" asked Leona.

Ember hadn't spoken since she told us she was Rhea's sister. Orion and Leona had told us the story of how Rhea came to be at the estate. My blood boiled at the thought of Nadia orchestrating the kidnapping of those girls. She had told me they had been volunteered for her testing, that their families had been richly compensated. Ember had only stopped shaking a few minutes ago, but I could still see the wetness of tears in her eyes.

Finn nodded. "But it's entirely possible we don't have a lot of time. Delta told me they can't keep them under much longer before they risk... losing them."

His voice trailed off and he mumbled the last few words, words I knew he didn't want to say. I saw the tears tumble from Ember's eyes as Leona wrapped her arms around her friend. Beside me, Jude too was wiping his eyes.

"Hey man, why are you crying?" asked Orion.

"Jude and Rhea were... friends," I said. I didn't know how much more I could say, and it didn't appear as though Jude wanted to answer himself.

"Why didn't you get her out of there, then?"

The question hung in the air like smog, dirty and choking.

"Orion," said Leona, in a warning voice.

"It's ok," said Jude. "I went to get help, but as we were leaving, an avalanche covered the estate. I thought they died. I didn't know Rhea was alive until Finn arrived a few days ago."

"He fully underestimated my digging abilities," said Finn, flexing his muscles.

Rebekkah rolled her eyes.

"I think we need to go there," said Leona. "We could ask the tribe for help if the Shepherd won't."

"The Amazons have never been friends of ours," said Jude.

I knew he was thinking about Phoebe, and Dutch—and neither of us would ever forget his own injury, and the basket of baby boys being used as bear bait.

"They're not the same as they once were," said Leona.

"How do you know?"

"We just came from there," said Orion. "A few months ago."

I knew from the silence between them that there was much more to the story, but I didn't want to ask.

"It's a long story, but my mother and father lead the tribe now. Asari, the original leader is dead, and they..."

"Don't really shoot at people anymore," said Orion, finishing her sentence.

"Your parents?" I asked, "Isn't Elias...?"

"Yes," said Leona.

"Long story," said Orion.

"I still think I need to go to the military base," I said. "If there is any chance they survived and are holed up there, their help would be invaluable."

"I agree," said Jude. "Do you have any maps around here?"

Orion nodded. "If you know where it is, I can probably help you find it."

"If we are where I think we are, we'd need to go in the opposite direction to find the bunker. The tribe falls somewhere between here and the mountains."

"So we split up?" asked Jude.

No one answered. It seemed like a terrible idea to split up such a small group, At the same time, taking over the estate was such a giant, looming, terrifying idea that the notion of having military support was tempting.

"I can go alone," I said.

Jude shook his head. "Not going to happen."

"It makes perfect sense, Jude. That way if I don't find them, or if no one is there, you still have your numbers."

"I'll come with you."

I shook my head. "You and Finn both know the estate better than anyone here. No one else would be able to get in and bypass the security systems. You have to go with them."

"Do you know how to ride?" asked Orion, "We can get you a horse."

"It's been a while, but I grew up riding. See Jude? I can make it there and back faster if it's just me on a horse. If no one is there I can come back and catch up with you."

Jude didn't seem convinced, but everyone else was nodding.

"You honestly think we should let you, the President, go off on your own wild goose chase. Just come with us, we can do this without the military."

"But it would be a whole lot easier with them."

He couldn't argue with me there.

"It's not safe."

I couldn't argue with him either, but I could feel the hard lump of my handgun where it was holstered under my arm. I wore it night and day, hidden beneath the bulk of my warm clothes.

"Ok, we'll get Meredith some extra gear, some provisions and a horse. Everyone else comes with us to the tribe."

Orion spoke with authority, and everyone else nodded, though I noticed some hesitation on Jude's part.

"It will take us all day tomorrow to get what we need without attracting attention. Lay low, get some rest, and we'll leave tomorrow."

"You think you'll be able to get what you need without anyone noticing?" asked Jude.

Orion and Leona laughed, and Orion stood and reached his hand out to help Jude to his feet.

"This ain't our first rodeo, Jude," he said. "Watch and learn."

I STAYED BEHIND AFTER everyone left. There was something so soothing and yet so painful about this place— somehow being surrounded in the visible losses of others made my own seem less suffocating. It was easy to focus on the immediate in times of crisis, the day-to-day issues that never ceased to pop up. That's what it was, I supposed, a time of crisis—a very long time of crisis.

I closed my eyes and breathed, trying to internalize the struggles of people I had never met, trying to absorb their pain so I could understand my own.

I didn't hear her come back until she coughed.

Opening my eyes, I turned to see Ember standing by the door.

"I'm sorry to interrupt," she said. "I just wanted to ask you something."

"Of course, come in," I said, patting the floor in front of me.

She came and sat down. I could tell she was nervous and unsure of herself. I let her make herself comfortable and waited patiently as she chose her words.

"Did someone do it to you too?" she asked.

"Do what?" I asked.

She pulled her hair back from her face so the thin line that marred her perfect face was fully visible.

"Oh," I said. "No, dear. I chose that myself."

She nodded. I could see tears brimming in her eyes.

"You didn't have that choice, did you?"

She shook her head.

I reached out, placing my hand on hers and waited. If she wanted to tell me, she could, but I wouldn't ask.

"My parents," she said. "They were scared."

Knowing what I knew about her sister's disappearance and subsequent struggles at the estate, I answered.

"They had good reason, child."

"I know," she said, nodding. Tears were now flowing freely down her face.

"It wasn't right for them to take it from you, but sometimes we don't get the luxury of a right choice. Sometimes all we have to choose between are two wrong ones, and you need to hope you made the best choice."

"Was that how you chose?"

I wanted to tell her exactly what I knew she wanted to hear, but it wasn't the truth.

"No, Ember. I made the right choice. There was probably a time in my life where I could have convinced myself that having children was the right thing for me to do, but if I had been truly honest with myself, I knew this was my path."

"How?"

"If I had chosen to have children, I wouldn't have been the President—and me being the President is probably what's going to help us save your sister."

I paused before continuing, trying to swallow the lump that had begun to form in my throat.

"And if getting your sister back is the only reason for me to be where I am, it would have been enough."

THE NEXT DAY DRAGGED more slowly than I could have imagined possible. We didn't have anything to do but sit around, which was good because it gave us an excuse to rest without anyone wondering. We piled our gear in the classroom since there were no classes that day. While we were given leave to wander the halls, I felt weird doing it. I didn't want to gawk at other people in their home—it reminded me too much of when they held tours through the White House. I also didn't want anyone to recognize me; even though I was sure I looked very different than the last pictures or videos anyone here would have seen. Jude, Finn, Rebekkah and I had mainly chosen to lay low in the classroom. Finn and Rebekkah were asleep curled up together on the floor.

Fernie and Gibs had taken the younger boys, (Renny included) outside to practice their knife throwing and most of the rest of the group had gone out too. The sun was shining and it wasn't too cold, so it was nice to get out of the stale, stifling air. Rayne had told us at breakfast that we would be headed back to the hospital tomorrow to regroup and figure out our options. He didn't really sound like he had a lot of ideas. Jude and I had discussed whether or not to tell Rayne, and bring everyone, but we had decided to go to the tribe first. Neither of us trusted the women, and though Leona and Orion insisted they were reformed, it seemed like a bad idea to head over there with a large group of unruly young men. If they did decide to help us, we could always send a messenger back to the hospital and have them meet us on the way. The more people we had at the estate, the better.

"Jude," I whispered.

He was lying on his back on the floor, one arm over his face. I spoke quietly enough that if he were asleep, it was unlikely he'd notice.

"I'm awake," he said, not bothering to move.

"I need you to do me a favor."

He pushed his arm up so it covered his forehead instead of his eyes.

"If I don't make it back to the estate, I need you to kill Nadia."

He snorted and dropped his arm back over his eyes.

"What?" I asked, puzzled by his response.

He laughed out loud.

"That's your favor?" he asked, snickering. "I've been planning that from the moment I found out what she was up to. I was rooting for Red when he went on that rampage, and if I had stayed at the estate, I would have done it myself if given the chance. So yeah, sure, as a favor to you, I'll off her."

Right.

"I guess I didn't think it through," I said. "Can we blame sleep deprivation?"

He smiled and pushed himself up on to his elbows.

"I'm sorry, I didn't mean to be harsh about it. Would it make you feel better to know that I'm very happy I won't have to apologize to you for killing your sister?"

"Half-sister," I said, smirking. "A very small half."

"Honestly though, I'm glad you came to that point," said Jude. "It couldn't have been easy."

I shook my head. "I'm still not sure I'd be able to bring myself to do it. She looks much more like our father than I do."

"She's dangerous."

"I know," I said. "And if given the opportunity, she'd quickly kill me first."

"I won't let that happen," said Jude.

While I appreciated his words, I knew in my heart that he might not be able to keep his promise.

# SEVEN

NIGHT FELL ON THE caves. I watched the last hints of light disappear from the windows above us as we readied ourselves for bed in the gardens. It wasn't terribly late at night, but everyone seemed ready to be done with our time here and get home. Going to sleep early seemed like the quickest way to make that happen. Jude, Finn, Rebekkah and I had found places near the door, and while they all looked asleep, I was sure they were as awake as I was. My heart hammered with anticipation and anxiety. Once we could be sure everyone was asleep and we could slip away without being noticed, we'd be on our way. Every minute seemed to stretch into an agonizing wait that reminded me of being stuck in rush-hour traffic when I had somewhere to be. I was at the mercy of time, and it wasn't doing me any favors.

I inhaled and exhaled slowly, focusing on lengthening my breaths in hopes that it would spur the passage of time. It had the added benefit of making it appear as though I was asleep. I counted my breaths in my head, leaving little room for the other thoughts and fears that plagued me. The air was thick and green, scented with damp soil and tomato leaves that seemed out of place in the stale air of the caves. I could remember those smells from my youth, always mixed with breezes and sunlight and the smells of summer.

By the time I had counted to a thousand breaths, I could hear Finn moving. He and Rebekkah would leave under the pretense of her need to use the restrooms, and shortly after that, Jude and I would slip out one at a time. I counted a hundred more breaths, and opened my eyes to peek at Jude. He was watching me. I nodded my head toward the doors, signalling that he go first. He nodded once and silently pushed himself to his feet and slipped into the dark hallway. The bags we had with us in the gardens were decoys, emptied of their useful supplies and stuffed with extra blankets Ember had brought for us. Whatever outdoor clothing we needed beyond what we were already wearing would be waiting for us in the stables. It was unlikely anyone would suspect us of leaving with all our belongings still there. I counted again, listening for the slow, steady sounds of slumber.

Slowly I rose and carefully stepped toward the doorway and into the hall. One small light down the corridor cast an eerie glow. They didn't use much light here, but it was still more than I was used to from the hospital. Electric light seemed like such a luxury after surviving for so long with little more than fires and torches. The light buzzed as I walked beneath it, hurrying to get back into the shadows. I turned the corner and moved as quickly and silently as I could across the hard concrete floors.

Someone moved in the hall ahead of me and I pressed myself into the shadow of a doorway, but just as I stopped moving I heard rummaging from the direction I had come. As I waited for a man to enter the restrooms, I peeked back to see if someone had followed me, but everything was still. Continuing on, I closed the distance quickly and found myself on the stairs. I took them two at a time. I could feel a cold breeze as it rushed downward from the door. I was out of breath by the time I reached the top of the stairs, but I pulled my hood up over the ski cap I was wearing and stuffed my hands into the deep pockets of the thick sweatshirt I wore. It wasn't enough for the cold, but I just needed to make the short dash to the stables. I listened as the door groaned and then clicked shut behind me and I ran through the shadows to the stable. There were probably sentinels in the towers, but Orion had told us not to worry about them. The packed snow squeaked under my boots and as I slowed to a stop at the stable door and reached out to open it, my heart lurched. In the silence I heard the same groan and click of the door I had just come through.

Panicking, I pushed open the sliding metal door and hurled myself into the humid warmth of the stable.

"I've been followed."

The others stopped what they were doing and Orion motioned for us to move back from the door as Ember's husband Rowan moved to stand between us and the door, shielding us in case the intruder was lucky enough to make it past Orion. The flashlight Leona carried clicked off and we were plunged into darkness. My heart pounded as I strained to hear footsteps. Orion stood silently beside the heavy metal door. We could hear them coming, whispering and crunching through the snow.

Slowly the door slid open and as soon as it had opened

wide enough, Orion flew through the opening.

I could hear a struggle, and grunts, but in the darkness could see nothing.

"Leona."

The light flickered to life and Orion stood by the door, his massive arms each wrapped around the neck of a flailing character.

"Let us go you great galoot!"

"Anyone you know?" asked Orion.

"Dutch, Olly, what are you guys doing here?" said Jude, stepping out of the shadows. "Orion you can let them go."

"Yeah, let us go."

Orion smirked and gave them one more squeeze before dropping them in a wheezing heap on the floor.

Dutch swore loudly as he pulled himself to his feet, but Olly just sat on the floor looking stunned.

"You think you were going to run off without us?" asked Dutch. He was dressed for outdoors.

Jude shrugged.

"So where are we going?"

I laughed out loud. "To the Amazons. Still want to come?"

Dutch's eyes widened.

"Whatever for?"

"It doesn't matter now does it?" asked Orion. "You're committed now. I ain't about to let you go back in there and sound the alarm, so get ready, we leave in ten."

Dutch glared at Jude, who shrugged and laughed.

"I knew from the moment I met you that you were trouble," muttered Dutch as he went out into the yard to collect the bow and quiver he had dropped in the struggle.

Olly still hadn't said anything, though he was now standing and brushing himself off.

Orion walked to one of the stalls as I pulled my snow pants over my jeans. He opened the door to one of the stalls and led out a large black horse, already saddled and ready to go. I zipped up my parka as he brought the beast to the door.

"This is Thor," said Orion, patting the mammoth horse. "He's a bit skittish, but of all of them, he's got the least temper. As long as you're firm with him, he'll take you where you need to go."

As he spoke, he patted the horse's nose.

"Do you have your maps?"

"They're in the pack, the big pocket," said Rowan, holding out a large black knapsack. It was much like the one I'd left in the garden. "There's enough food in here for a week if you're careful, so that should get you there and back if necessary."

I nodded.

Leona reached for Thor's reins as Orion turned to get another horse. Rebekkah would be riding too.

"Are you sure your dad isn't going to freak about us taking horses?" Leona asked Ember.

"He won't," spoke a harsh deep voice from the back of the stables. Orion turned sharply, causing the horse he was leading to toss its head and pull back on the reins.

"Hush," said Orion, reaching to touch the horse, his first

instinct to calm the startled beast.

"I had to tell him," said Ember, her voice meek and apologetic. "How could I not?"

From the shadows stepped the man I recognized from when we arrived, Archer. If he was Ember's father that meant he too had a vested interest in finding Rhea.

"I'm coming with you," he said.

No one objected. He was dressed and ready, and we needed to go.

Finn and Orion helped Rebekkah onto the brown horse Orion had and Leona held Thor as Jude gave me a boost into the saddle. I wasn't used to riding such a tall horse, but as I grasped the reins, I could feel him respond to me, and I to him. My years of riding came flooding back as my body moved by muscle memory rather than thought.

"Let's go find them," I whispered to Thor, who flicked his ears in response.

Archer led the brown horse, and Thor followed obediently as Orion opened the gate. One by one we filed through the opening, first the people on foot, and then Archer with Rebekkah's horse and finally Thor.

"I'll see you soon," I said to the others. "And with any luck, I'll be bringing the cavalry."

"Good luck," said Jude. "Don't do anything stupid."

I laughed and squeezed my legs into Thor's sides. He pushed off and within seconds we were alone, the compound disappearing into the darkness behind us, and nothing but the unknown ahead.

# EIGHT

## *Athena*

WE MADE LOVE THAT night. I didn't really feel like it, but I never seemed to be able to object when it came to Torren. He fell asleep as soon as we were done, though I lay awake in our hut, watching the light from the fire dance on the bundles that hung in the rafters. There were bundles of skins I had tanned, waiting for someone's quick fingers to stitch them into mittens or moccasins. I didn't have quick fingers. Not when it came to sewing at least. Asari had been more interested in teaching me hand-to-hand combat. I was next to useless as a wife, but what I lacked in ability, I made up for in obedience.

I couldn't think of a time I had said no to Torren, which seemed strange to me, especially considering some of his inane requests. I rarely agreed to anything at the first request, unless that request came from my aunt, but that was less about obedience and more like "self-preservation". Asari didn't ignore challenges to her authority.

Maybe love really does change a person.

Did I even love Torren?

Pregnancy had changed me for sure. Maybe that was it; some deep need to build a home, make a family. It had never really been part of my plan, though it's not like we had suitable partners growing on trees around camp. It was a wee bit imbalanced if you asked me. Buck was nice on the eyes, but...

That wouldn't have worked.

Nothing about that would have worked, though that truth didn't stop me from raising an eyebrow at my "sister". I didn't want him, but I didn't want her to have him either.

Irritated, I pushed myself from our bed on the floor and wrapped a soft, thick wolf-pelt around my shoulders. It was the last wolf I had killed, skinned and tanned. Wolves weren't all that useful around camp, since their meat wasn't terribly tasty, but every so often I liked to drag one home, just for me. Their fur was soft and luxurious, and there was nothing like reminding yourself of your spot at the top of the food chain. It was chilly in the hut, but between the fire, the fur and the soft, lined buckskin moccasins I wore, I was comfortable. Torren snored softly; if he got any louder I might just throw a stick at him. I wouldn't really, but the thought amused me. There was a low stool near the fire, and I sat on it, wrapping my arms around my knees. I wouldn't be able to do that much longer, I could already feel the hard, swollen lump in my belly. Not much longer and just sitting on something so low was going to be difficult. I pulled the fur more tightly.

The hummingbird on my wrist peeked out from under the long cotton shirt I wore. The wings were high, a visible testament to the growing life inside me. My mother had given me that. There were marks all over my skin. She had cellutated me too, as a child. That was before we ran out. Only five of my sisters had received the inoculations—six of my sisters, if I included Leona, though I usually didn't. The rest of them were born after my mother had run out of the medicine. The cellutation kept us from being as fertile as we could be, but this hummingbird, it was the answer. I was pregnant within two months of the first time I spread my legs for him. I hadn't bled in four.

I heard the chatter of voices in the camp, faster and louder than they should have been for the middle of the night.

"Torren."

He grunted and rolled over.

I said his name again, louder this time.

"What?" he mumbled, the irritation pushing past the groggy fog of sleep.

"There's something going on."

"Huh?"

I wanted to roll my eyes, but didn't. Why I bothered to wake him up at all was a mystery to me. I didn't need him to find out what was going on.

"Just listen."

He sat up, pushing the furs back so his bare back and shoulders were visible, pale and rippled in the glow of the fire. I had given him a tattoo after we'd married, a wolf and a mountain lion locked on each other, entwined in a circle of anger and heat and passion over his right shoulder blade. It was probably my best work.

He had great shoulders. I bit my lip and drank him in.

As soon as he stopped to listen, the last vestiges of his

dreams drained off him like water pouring down his skin. He knew something was happening, as I did. He stood, letting the furs drop from his naked body, and pulled his buckskin pants on. Such a difference from the ill-fitting wool trousers he had come here in. Nothing fit a man like leather. He didn't bother with a shirt, but yanked his coat from where it hung on a low hook by the door, pushing his way out of the flap with little more than a second glance my way.

"Stay here," he said.

I did.

A cold breeze blew in as the door flap closed behind him, chilling my knees and waking an army of goose bumps that marched up my thighs.

I waited on that hard stool by the fire until he came back. I doubt he would have at all if he had been better prepared when he left.

"What's going on?" I asked as he let his coat fall off his bare shoulders onto the floor, and began to collect more clothing.

"There is a party within our borders," he said, pushing his head through his soft, tanned leather shirt. I stood to help him tie the laces at his neck, but he brushed me away. Instead I helped him gather his outerwear, the long rabbit mittens that covered the sleeves of his coat to his elbows and the fox-fur hood I had tried to make before my mother, my frustrated teacher, finished it for me.

"Do you need my help?" I asked, though I didn't need to wait for the answer.

"Stay here," he said, pulling me toward him and pressing

his rough, unshaven lips to mine. "I'll be back soon."

And with that, he was gone.

At least I wasn't alone.

THEY DIDN'T COME BACK until the pink light of dawn came streaking across the sky. I hadn't slept, rather spent the rest of my night pacing the hut, waiting.

I didn't worry about Torren, he was strong, fierce. He would come back. Instead it was something deeper and more ominous that kept me from sleep. I could feel a powerful change in the air. I didn't know what it was, but I could feel it pushing its way in like the spray of a skunk—potent, infiltrating.

I heard their return to the camp. I had dressed hours before and stepped from the hut to greet them.

I saw Torren leading the group with Orion behind him. He was as beautiful as the day he left camp, though significantly less ragged. He sported an unshaven face like his younger brother, and his hair was still long, but it had been trimmed recently, and was tied back under his cap.

These were no enemies, though I spotted Leona's green cloak among them and tensed. I recognized a few faces from when they had come before; the girl with the smoldering eyes and her staid male sidekick. There were others I didn't recognize, like the lanky broomstick with the high-tech winter gear, and the similarly-dressed girl on the horse. They weren't from the caves.

I followed the crowd of visitors and comrades to the large hut that stood in the center of the camp. My parents were at the door to the main gathering area, where I had first seen Leona, unconscious and half-frozen. My mother's wolf stood at attention beside her, always ready to protect her from intruders. Leona ran to our mother and they embraced. It was awkward and strange to watch. She made no move to touch our father, but he greeted her with a stiff squeeze of her shoulder. They spoke too quietly for me to hear them, but my mother nodded and welcomed them all through the flaps and into our home. The tall guy in the fancy clothes lifted the girl down from the horse and carried her with him, ducking into the hut. Torren and a few of the other women followed them.

Most of the women around me went back to their work, seeing no threat. I had no work to do, so I simply followed them through the door and down the few steps into the large, open room. I found a place near the wall where I could sit and listen. Apparently I wasn't the only one that didn't have anything better to do. Mila's slim frame plopped down next to me. She was barely a teenager and I swore she had grown a foot in the last week. She was all legs and elbows and so fair she could have disappeared into the snow without much trouble.

"Did I miss anything interesting?" she asked, nearly spilling over with excitement. People didn't come to our camp very often, with good reason. We had tamed it down a lot in the last few months, but we were still an intimidating lot. We were strong, heavily armed and fifteen-plus years of attacking everyone who came near us had built an impenetrable wall around us. The women here induced fear in our neighbours, and other than Leona, Orion, and the friends that had been here before, the others with them were noticeably wary and watched carefully. I could understand it. We tattooed our faces, and carried spears. Other than Torren and Dax, there were no men here. There was no balance. We knew only force.

I shook my head.

"I haven't heard anything yet."

"Hey look… it's Buck!"

I grabbed her arm and held her to keep her from jumping up to say hello.

"Not the time, Mila."

She slumped.

"I like Buck," she said to no one in particular.

"Don't we all," I muttered.

"So what brings you here?" asked Nova. Her wolf lay on the ground beside her, as he always was.

"A few days ago we had a group of people join us at the caves, and they came with terrible news."

The girl from the horse raised her hand.

"I think I can help explain this. Nova? Do you remember a girl named Isis?"

Leona turned, surprised to hear this other girl speaking. "How did you know my mother's name?"

"Isis?" My mother's words were almost a whisper.

The girl nodded. "I'm sorry for what happened," she said.

"There is so much I should have told you."

"But instead you disappeared."

The girl nodded. "I had to. I no longer use that name, either, I go by Rebekkah now."

Nova nodded, still confused—and there was something else in her eyes. Fear? Anger? I couldn't place it.

"I hope you'll let me explain," Rebekkah said.

Nova softened. "I'm not angry with you, Isis... Rebekkah. Just surprised. Please, continue."

"That morning..." Rebekkah said, "I didn't just bail. I couldn't come to you."

Nova nodded, waiting patiently for the story to unfold.

"I had been threatened, coerced into receiving your serum and bringing it back to the government labs, so they could analyze my blood and let them replicate it."

None of this was making any sense to me, but my mother seemed to understand.

"I'm sorry to have put you in that position, Rebekkah. Had they just come to me, I'm sure we could have worked something out for distribution of my serum."

"There's more," said Orion, his deep voice little more than an ominous rumble in the room.

"He's right," said the beanpole, he had taken off his ski cap and his brown curls were shooting out from his head in every direction.

"We came from an estate in the mountains where Nadia Black and other high-ranking members of the government are holed up, including a number of young women who are being held in medically induced comas and being used as breeders."

"They have plans to start a new society when the frozen days are over," said Rebekkah. "Where some women are nothing but breeders—leaving the others free to live without the bother of child-rearing."

The look of pain on my mother's face was obvious. She had lived for years under the control of my aunt, her sister-in-law, Asari. She had been a "breeder", as had my father.

"Whoa," said Mila quietly beside me.

I nodded.

"I notice you speak only of our vice –president," said Dax, interjecting. "What of Meredith Kroeker?"

The visitors looked at each other, unsure of something.

Leona was the one who finally spoke.

"She's not there, she didn't agree with the others, but couldn't stop them."

"Where is she?"

"Finding a way to stop them," said one of the young men I didn't recognize.

"Which is also what we're doing," said Orion.

"They have my sister, Nova." said the girl with the fiery eyes. "They were the ones who took her."

Even from the far side of the room, I could feel her emotions radiating through the crowd. My mother closed her eyes.

"They took her from our house and they are keeping her in a coma, like some kind of machine."

She broke down then, unable to say more. I watched as Nova stood from the edge of the wooden platform she was sitting on and sat down beside the girl. She pulled her into an embrace, enveloping the weeping girl in her arms. I could see her lips move as she whispered something, words of comfort, perhaps.

They stayed that way until the others began to talk quietly amongst themselves. Torren had found a seat next to Dax, and they were talking, their heads angled toward each other.

Nova stood and walked slowly back to the platform, leaving the girl to be comforted by Leona and Orion.

"What is it that you need from us?" asked Nova. Her wolf followed her with his eyes as she paced slowly in front of her guests.

"Force," said one of the young men.

The others nodded in agreement.

Nova said nothing. She was nothing like my aunt. The idea of taking down the government would have sent a surge of adrenaline through her until she could taste the sweetness of power on her lips. Asari liked nothing more than the taste of the blood of anyone who stood in her way.

"What did the Shepherd say? I assume you asked him."

Leona nodded. "He wasn't much help."

"And you thought I would think differently?"

"I thought you would do the right thing."

Nova's eyes closed and the look of pain on her face was evident.

"There are women and children here..."

Orion laughed out loud, his booming voice carried through the room.

"You make it sound like you are helpless!" he said, standing to face Nova. "Your 'women and children' are warriors. There is nothing helpless about this tribe."

As if on cue, my mother's wolf stood beside her and let out a subtle but menacing growl. She reached out her hand, silencing him.

"Asari isn't here anymore. She was the warrior."

"And you?"

Nova shook her head. "I ask for peace from these women, not war."

Orion's voice softened. "Please don't misunderstand me, I appreciate what you have done for me and Leona, and there is no one I feel better suited to lead this tribe but you. But right now we need warriors."

"How can I ask that?"

"If you lead them, they will follow you."

"I'm not equipped for violence," she said, desperation creeping into her voice. "I am not Asari."

Dax stood. "No one said you had to be."

Orion nodded slowly. "Part of striving for peace is removing those who oppose it. There will be no peace if they have their way. Your daughters and their children will be taken. I can't let that happen."

I could feel the battle cry stirring inside me as he spoke. I could almost hear my blood rushing inside my body, stirring me and invigorating me. I would stand with them. Hand me a knife, and a bow, and just try to stop me.

"I need to think about this," said Nova.

What was there to think about? I could feel my hands clenching and the words on my tongue, but I couldn't force myself to my feet. I couldn't push the shout through my lips. I growled like a caged animal, but no sound escaped me.

"Please stay with us. We will find room for you."

"Nova..." started Orion.

"I need time," she said. Her voice firm, but her eyes were sympathetic.

He nodded.

"Athena," said Torren. "Go find them a place to stay."

I swore at my muscles for betraying me as I rose to my feet and nodded.

"Can I help?" asked Mila. Her eagerness infuriated me.

"Don't you have someone else to take care of?"

The smile fell from her face like a dead crow, speared by an arrow, crashing to the ground. I knew I had hit my mark.

Her eyes welled with tears and she ran from the hut—a blur of white-blonde hair flying behind her.

# NINE

## *Mila*

SOMETIMES I HATED ATHENA.

I pushed back the flap of my hut and ducked inside. I could hear singing as my eyes adjusted to the dim light. She always sang—at least for as long as I could remember. I had heard the whispers, I knew she hadn't always been this way. They had broken her into nothing more than a shell of what she had been.

Her hair was pale like mine and tied back in a tight braid. She didn't like it when I braided her hair, but if I didn't, she was more likely to chew on it and then it was a mess to comb through. As it was she still chewed on the ends, but if that got too bad, I could always trim it off.

"Hello mother," I said, though it was rare that she acknowledged me.

I sat on the furs that made up my bed and watched her. That was my job, mainly. Make sure nothing happens to this poor, half-melted, shattered person.

She was humming a tune that was only familiar to me from the number of times she would hum it. If it had words, I didn't know them, and truth be told, I would have made her stop if I could. If I looked at her from the right side, she was a truly beautiful woman. They told me I would look like her. When she turned toward me, my stomach ached, as it did every time I looked at her scars.

I was too little when it happened, I wasn't there, but I didn't know where else I would have been. They had taken me from her and the next time I saw her, the mother I knew was gone. She toted me around like I was some kind of doll, mothering, but completely detached. I could still remember her lying in her bed, her face and arms wrapped in bandages, the smell of her singed hair. It wasn't until I was much older that they told me what happened. It was Athena. In her cold, unfeeling way, she told me how my mother had gone crazy, her senses had left her and in a moment of darkness, she had thrown herself onto the fire in an attempt to kill herself. To be free. They had doused her with water, and bandaged her up, but the person who was left was not the woman who fought them every step as they dragged her to this place.

"No one has the heart to kill her now," Athena had said. "She's simple, it would be like killing a child."

Not that they'd had any problem with that in the past.

This tribe had taken everything from me, but there was nowhere else I could go.

"Angela, is that you?" she asked, her voice childlike and sincere.

She asked for Angela a lot.

"No. It's me, mom... Mila."

She thought for a moment.

"Do you know how Jude is feeling?"

"No mom," I said. Apparently we were doing this again. "I don't know who Jude is."

There were times when she seemed to know who I was, but it was in those times that I could see the depth of her despair. It almost wasn't worth partaking in her pain for those seconds of recognition. Some days, though, I would have sold my soul to see my mother again.

I barely remembered her anyway.

I curled up in a ball on my bed and closed my eyes, trying to block her song out, but the tune was so ingrained in who I was that I doubted there would ever be a time I could separate from it.

"Do you want to come for a walk with me?" I said, sitting up suddenly. What was the point in sitting in this dark hole when things were happening outside? Visitors were here, bringing tidings of scary places I had never heard of.

She didn't object, so I took that as agreement and found her outdoor clothing. When she was dressed for the cold, I pulled my warm mittens back on and we ventured into the camp.

For the most part, it was like any other day, but there was an undercurrent of uncertainty that buzzed through the camp. There were more low voices, more furtive glances than usual, less laughter and jocularity.

They weren't hard to find, and as we strolled past them I could feel their frustration. They had dropped their packs on the ground and some of them were using them as makeshift seats, obviously exhausted from the journey. Others were having what seemed to be nearly-silent heated conversations. I could hear the hiss of their whispers. Athena was there too, carrying a large wooden bowl full of dried meats, and yesterday's bread. They would eat with us soon, I was sure, but they were probably hungry.

"Who are they?" asked my mother, holding on to my arm as she usually did when we left the hut.

"I don't know," I said. "Except for Buck, and Leona I guess."

"Buck is here?"

I pointed to him, though it seemed silly. Buck always stood out in a crowd.

My mother smiled, as if she was remembering some secret joke they had.

"Jude," she said, barely louder than a whisper.

"I don't know how Jude is feeling, mom."

She didn't respond.

"JUDE." Her voice was louder this time. I pulled her arm, hoping to drag her back to the hut before she had an episode out here, but before I could, one of the visitors came running over. He reached out and placed his hands on her arms, taking stock of my mother and looking her in the eyes.

No one looked my mother in the eyes.

"Phoebe?"

She nodded.

"How do you know my mother?"

"Mila?"

He seemed shocked as he looked at both of us, flitting from one to the other.

"I had given you up for dead."

"Who are you?" I asked. "How do you know my name?"

"I'm Jude," he said as my mother crumpled into his strong arms, shaking and crying. He held her on her feet and when it was obvious she wouldn't regain her footing, he scooped up her frail frame and carried her back to where his group was gathered.

I followed as he pushed his way past the crowd and into the large hut they would be staying in. Buck and Leona followed him, and I pushed past them both.

"What's going on kiddo?" asked Buck.

"I don't know," I said. "I think they know each other."

Jude nodded. "We do." He had placed her on the floor next to some of the bedrolls someone, probably Athena, had stacked in the center of the room.

He knelt in front of her, slowly and carefully brushing the hair from her face, and wiping the tears from her scarred cheek with his thumb.

"Oh Phoebe," he said. "I wanted to come after you."

"I'm glad you didn't," she said, her voice wavering in the hushed silence of the room. Almost everyone else had gathered behind us, including Athena. We stood and watched as for the first time, my mother seemed completely coherent. "They would have killed you all."

"But... this..."

She placed her tiny pale hand on his much larger one that

was still resting gently on her cheek.

"You came now," she said. "And that's enough."

A tear fell from his face.

"Who are you?" I asked, realizing I had begun to drown in the reality that was setting in. Was this man my father? Where did he come from?

"My name is Jude, Mila," He said. "You probably don't remember me, you were very young the last time I saw you."

"A baby," said my mother.

"Are you..." the words caught in my throat.

His eyes opened wide as he realized what I was asking.

"No!" he said. "I'm not. I was a friend of your mother's, a long time ago."

"You're still my friend," she said. "You came."

I had never seen my mother this lucid. It was as if some kind of shroud had lifted from her, like she had hidden herself away, just for this moment. I wanted to grab this moment and hang on with everything I was worth. Tears filled my eyes as for the first time I saw her.

"Angela?"

"Alive, safe," he said.

She smiled as her tears made crooked paths down the bumps of her scarred skin.

"What happened to her?" I hear Leona whisper to Buck.

"Too much," he said, wrapping his long arms around her shoulders.

I could hear them talking behind me, Buck telling Leona

the story of my mother—a story I had heard in tiny pieces and puzzled together. How the tribe had stolen her, presumably from wherever it was that Jude knew her from. How she had been one of the first breeders for the tribe. He detailed her descent into madness, culminating in her desperate act, throwing herself into the fire in hopes of ending it all.

Tears glistened in Leona's eyes.

"Were you..." she asked.

He shook his head. "I wasn't here then. I just heard the story told many times. Phoebe was a cautionary tale to the other girls."

Jude had gotten comfortable leaning back against the furs with my mother curled into the hollow of his shoulder. He held her close to him, and for a moment, I could picture her being the mother I needed. I could envision a family, with parents and children, little brothers chasing each other around. I couldn't see her scars from where I stood; she rested her face against his chest. Secure for a moment.

I looked away. It was almost too much. I couldn't see her like this—have this moment—because when it was gone again, it would hurt too much.

# TEN

## *Meredith*

WHAT HAVE I DONE?

It wasn't the first time I doubted myself on this trip. Being out in the cold with no one but yourself to talk to played tricks on your mind. The trees whispered amongst themselves as we passed. Just me and Thor on a fool's errand. We had to be getting close, but to what? Was anything left of the place I once knew? Had the winter taken them, scattering their bones like a scavenger?

My fingers ached from the cold and holding the reins and I was exhausted from staying upright in the saddle for so long. My body wasn't used to riding anymore. It hadn't been for a long time. I cursed it. I was stronger than I had been in so many ways, yet this was a whole new ball game. My muscles ached and protested, but I soothed them with kind words I didn't believe. Thor flicked his ears when I spoke to him, and as time passed I grew certain that he completely understood.

"Do you think we're almost there?" I asked the horse.

"I know... I'm cold too." I responded to his obvious reply. "You realize I'm talking to myself here. People are going to think I'm off my rocker."

Thor flicked his ears and turned his head to look at me

with his soft black eyeball.

"Don't roll your eyes at me," I said.

It was getting late, the colored streaks that painted the sky were slowly disappearing, devoured by the hungry and ever-growing darkness.

"I don't think we're going to make it tonight," I said, more to myself than to my silent company. I wasn't sure how far we still needed to go. For all I knew our destination was around the next bend, but we would make camp for the night anyway. It was too dangerous to travel in the dark, especially without sure footing for Thor. The snow was still melting slowly during the day, but as the sun set it hardened, creating a slippery and uneven surface, shining in the moonlight. I pulled the reins gently and guided Thor off the main path and into the woods. Once we were within the shelter of the giant conifers, I slid from the saddle and stretched my legs. I was already sore, which didn't bode well for the next few days. My thighs quivered, and my legs felt like they could barely support my weight. My toes and feet were numb but I stomped until they began to tingle and ache.

Thor waited patiently while I dug through the saddlebags and pulled out a small sack of grain. There probably wasn't enough left to curb his hunger, but it was all we had. Hopefully we would arrive tomorrow. Hopefully there was still someone there. Hopefully they would be able to help. I smiled and rolled my eyes as I set the sack on the ground and opened it so Thor could eat the grains inside.

"There are a lot of 'hopefullys' in there," I said, as if Thor was privy to my internal monologue. He said nothing, happily munching on oats.

I busied myself starting a small fire and pulling some thick boughs from the evergreens to fashion an acceptably comfortable bed for myself. I heated some water to make myself some tea, and chewed slowly on what was left of the bread and beef jerky I carried. I had a little bit of dried fruit left too, but that would serve as an acceptable breakfast.

Alone in the dark, I let the tears fall—let the feelings of failure wash over me as I wept silently. I should have been able to do something, somehow keep everything from snowballing out of control, but I had been powerless to stop it.

I was weak, a disappointment.

I brushed my wool mitten across my eyes, wiping away the tears before they froze to my eyelashes.

"I'm going to make it right, Thor," I said. "I'm going to find a way."

He said nothing.

# ELEVEN

## *Meredith – 20 years earlier*

"I DON'T REALLY KNOW what to make of this information," I said, "Forgive me Mitchell, you'll need to simplify it for me."

He had been insisting on an audience with me for years, I knew his type, a trained meteorologist with visions of the apocalypse, seeing doomsday around every corner. This meeting was nothing more than a favor to some powerful friends. Some days it felt like I needed to gather each and every vote myself, one at a time, begging and pleading for people to care.

"The ice sheets in Greenland are melting," he said. "Giant slabs of frozen water, fresh water, not salt water."

"I understand," I said.

Not really.

"We have been monitoring them and the volcanic activity beneath the sheets is increasing. If those sheets were to melt suddenly and flood the oceans with fresh water, the cooling trend in the northern hemisphere would be dramatic."

"That's a big 'if', isn't it?" I asked.

"In some ways, yes," said Mitchell, obviously irritated by my lack of alarm. "But combined with the recent lack of sunspot activity, it could potentially create a rather drastic situation."

I had learned many years ago about the link between sunspots and cloud cover, though I couldn't remember exactly how it worked. I did know that less sunspots equalled more cloud cover, and therefore more insulation from the sun's warming rays.

"So, more clouds—less warmth from the sun, plus melting ice sheets—less warmth from the ocean," I said.

"It's an oversimplification," said Mitchell, "but yes."

"So we're potentially looking at cooler weather?"

Mitchell did his best to maintain his professional demeanor, though I could tell it was cracking.

"Madam President," he said. "Weather is kind of like a light that works on a switch and a dimmer. You can make it brighter and dimmer slowly, but you can also flip the switch, and plunge yourself into darkness in an instant. It may be a gradual change, but I feel we really need to be prepared if the lights go out suddenly."

I nodded out of habit.

"Thank you for coming, Mitchell," I said. "I will pass your report to my advisors and we'll see if we can't come up with some kind of plan to deal with this."

I patted the thick stack of bound papers he had brought for me. It was unlikely that I would understand much of the information contained inside, but I had people who could translate it for me.

He nodded.

"Thank you, Madam President," he said, taking his leave.

Arianna appeared at the door, to guide him through the maze of hallways to the exit. I smiled at her and she rolled her eyes at me before leaving. She heard much of what happened in my office, and often offered me a sympathetic glance when my guests couldn't see.

I smiled and nodded to her as she left. I stood and picked up Mitchell's heavy report and carried it from my office, dumping it into Arianna's in-box. She would find a place for it, I was sure. I went back into my office and closed the door most of the way. Leaving enough of a crack that Arianna would know she could interrupt me, but not so much that it was an open invitation to anyone.

I did little more than shuffle papers around on my desk. There were documents that needed to be signed, though very little of any importance. It was mind-numbing, but after my meeting with Mitchell I was in no mood for anything intense.

"Arianna," I called.

Her face appeared at the door.

"Do we have anything from the Greetings Office?"

She laughed. "The meeting was that good, huh?"

There was always a stack from the Greetings Office, a department solely devoted to taking requests for celebratory cards from the presidency. We acknowledged milestone birthdays and anniversaries, retirements, bat mitzvahs, and the like from American citizens. Difficult days always included some time with the greetings pile. It required nothing more than a signature from me, but it reminded me that there really were people out there, living their lives and celebrating their milestones.

"I'll get you some," she said, disappearing for a moment before reappearing with an elastic-bound stack of cards. They were all addressed and written, just waiting for my signature.

I signed cards for over an hour, and barely made a dent in Arianna's supply. She would take them back to the Greetings office where they would be sealed and mailed to hopeful citizens. My hand had started to cramp from the tedious but heart-lifting work when the tablet on my desk that normally showed an image of the Presidential Seal blinked over to Arianna's face.

"Madam President, the Secretary of Homeland Security," said Arianna.

"Send her in."

I dropped my pen on the desk and stretched my hand, pushing the stack of cards away to clear a section of my desk. I didn't like to have work cluttering my desk when people came to meet with me, I preferred to give people the appearance of my undivided attention. It was rarely more than a facade, since it was impossible for me to fully clear my mind, but it was the best I could do.

"Eloise," I said, standing as she entered the office.

"Madam President," she said with a curt nod. She was dressed in a smart and well-tailored suit, her hair pulled back from her face into a tight ponytail at the nape of her neck. She had hair like mine, impossible to control without severe measures. Even still, a few of her tight curls were on the verge of escape. I ran my fingers through the hair on the side of my head self-consciously, tucking any strays behind my ear.

"What brings you here, Eloise?" I said, gesturing to the chair in front of my desk, as I sat down again.

"The relationship between you and the Vice President."

I raised an eyebrow.

"Not mincing any words, huh?"

"You know as well as I do that this is a strained situation."

I did. There were rarely days that I didn't regret taking the presidency with Nadia at my side. It had seemed like a brilliant move at the time, we each held the unwavering loyalty of a large segment of the population, so it seemed like everyone was happy. As time progressed, however, it started to feel more and more like we had led the country into one giant family feud. We agreed on almost nothing and I knew Nadia resented my power.

"We only have two more years until another election."

"May I be blunt, Madam President?"

"Always."

Eloise cleared her throat. "Recent intel would suggest you won't finish your term."

"I'm not sure what you mean by that," I said.

"We worry for your safety."

*Oh.*

I swallowed hard. Somehow I knew this day had been coming. Nadia was a ruthless and hungry person, though I had pushed those worries back, making myself believe that she wouldn't resort to such a cowardly action. I knew in my heart I was deceiving no one but myself.

"So what do we do?" I asked, my heart fluttering in my chest. Knowing Nadia's capabilities was one thing, hearing them from someone else was an entirely different experience that I wasn't sure I was ready for.

"We have established a safe house for you, not far from here, but as far as the government is concerned it doesn't exist. Nadia knows nothing about it, and if all goes according to plan, she never will."

I nodded.

"The only other member of top-level personnel that has been briefed on this is the Director of the Secret Service. She will be coming by later to brief you on your panic code, and the details."

I nodded again.

"Do you really think Nadia would kill me to take over the presidency?" I asked.

"Forgive me, Madam President. I think this is less a question of 'if', rather of 'when'."

"This safe house is fully staffed?"

"Of course," said Eloise, "with a special-ops military regiment with enough brute strength and firepower to guarantee a solid win against anything Nadia could pull together. If she were able to find you at all."

That was somewhat reassuring.

"Thank you, Eloise, for all you do." I caught her eye as she stood to leave. "Out of curiosity, have we done this before? It doesn't seem to fit with standard protocol, yet you seem to have it organized so well."

"We prepare for all scenarios," she said, "Even the unbelievable ones. I would be lying if I said this has never been considered, or even executed before."

I nodded. How many presidential terms in the past had been riddled with this level of mistrust?

"Could you do me another favor?" I asked.

"Of course, Madam President."

"Ask Arianna to give you the contact information for a man named Mitchell Ramirez. He has another unbelievable scenario for you, and I think it might be wise to consider, and perhaps even prepare for."

"Yes Ma'am."

I sat down in my chair as she left the room, swivelling it so I could look outside over the freshly mowed lawns and gushing fountains. The sun was shining and the sky was blue, and in that moment I wanted nothing more than to be out there with my bare feet wiggling in the grass and the beating sun warming my shoulders.

Instead I was here, in my thermostatically perfect office, with the distinct feeling that I would never be warm again.

LESS THAN A WEEK had passed before I found myself on Marine One with Renee, the Director of the Secret Service. I had no idea what excuse they had given to whisk me from my office that day, but there I was, under the beating rotors of the helicopter, making my way to a bunker that didn't exist.

We stayed low over the trees, and though I had headphones so I could hear Renee and the pilots, I had turned them off, so they did nothing but muffle the sound of the motors. I watched in silence as we skimmed over treetops lush with green leaves and rivers teeming with fish and waterfowl. It was a painting, as beautiful as any that graced the hallways and offices of the most powerful government in the world, but it struck me that this view was not as pure and untouched as it seemed. Somewhere under the light and the life was a place to cower, a place to hide from the darkness that was seeping in, lest it overtake us completely. I wished that none of this was necessary, though I knew it was and was grateful for it.

I could tell we were about to land, though I didn't see our destination. There was a small clearing in the woods but no sign of a building of any kind.

Rolling hills rose up on either side of us as the helicopter landed gently. The doors slid open and I unbuckled myself and followed Renee into the long grasses, the wind from the rotors tossing our hair in all directions as we ran with our heads low to clear the helicopter.

"Where is it?" I asked once we were far enough from the helicopter to talk without shouting.

"You'll see in a minute," she said as I followed her into the trees. A small hill loomed in front of us. It wasn't high, but the side facing us had a steep rock face. I was about to ask Renee about it when I heard a grinding sound. The rock itself was pulling backwards, sucking into the hill. It was amazing. I hadn't noticed anything that seemed manmade in any way, yet before my eyes the hill was transforming, and from behind the rock appeared a tall man in fatigues with a dark green beret perched on his head.

"Madam President," he said, with a salute.

"At ease, soldier," I said.

"Madam President, I'd like to introduce you to Sergeant First Class Leif Scott," said Renee. "On the books all members of this unit are retired service members, but as you can see they are still on active duty. This bunker was a leftover from the Cold War Two, and listed as fully decommissioned and destroyed. Nothing about this place exists. After you, Ma'am."

She pointed to the opening in the rock and I stepped toward it. It seemed like a small opening from where I stood, but as I walked closer I realized how large the door was, which made sense since Sergeant Scott was not a small man.

They followed me through the door and I heard Sergeant Scott give the command to close it behind us. The scratching and grinding of the rock door echoed through the surprisingly well-lit hallway.

"Welcome to Operation Hide-the-President," said Leif.

"Well, that's clever," I said, laughing. "Not obvious at all."

"If it doesn't exist, we can name it anything we want, Ma'am," he said, smiling. "I wasn't feeling terribly creative that morning."

"All good, Sergeant." I said. He was an incredibly handsome

man. The depth of his olive skin contrasted perfectly with eyes that were so pale and blue that I was reminded of sea glass sparkling in the wet sand. I had difficulty meeting his gaze and thanked the heavens that my skin was dark enough to hide a blush.

I could hear Renee describing the details of the bunker as we walked, but I wasn't listening. There was no doubt in my mind that they had thought of everything and taken every precaution.

"There is enough food here to last approximately twenty years without rationing. The majority of it is in freeze-dried rations to save space, but there is a fair amount of shelf-stable and frozen ingredients for simple cooking as well."

"Twenty years?" I said, startled back into listening, "Why so long?"

"It's easier to stock extra than try to obtain more supplies down the road. The less paper we can leave behind the better. A few trucks of military rations may disappear once and not many will notice. A constant draining trickle is easier to track."

"You're not going to be down here for twenty years, Ma'am," said Renee. "But at the same time, if disaster strikes while you are, we believed it was best to be prepared."

"How many people are down here?"

"Thirty-six in total, on two 18-body, 12-hour rotations," said Leif as he opened a solid metal door.

"Welcome to the brain," he said as we walked through the doors into a large room filled with people and computers. A woman stood from her desk and joined us, saluting when she stopped.

"Welcome, Madam President," she said.

I nodded to her.

"This is Sergeant First Class Emily Watson," said Leif, "She is in charge of Communications and Intelligence."

"Nice to meet you," I said.

"Thank you Ma'am, a pleasure to meet you as well," she said.

Her hair was dark and thick and tied in a braid down her back, and the way she held herself reminded me so much of Delta. A younger version at least. It was comforting to me in a strange way. Delta was one of those people who made every place feel like home. She carried herself with a certain confidence and understated dignity. Though she was only a few years older than I was, I saw her almost as a mother figure. She was a mother—sort of—many times over in fact. Though she'd never had a child of her own, she had adopted a whole herd of boys who would have otherwise grown up alone. I smiled as I thought of her kind heart and giving soul. We could all learn a few things from her.

For the next two hours, Renee, Leif and Emily briefed me on the protocols, panic codes, and procedures of Operation Hide-The-President. The level of detail involved in the operation amazed me. The hillside hid trucks and tanks and vehicles for almost every situation. There was even a helicopter hidden in a secret room beneath the clearing.

"It's for emergencies only," said Leif. "Once we open the ground above it, it would be next-to-impossible to hide again."

"It's basically just for evacuation," said Renee. "I hope we never need to use it."

I agreed, though the same could be said for this entire operation. I tried to absorb the things they told me, but it was difficult to separate the details of the operation from the fact that my own half-sister was a threat to my well-being.

But if I was honest with myself, there was never a time that she wasn't.

# TWELVE

## *Mila*

I DIDN'T SLEEP THAT night. My body felt heavy and
sluggish, and my eyes ached, but there was nothing I could do to
shut off my mind and allow a descent into slumber. My mother
was back, not that I had ever known her this way. If I slept, I
might lose her again. I doubted she was sleeping either. She had
always kept odd hours. Waking in the night and sleeping during
the day whenever she didn't have chores to do. I got used to
staying away from the hut during the day—I didn't like watching
her escape that way. I wanted her to be present. I wanted her to be
my mother, but until now I didn't know who that was.

I had cried until I ran out of tears. Whether they came
from being happy or sad I couldn't tell. I was angry at Jude. Who
was he to hold the key to my mother? Why did she need his key
to unlock the door I had been pounding on for years? I was her
daughter. She should have opened it for me.

The furs were warm and soft against my skin and I
snuggled down deeper, until not much more than my eyes were
showing. Their scent was rich and musky, the smell of tanned
leather and human sweat. The fire was low, little more than a few
flames and some glowing red embers. Every so often it crackled

and popped, sending sparks sailing toward the open hole in the roof. This hut should have slept four or five women, but most of the tribe didn't want to stay with us. For the most part they avoided us altogether. I got it. My mom was weird and her very presence made people uncomfortable, until today.

I watched the fire as it moved and changed, and as always tried not to imagine what it would have felt like to fall into the flames. Tears trickled from eyes I thought were empty. She needed Jude, for whatever it was that she needed. He brought her out of that despair and how could I fault him for it? I pushed the anger down, the voice in my head that told me that I should have been enough for her, that I should have been the one to find her, that she should have held on, if only for me.

But it wasn't the truth.

I heard my mother move before I saw her. She moved slowly and I knew she thought I was asleep. I closed my eyes and listened as she crept through the hut, pulling on her boots and wrapping her long fur cloak around her shoulders. I waited until the flap closed behind her before getting up and pulling on my own boots and coat. I knew where she was going, but somehow I needed to see it. I hurried through the door and up the few steps into the camp. The moon was bright and cast eerie shadows across the snow in a pale blue glow. I could see my mother jogging between the huts, her cloak billowing out behind her as she slid from shadow to shadow. I followed her, my buckskin moccasins silent on the hard snow. If she knew I was following her, she gave no indication, creeping quietly into the hut Athena had offered

Jude and the others for the night.

I stood in the cold, clean air. It was silent, except for the faint breeze whispering through the treetops and kissing my bare cheeks. Smoke from each hut drifted upwards in a lazy climb, and no one moved. The village was asleep. I bit down hard on my lip as hot tears gathered in my eyes. I refused to guess what was happening in that hut, though I found it difficult to banish the thought from my mind. I resisted the urge to follow her into the hut, demanding that my feet turn me around and return me to our own. I swallowed hard to force away the lump that threatened to take control.

Slipping through the flap into the warmth of the hut I should have been sharing with my mother, I let my coat drop from my shoulders onto the hard earth floor. The fire was dwindling, and though I knew it would be fine until morning, I plunked a few dry logs onto the small pile of red embers, sending a torrent of sparks up through the hole in the ceiling. Athena would snap at me if she saw. I had learned the dangers of fire as a child, especially indoor fires, and it didn't take much more than an errant spark to cause damage. I rolled my eyes in defiance to the imaginary lecture and then glanced around to make sure none of the sparks had actually found a place to smolder.

With the fire ablaze once more, the chill was chased from the hut, and I let the warmth creep back into my icy extremities. I watched as the flames devoured the wood I had added, and wondered—not for the first time—what it would have taken for my mother to throw herself into them. I shivered at the thought, and felt immediately ashamed. I should have been thankful to Jude for bringing her back, thankful for finding the person she had been under the mountain of scars she carried. He had given me my mother, and in the same breath, he had taken her even farther away.

# THIRTEEN

## *Athena*

WE ALL WAITED, SOME less patiently than others. I could
feel the buzz of anticipation around the camp. It was palpable,
electric. Everyone knew the stories by now, it had spread in
whispers and nods around the campfires the previous night. It
seemed strange to me that the women I had grown up with were
so enthralled and interested by the story the outsiders brought.
How was it so different than what we had done? Perhaps that was
what made it interesting. Maybe they thought we were alone, the
only ones who thought far enough ahead to make plans. They
had followed Asari almost blindly, drinking in her lust for power
and following her orders. We were strong. So strong. I would have
followed her forever.

Things had changed when my parents had assumed
control of the camp. What had once been a rule of strict
command—a bloodthirsty army bent on having its way—became
a more peaceful society. Our rabid hunger was replaced with
something different. We were still steadfast, determined, but it was
as if the burning intensity had deflated.

It was better, I supposed, but there was something inside
of me. A fire in my belly that had yet to be extinguished. It was

small, barely more than a spark but given the right circumstances I knew I could fan it to the bonfire it once was. However, since marrying Torren I had felt wrapped in some kind of damp cloak, threatening to snuff out that tiny flame.

I fought it. I pushed it back. Kept the fire alive.

For what? Did I even need it any longer?

"Has Nova said anything yet?"

Mila had joined me by the cooking fire. The sun was bright and it was almost a pleasant temperature. The snow was glistening underfoot, melting slowly in the blinding light. I found it almost too warm under my coat by the fire, but I wasn't ready to take it off.

"Not yet," I said.

I had hoped she would have come to a decision by now. Since the sun came up, everyone had been milling around and watching her hut for a sign of movement. But even now at nearly afternoon, the door flaps lay still. The outsiders had built themselves a fire on the outskirts of camp, cooking their own food and melting snow to drink. It hadn't escaped my notice that Phoebe had crept from their hut in the wee hours, and I doubted Mila had missed it either.

"Asari would have made a decision by now."

I rolled my eyes.

"Of course she would have," I said. Asari had been nothing if not impulsive, guided by her gut. "Look where her decisions got her."

"Oh yeah," said Mila.

"She'll make the right decision," I said, not sure who I was trying to convince.

Picking up the long-handled wooden spoon I gave the stew in my pot a quick stir. There would easily be enough for everyone, even the outsiders if they wanted. The cast-iron cauldron always had something in it. Today it was bear. Better than squirrel or racoon I mused. It was starting to stick to the bottom, so I scraped as I stirred, hoping to keep the stew moving enough to avoid burning. Burned bear stew was awful, but there was no such thing as wasting food.

Mila nodded. Her fair head bobbing up and down, less likely because she believed me, and more likely because of habit. She had found herself a seat on one of the logs we used as chairs around the fire, and had pulled her knees up to her chest. She looked cold, but I doubted that's what was bothering her.

"I kind of want them to go."

I raised an eyebrow. Mila would tell me what she wanted to whether I responded or not.

"Your mother seems a lot less nuts with them here."

She glared at me. "Shut up, Athena."

I shrugged. "It's the truth."

She couldn't disagree.

I glanced across the camp to where the outsiders were talking quietly by their fire. I could see Phoebe there; her pale blonde hair was difficult to miss. She was sitting next to that Jude fellow, a little closer than average acquaintances would sit. She wasn't part of the conversation but she had a strange, drifting smile that played across her lips. Her eyes looked distant, as though she was playing back some kind of happy memory in her brain that no one else could see.

"You're jealous," I said to Mila.

"Wouldn't you be?"

"Probably."

So we had more in common than I had originally thought. Sitting by that fire was someone who had stirred a jealousy in me too, but I wasn't about to admit that to Mila. I had grown up with a handful of sisters, but as the eldest I had enjoyed a certain level of authority. Finding out now that I had an older sister was a source of constant irritation to me, grating on my nerves like a whetstone sharpening steel. I would be lying if I said I didn't think about that often while sharpening my own blades. I hadn't spent enough time with Leona to assess what kind of threat she was. I hadn't even spoken to my mother—our mother—about her yet. Once she left I found it easier to pretend she had never come at all, yet there she was. If we stood next to each other, it was doubtful that anyone would know we were sisters. Her looks favored our mother, her auburn locks mimicking Nova's once red mane. My looks came from our father, Dax, and while I prided myself on my dark waves and had never once been self-conscious about my looks, feeling compared to her was frustrating.

"I want them to go too," I said, my voice low. "Do you think your mom would go with them?"

It was a valid question, however mean and inappropriate.

"Probably."

I had expected a snotty, petulant answer from Mila, so I was surprised to hear her concede.

"She seems happy, if that's any consolation."

"Happier than with me."

Now there was the self-absorbed teenager I knew and loved.

"Your mom hasn't had it easy, you know."

Everyone knew Phoebe's story. The only reason she was still alive was because no one could bring themselves to slaughter such a broken soul. We had broken her, and she was our burden to bear.

"I know," said Mila, watching her mother by the outsiders' fire.

"You should be happy she's back."

"I get it Athena," she said, sullen. "I'm selfish and stupid and annoying, you're not telling me anything I haven't told myself."

I put down the spoon and turned to face her directly. Raising my hand to her chin she flinched, figuring I was going to slap her. I didn't fault her for it.

"You have feelings," I said, not entirely sure if I was talking to her or myself. "You are allowed to have them and no one should say you're not. But, if I can give you one piece of advice: suck it up and go get to know your mother. You never know how long she'll stay like this, and you'll regret it if you don't."

Tears were brimming in Mila's eyes, though I knew she was doing her best to control them. She nodded with my hand still on her chin. I slapped her cheek gently.

"Go," I said, nodding toward the outsiders.

She hesitated.

"Don't make me have to drag you there by your ear."

She stood and with a sideways glance at me, left. I watched as she made her way to the other fire. Buck stood to leave the space beside Phoebe open for her to slip into. He placed a hand on her shoulder for a second and found another place to sit.

I went back to my stirring.

I didn't have to look up to know that Torren was on his way over. I recognized the sound of his gait on the snow.

"Yes, husband?" I said.

*What could you possibly want now?*

"Could you sharpen my knife?" he said, dropping it and its leather sheath on the log beside me.

*It's not my fault no one taught you how to do it properly.*

"Of course," I said. "After lunch."

"Super," he said, sliding down onto the log beside me, his legs straddling it.

"How's the baby?" he asked.

I shrugged.

"Good I think," I said.

*Because I can see inside my belly and ask it, right?*

"Good."

His arm settled around me and rubbed my back. I relaxed into his touch. It was comforting. Physical contact wasn't all that common around here, and even though Torren grated on my nerves sometimes, it was nice to feel wanted.

"Any word from my mother?" I asked.

He shook his head. "Nothing yet. I'm going to go talk to the others."

I watched him as he stood, his lean tight frame stretching to the sky beside me like the trees that surrounded the camp. He blocked out the sun and I looked up into his silhouette.

"See you later?" I said, with a teasing face.

"Of course," he said with a wink.

And then he was gone, and I was in the sun again.

# FOURTEEN

## *Meredith*

The fire was out when I opened my eyes to another frosty morning. I cursed under my breath. A nice hot cup of tea would have been a nice way to start the morning, but the idea of gathering wood and re-starting the fire just to boil some water seemed far too daunting. I sat up pushing back the bedroll Ember had packed for me and groaned. Every muscle in my body protested as I got myself to a sitting position and yawned.

"This had better be the last night out here, Thor," I said to the horse. He flicked his ears, looked at me and said nothing, which I took as a good sign.

"If you start talking back, I'll know I'm in trouble."

We were close, of that much I was sure. I had consulted my map by the firelight the previous night and if my calculations were correct, there were less than a few miles to go, provided of course the place I was looking for still existed. I knew they had enough supplies to make it this long, but anything could happen in nearly two decades. *Decades.* Had it truly been that long? I wouldn't have blamed any of the people staffing the bunker for fleeing to their families, but I had to hope that at least a few of them had remained. They would be safest there, realistically. If there was any place to wait out this winter—could it even be called a winter?—it was there. The bunker was stocked with food and water, the latest technologies, everything someone would need to stay alive. Like "the caves", the bunker was mainly underground, safe from the harshest winds and easy to keep warm enough. I shivered at the thought of warmth. How long had it been since I was truly and completely warm?

Before standing, I dug through the pack. There were no more grains left for Thor, and only a good sized handful of dried fruit for my own breakfast. It would do nothing to rid me of the persistent rumble in my stomach, but I had lived with less for so long that I barely noticed it anymore. Pulling out the small muslin sack, I poured half of what was left into my hand and held it up to the horse that was now towering over me, hoping for food.

"You'll need it as much as I will," I said as his warm lips pressed against my stiff, cold hand.

When he was done and my hand was empty, I poured the rest out and shoved it all in my mouth at once. It was cold but sweet and chewy, and full of nutrients I knew I would need.

Thor protested and nudged my head with his nose.

"I don't have any more, you big lug," I said with my mouth full to bursting. I probably should have taken my time eating it, but I didn't feel like being out here a moment longer than necessary. I held onto Thor's bridle as I struggled to my feet, my legs afire with pins and needles. When I let go, he pressed his nose into my chest, nearly knocking me off balance.

"Quit it, would you?" I said as I steadied myself on a tree, pulling on my mittens.

He was probably angry that I had no food left to give him, but being pushy wasn't going to help either of us. I was tempted to wrap the sleeping bag around my shoulders as we rode, but it would probably be more of a bother than it was worth, so I rolled it up as best as I could with stiff, aching hands and shoved it into the pack. I grasped Thor's reins and walked out of the trees, hoping to get the blood moving in my legs again. Thor followed. Once we were out from under the cover of branches, I swung myself into the saddle, groaning as my bruised thighs and buttocks found their place on the frosty, hard leather.

"We're almost there, Thor," I said, hoping I wasn't lying. I squeezed my legs together and guided him in the right direction. I didn't need to check my map, because I could feel the pull of it from the deepest part of me, a part I had been pushing back for years, a whisper I refused to acknowledge because I knew merely speaking his name would break me.

"I'm coming Leif."

# Fifteen

## *Meredith – 19 years earlier*

IF THERE WAS ANY benefit to being the President, it had to be the sheets. I could feel them wrap around me, caressing me as I rolled over, as soft as the dream from which I was slowly waking. The sun trickled in and sliced across the room in shining slivers through the wooden blinds. I closed my eyes again and murmured as hands pulled my hair back from my shoulders and soft lips kissed the place where my neck met my shoulder.

"Good morning, beautiful."

I sighed and didn't answer as he kissed my neck all the way to the hollow behind my ear.

There were days when I couldn't believe a year had passed since I had first laid eyes on Leif Scott, and other days when I could have sworn he had been part of me forever. I could barely remember the time before him, as if my life had been segmented into two separate volumes. The one from before had long since grown dusty on the nightstand. It had started innocently enough, as it always does—a few furtive glances, a conspiratorial smile during a briefing session. Leif and Emily travelled from the bunker often to meet with Renee and discuss Operation Hide-the-President. They came under other pretenses I was sure, because only a select few were aware of their true purpose. Renee would assign them to different stations in the White House for certain periods to be familiarized with the goings-on and my personal schedule. Though I had never bothered to ask. I began watching for him, wondering where he was when he wasn't here and what he was doing. It became a type of obsession. I found myself growing jealous when he wasn't there, or being strangely giddy when he was. Even Arianna had started wondering what was coming over me.

It was she who had figured it out, and I started noticing our schedules began to overlap more and more. Without ever discussing it with me, she made time for us, built moments with Leif into my schedule.

"I really need to give that girl a raise," I said.

"Hm?" said Leif.

"Never mind," I said. "Just making a mental note."

"I'm not sure if I should be insulted," Leif said, his voice playing as his hand swept through my hair. "You're thinking of other things."

"I always think of other things," I said, rolling onto my back so I could look into his icy blue eyes. "I'm a woman, that's how we do it."

"That's what makes you good at what you do," he said. "If I was in your place, I wouldn't be able to concentrate on my work."

"It goes both ways," I said, laughing. "It means I can also think about you when I'm working."

"You think about me?"

"More than I'm willing to admit," I said.

"I'll admit to thinking about you," said Leif, "Like, right now, all I can think about is..."

"Is that all you can ever think about?"

He stopped, with fake indignation, "I was going to say that I was thinking about how hard you work keeping this fine nation working at its best."

I laughed out loud.

"Malarkey," I said.

"I can keep my mind above your breasts, you know," he said, then whispered "though staying there is fun too, I'll admit."

I rolled my eyes as he kissed me lightly on the lips.

"You need to get out of here," I said, glancing at the clock on the bedside table. "I have a ridiculous amount of meetings this morning, and it won't be long before Arianna shows up with my itinerary."

"Arianna wouldn't be surprised to see me in here," said Leif, still kissing my neck.

"I know," I said, "but the hallways are clear now. They won't be soon."

He nodded and groaned as he rolled from the bed.

"It's frustrating to have to leave you, you know," he said.

I knew all too well.

I watched him as he pulled on the uniform that he had neatly hung over the plump stuffed chair. It was a habit of his when he came to see me. Considering how starched and pressed he looked normally, it would be too obvious to be wandering the

White House with a rumpled appearance. I knew I too should be climbing from the enveloping warmth and comfort of my bed, but I couldn't help but watch him as he buttoned each button of his shirt, his large hands surprisingly nimble.

"Marry me," I said.

It was impulsive. The words were barely formed in my mind before they spilled from my mouth. It caught me off guard, and I could tell it had the same effect on him. He paused mid button and his eyes crossed the bed, followed the curve of the blankets that barely concealed my form until they rested on mine. I met his gaze, letting myself be swallowed into the pale blue.

"Are you serious?" he asked.

I swallowed and nodded. Suddenly I was afraid, and it took every ounce of self-control to not immediately recant my words, stumbling back over them in an effort to run away from what I knew to be true. I held my tongue and nodded again, searching his face for some indication that he felt the same way I did.

When I saw the tiniest flutter in the edges of his lips, I knew I said the right thing. His face broke into a smile and relief flooded through me. He crawled back onto the bed, on his hands and knees, until his face was level with mine. I could feel the happiness and excitement in the room, and I laughed because I couldn't imagine a moment where laughter was more appropriate.

"Do you have plans for today?"

"Dang it, I do," I said. "But I can have Arianna clear my schedule for tomorrow."

"Tomorrow," he said.

I reached up and cupped his face in my hands, the beautiful olive skin and searing blue eyes. Mine.

"You haven't answered me," I said with a smile. I knew his answer as well as I knew my own, but I wanted to hear it. I wanted to hear the words come out of his mouth and be written on my heart.

"Yes, Meredith Kroeker," he said. "With every thought in my mind and every beat of my heart. Yes."

"Tomorrow," I said.

He kissed my lips and lingered there.

"Tomorrow."


"I'M GOING TO NEED you to clear my schedule for tomorrow afternoon," I said to Arianna after she had briefed me on my day's itinerary. I was leaning back in my desk chair, having asked her to meet me at the office rather than my quarters. I needed the time walking the hallways to work out the excited jitters. Without it, I doubted I'd be able to sit still for long.

"It's not going to be easy," she said.

"I don't care, it needs to be done."

She studied me over her glasses, her hand paused in midair over her tablet, as if she was waiting for me to tell her I was joking.

"Do you want me to schedule something in place of everything I'm cancelling?"

I smiled, knowing that she was digging for an interesting tidbit. I had never before asked her to reschedule an entire afternoon without giving her some kind of explanation.

"I'll be attending a wedding."

"A wedding?"

"Yes," I said. "Mine."

Her face lit up and her mouth formed an impossibly tiny circle.

"You're getting married?" she whispered.

If there was any chance of controlling my excitement, it dissipated with her perfectly surprised reaction. I laughed.

"Yes," I said. "Though, if we could keep it from becoming common knowledge, I would appreciate it."

"Of course," she said, suddenly making a few hasty notes on her tablet. "I will move everything around with the utmost discretion."

It wasn't unusual for my meetings to be rescheduled to favor the most important ones, and I didn't think I had anything that was terribly pressing on the calendar for the next day.

"Who am I seeing first this morning?" I asked, as much as I wanted to revel in my own happiness, I needed to get my head on straight. I still had a country to run.

"Eloise will be here in ten minutes to brief you on your trip to the medical labs."

I groaned. I wasn't looking forward to this one. It was necessary, but any conflict with Nadia was low on my list of fun things to do. I had given her the task of overseeing the fertility trials. Population had been dropping for the last decade, due in part to the effects of the cellutation vaccinations. We had scientists working for years to figure out a way to combat this side-effect, but so far, they had not been fruitful. It had seemed like a giant project at the time, and asking Nadia to take care of it fulfilled a selfish purpose: getting her out of my hair. If I could keep her busy enough working on something I had little interest in doing, we could get twice the amount done and never actually need to work together.

It was a great plan in theory. In practice, it was making me grasp giant handfuls of my already unmanageable curls in a constant desire to rip them from their roots. I had somehow, perhaps conveniently, forgotten that Nadia was typically short on ethics. The prize was won no matter how she chose to play the game. Rumors had been coming in recently about those ethics, namely that she was working on a plan to steal a serum from another private medical lab, MedTech, by threatening their first human test case. It was ridiculous, especially since we had the resources to work together with MedTech and, if the serum worked, give them national exposure. It didn't matter to me who invented a solution to the problem, as long as it would become available to my citizens.

But Nadia didn't think that way.

It was a race—a contest—and she needed to win at all costs.

As usual, I was the one who had to pull the plug.

"Thanks Arianna," I said.

One more day. One more day of frustrations and Nadia and hair-pulling and tomorrow would come. Tomorrow would change only a small part of my life, but knowing Leif was in my corner would change everything.

Tomorrow was for me.

I leaned back in my chair and watched as she left, still swiping things on her tablet and making quick notes.

Eloise was right on time, as usual. I often wondered if her internal clock was infallible or if she typically just arrived early and waited in the halls for the exact right moment. I should remember to ask Arianna.

"Good Morning, Madam President," she said "Are we ready for our trip?"

I rolled my eyes. She knew well enough that I would never be fully ready to confront my half-sister.

"I assume you have made the necessary preparations?" I asked, ignoring her thinly veiled jab. As Director of the Secret Service, Eloise was very familiar with Nadia, and she didn't need me to tell her that this morning wasn't going to be fun. While I typically had the same core staff of secret service members, Nadia's changed on a regular rotation, at my orders. I couldn't trust people around her for very long, she had a way of getting into heads and making otherwise reasonable people understand and sympathize with her unreasonable ways. As it was, there were key members of the government who I knew would side with her against me if it came to that.

Eloise nodded. "We will take you to the car in an hour."

"Perfect," I said. "Thank you, Eloise."

After the door closed behind her I stood from my desk and walked to the window. It was a beautiful summer day, the kind where normal people considered ditching work or school and finding the nearest beach or poolside. I unlatched the window and pushed it open so the warm summer breeze could find its way in and brush my face. My thin blouse was almost too heavy for the weather, but it was rare that I was seen outside my quarters looking anything less than properly put-together. While I dressed in the latest fashions, I had to maintain an image that was appropriate for a woman in my standing. I inhaled, sucking the warm air into my lungs and closed the window, revelling for only a second about how lovely it would be to shed my armor and step, bare-shouldered and bare-footed onto the lawn.

I distracted myself with the work on my desk, and did my best not to watch the seconds tick by.

Eloise and my Secret Service agents arrived at my door five minutes before they said I would be in the car. We walked together through the hallways. People moved out of our way, and I could hear them greeting me as I passed. I smiled and nodded but didn't really pay attention to those who were speaking to me.

It wasn't until we stepped through the front doors that I realized the sun had disappeared behind a thick bank of grey clouds. A cool breeze met me as we descended the steps to the waiting cavalcade.

"Wasn't it just warm and beautiful outside?" I asked Eloise, wondering if my personal excitement had somehow dreamed those moments breathing through the open window.

"It was, Ma'am," she said.

"It's cold for this time of year."

"Agreed, Ma'am."

I pulled my jacket closer around me and hurried to the car Eloise guided me to. A stiff wind blew my skirt as I climbed into the backseat.

"Would you like an extra coat, Ma'am?" asked the man holding the door.

"Yes please," I said. They carried any number of supplies in my cars, though I couldn't remember ever needing the spare coat in July.

We drove through the streets to the medical labs, and as I watched the people on the street it was becoming increasingly obvious that I wasn't the only one confused by the weather. Hot-dog vendors were struggling to dismantle their umbrellas lest the wind blow them away. Tourists huddled together on street corners waiting for the lights to change so they could race back to their hotels and change out of their shorts and t-shirts.

We pulled up to the medical labs and as I stepped from the car into a wind that was even colder than only minutes ago, my heart sank as I realized exactly how wrong it all was.

It was snowing.

# Sixteen

## *Mila*

OUR BELLIES HEAVY WITH bear stew and our
conversation light, I sat by my mother at the outsiders' fire.
Athena had offered them all some stew and they ate their fill, not
wanting to be impolite. Buck—Orion, it was still hard to think of
him as that—and Leona visibly enjoyed the thick meaty sludge,
though they were well accustomed to it. The two younger men,
Dutch and Olly, as well as Jude, Finn, Rowan and Ember's father,
Archer were hesitant at first, tasting slowly before digging in—the
warmth and hearty protein drawing them in quickly. Ember
seemed uninterested, too preoccupied to eat much more than a
few mouthfuls, but she did at Leona's urging. Rebekkah too ate
slowly, chewing each mouthful for longer than seemed necessary.
Torren had joined the group shortly after I did, and Athena now
sat beside him, swirling his knife on the flat piece of stone that sat
in her lap. She was brilliant with a whetstone; no one in the camp
could outmatch her sharpening skills. By the time she was done
with Torren's knife, it would be sharp enough to shave with, which
is probably the reason Torren's face was as neatly groomed as it
was. I hadn't ever seen a man's face without hair on it, none of
them bothered with it, but Torren regularly tidied up the edges of

his beard, rather than letting it grow wild like the others.

"Meat," said Finn, his mouth full. "I love meat."

The other men grunted in approval.

Jude nodded. "It's probably best we don't mention this to Rayne, he likes nothing better than a stomach full of meat." Silence fell over them. I didn't know who Rayne was, or why they would suddenly hush.

I watched as Rebekkah smiled at Jude, her eyes soft and sympathetic. Finn didn't seem bothered. Perhaps he didn't know who Rayne was, or he was more interested in the food than the conversation. Rebekkah inched herself down the log closer to Finn and whispered something to him. It fascinated me to watch her. Even without useable legs, she did what she needed to. Sure, there were times when Finn would carry her, and she had ridden here on a horse while the others walked. But the rest of the time, she just made do. Leona ate her stew with almost half her fingers missing. My mother, sitting between them both, smiled despite the thick scars that disfigured her face. Without realizing it, I stretched my fingers out and touched my own face, smooth and unmarred, I wiggled my toes in my boots and pushed my legs out in front of me.

While I had been watching the other women around the fire, the conversation had shifted—as it had done many times before—to the reason we were all here.

"I'm sure she'll agree to go with us," said Leona, "How could you not? Knowing everything that's happening at the estate."

"I don't know," said Orion. "If you think about it, how is it so different than what was happening here? More sterile, sure, but basically the same thing."

"But my mother had nothing to do with that," said Leona, protesting.

"I didn't say she did, just that given the circumstances here, it doesn't seem like such a crazy thing."

"You think what Asari made us do wasn't crazy?" said Leona, her eyes glaring at her husband.

"Whoa! Don't put words in my mouth that I didn't say. I never want to be in that situation ever again, and I would never wish it on anyone else either. No matter what Nova says, we're going to get Ember's sister and those other girls out of there. If we can't, I'm going to die trying."

No one spoke. We all knew the story of Leona and Orion. What happened inside their hut was never spoken of, but that they somehow managed to come out of it was a testament to Leona's strength. Orion was as much a victim as Leona was and though no one would have blamed her for hating him for what he did, she found enough strength inside her to forgive him. I didn't know if I had that inside of me.

"Don't die," Leona whispered.

"I'm not planning on it," he said and scooped another heaping spoonful of stew into his mouth.

"Besides," he added, his mouth still full. "I'm going in there with the sharpest shooter I know. What could possibly go wrong?"

Leona glared at him.

"You know I haven't gotten the feel of my bow yet," she said.

"You thought I was talking about you?" he said with mock surprise. "I was talking about Dutch."

Leona swatted him while Dutch laughed.

"Get me some knives and I'll show you who the sharpest shot is," Leona said, fierce with competition.

A knife flew through the fire and embedded itself in the log beside her, less than an inch from her hand.

"Use Torren's," said Athena, smiling.

Torren whistled and the others looked back and forth between Leona and Athena as they locked eyes.

"You'll find it's exceptionally sharp. Be careful with the fingers you have left."

"Athena," said Torren in a warning voice, and her eyes immediately dropped to her lap.

"Forgive me," she said. "I meant no slight."

That was not the response I expected from Athena, and looking around me, I wasn't alone in my surprise. Leona didn't seem terribly surprised and neither did Ember. Many of the others seemed, at the very least, disappointed that there would be no competition.

"Thanks Athena," said Leona, "but I think I've lost my appetite for competition."

She pulled the knife from the log and tossed it to Torren who caught it deftly and slid it into its sheath.

"Aw," said Dutch. "I was hoping for a little fun."

"I'll take you on, pup," said Orion.

"Really?" said Dutch, obviously excited about the prospect of a diversion. "Don't forget, you called me the sharpest shot."

"Don't you forget," said Orion, "that I was the one who took down that deer."

"He has you there, Dutch," Jude said, laughing and clapping his younger friend on the back.

"That was you?" said Dutch, his jaw dropping.

"If you'd listen to some of the conversation around the campfire, you would have figured it out too," said Jude.
Orion stood and stretched his massive frame. His longbow was leaning against the hut nearby, never far from reach, and Dutch still wore his slung across his back. Dutch crossed his arms, not fazed by Orion's confidence.

"Well, whatever," said Dutch. "No one can beat my shooting, especially not combined with Jude's arrows. I still have your perfect one, by the way."

"I should hope so," said Jude. "I don't make arrows so you can shoot them off into the woods."

Orion picked up his bow and quiver.

"I once heard," he said, "that it's a poor carpenter who blames his tools, I think it's a poor marksmen who relies on them. I don't need your perfect arrow, though you know, I wouldn't mind winning it off you."

"Like that would ever happen," said Dutch, confidence dripping off his words.

Around the campfire, we conferred and conspired, taking sides as the two men puffed and preened. They set off into the trees to create their contest with many of the others following to join in or serve as judges.

"Boys," said Athena, who was one of the few left at the fire.

I wasn't sure if she was merely commenting on their immaturity, or if part of her irritation was knowing she could have probably beat either of them. I opted for the latter.

"Why don't you go show them what you can do?" I asked.

"I have no need," she said, "and besides, I don't have time for that kind of buffoonery."

She got up and left. I let her go, indifferent to whatever kind of mood she was in. Plus the outsiders were more interesting. There were only a few of us left at the fire. Archer was still eating his stew, as if he hadn't noticed everyone else had left. Ember, too, still seemed distant. I couldn't blame either of them.

I sat in silence. There was something I had wanted to ask Ember, but so far I hadn't had the nerve. She had always interested me somewhat. Her dark eyes with their golden specks sucked me in, but I had wanted to ask about the thin tattooed line on her face. Tattoos were far from uncommon in the camp—almost all of the women here had them, on their faces too—but theirs were all pictures, and had meanings. Ember's was just a line. Nova's wolf tattoo, or Athena's intricate patterns were beautiful if not intimidating, but had a purpose. I couldn't understand what Ember's tattoo meant.

Finally I mustered the courage to ask. There were so few people around and it was such a simple question, no one would notice.

"Why do you have that line on your face?" I asked. I probably could have been less abrupt, but was there a good way of asking a question like that?

Archer immediately stood and left the fire. Ember frowned and watched him go.

"It means I'm sterile," she said.

"Sterile?" I had heard the word before. Nova used it when she was bandaging people's wounds, or trying to prevent illness. Ember's eyes settled on mine, as if she was analyzing me.

"It means I can't have children."

Her answer as strange to me. Most of the women in the camp couldn't have children. I must have looked confused, since Ember's eyes softened and she walked over to where I was sitting and sat beside me.

"The world before was... different," she said. "No one was having babies anymore, either because they couldn't, or because they didn't want to. Some people were starting to panic, so girls started disappearing."

"Like your sister?" I asked.

She nodded. "Right after my sister was taken my parents took me to a doctor and took away any chance I had to have a child. They thought it would protect me. It started snowing the same day."

"But why the line?"

"It's part of the procedure, it just appeared. I guess a lot of women wanted people to know."

"Why?"

Ember shrugged. "Maybe to protect themselves? Or as a status symbol? It wasn't terribly fashionable to have kids back then."

"And now?"

"Now it's necessary."

"That's why the tribe took my mother?" I asked.

She nodded. "And Leona, and Orion, even Nova. Asari knew they would never survive if they weren't able to produce children here. You need the young to take care of the old."

"And that's why they took your sister?"

"Yes."

It was starting to make sense. There was so little I knew of the time before. My mother had been in no state to explain it to me, and the rest of the tribe mainly ignored me.

"So do they all have lines like you under their tattoos?" I asked.

"I think so," said Ember. "Though some don't, like Nova and Athena."

But no one would know the difference.

With hoots and hollers the archers came back, Dutch and Orion looked irritated.

"Who won?" asked Archer, looking up from his stew as if it wasn't completely obvious that neither Orion nor Dutch had come away the victor.

"Rowan did," said Ember, smiling as her husband appeared from behind the others, carrying his prize.

Dutch muttered under his breath.

"Quit whining," said Jude to his younger friend. "He beat you fair and square."

Rowan walked to Ember and handed her the arrow, kissing her on the forehead as he sat down beside us. Ember turned and slid it into her quiver.

"Perhaps you should have made a big deal about your skill," she said to Rowan with her tongue firmly in her cheek. "You should always make sure people know how talented you are before agreeing to a bet."

Rowan chuckled softly, stretched out his legs and said nothing more.

He didn't need to. He had won.

# Seventeen

## *Shayna*

"HOW DID IT COME to this?" Delta asked.

I didn't bother to answer. We'd had this conversation so many times in the last years that it seemed redundant to reply. We both took turns asking, and we'd both given up answering. We could discuss the political atmosphere before the world froze, society's ambivalence toward children, even cellutation and its effects on fertility, but none of it meant anything anymore. Looking through the glass at the women who lay before us, bathed in blue light, their lives disappearing without them even noticing it, there was no reconciling any of it.

"I guess a better question would be, at what point did things like this become right? Or normal?"

"Those are very different things," I said. "Right and normal. What's normal isn't always right, and what's right isn't always normal. Far from it, actually."

People were often able to convince themselves that they were doing the right thing because everyone else was doing it too. It was one of the major flaws of humanity. Right and wrong got muddled into popular opinion and the lines were blurred. Suddenly it became less about what was right, and more about what each individual wanted for themselves. Once the focus turned to each individual, it was all too easy to forget that all those other people around you were also individuals. It was easy to forget that they too had rights and needs.

Nadia lived in her own movie, where everyone else played a part in her story. Everyone was expendable, subhuman. That's how we got here.

"I remember when I was in med school," I said, "I did a semester in OB-GYN, and the stories I heard, Delta, you wouldn't have believed them."

Delta didn't respond, still staring at the immobile women on the other side of the glass. We came here as much as we could. It didn't seem right to leave them alone, even if they had no idea. I continued without provocation, filling the empty space with my words.

"Years before I got to med school, and even as recently as a year or two before, they had big problems in the maternity ward. People, nurses mostly, were stealing infants. Apparently there was some sort of black market for them, girls specifically, that everyone knew about but no one spoke of."

I could clearly remember the stern lectures we had been given, not only to not be swayed by the massive amounts of money that could be made, but also to keep our eyes open for any of that sort of behaviour and report it. No one ever did though. It always seemed that they would find some poor, marginalized, often teenaged mother and everyone would turn a blind eye.

"How...? How?"

I noticed Delta was now watching me intently. Her face was white and her eyes were wide. It was unlike her to react to something like this. After all the terrible things she had seen in her life, I had figured she was immune.

"Um, let me see," I said, trying to remember. "I think in one case, there was a nurse—she was fairly notorious for this—she would usually time it when there was a child who had just died, or a stillbirth. She would keep the child warm in an incubator and if a baby girl was born the same day, she'd whisk them away to get checked out or something, and then bring the dead child to the mother, saying something had gone wrong."

Delta appeared to be having trouble breathing.

"Are you ok?" I asked, grabbing her arm and leading her to one of the chairs that sat on the other side of the room.

She didn't answer, and we never made it to the chairs,. Before we had moved even a few steps, her eyes rolled back into her head and she fainted in a heap on the floor.

"HOW ARE YOU FEELING?" I asked.

Delta was slowly coming out of her fog. After making sure she had only fainted, I had gone for a gurney. Vaughn and Harris had helped load her on so I could take her back to the clinic. She had always been a sturdy woman, but the years and the stresses were taking their toll on her. Sitting in the hospital bed, draped in pale colored sheets and her grey hair spread on the pillow, she looked almost frail. Her color hadn't returned save for a slight flush on the apples of her wrinkled cheeks. Her skin looked pallid and translucent, her lips bearing no color of their own to differentiate them from the rest of her face.

"How did I get here?" she asked as I checked the IV fluid bag I had hooked her up to, just in case she was suffering from some level of dehydration.

"I asked your boys for help," I said. "Don't worry, I assured them that you were fine. You are fine, aren't you?"

"Depends on your definition of fine."

I studied her face, though she avoided my eyes. She seemed fixated on the tape that held the intravenous needle in the skin on the back of her hand. She fiddled with it and picked at the edges with her fingernail.

"You can tell me if there's a problem," I said. "I can help you. Tell me what symptoms you're having and I'm sure there's something I could help with."

"Oh Shayna dear, this is a matter of the heart, but not the kind you can fix with medicines."

I pursed my lips, hoping my silence would make her feel the need to elaborate. It worked.

"Forty-one years ago, I had a child. A baby girl. Coralie."

I had no idea. All along I assumed Delta was unable to have children. She didn't bear the mark the others did, but even the cellutation inoculations made it extremely difficult if not impossible. In the years I had known Delta, I had also never seen her romantically attached to anyone, which could have

140

also been a factor.

"I was young and alone, and her father was out of the picture. I was stupid and rushed into bed with him, thinking we had something and then he was gone and I was pregnant."

Her words were starting to settle in my mind and a feeling of heaviness began to settle over me. It was as if I could tell the rest of her story, in fact I already had.

"They took her from me as soon as she was born, and they brought her back to die in my arms. I held her, or I thought I held her until the life drained from her. Did someone take my child?"

Her eyes were wet and searching my face for some answer I couldn't give her. A lump grew in my throat and before I knew it, tears spilled from my eyes as quickly as they were falling from hers.

"I don't know, Delta," I said, wishing I could offer something else, and failing miserably.

"All this time, I had no idea that even happened," she said. "I was so busy raising my boys that I never gave it another thought. And now, I'll never know."

The thought that her daughter might have survived childbirth was one thing. Surviving the freeze was an entirely different thing. Most people died when the world froze, or not long after. Between the looting and the killing and the cold, the number of people that were still alive was relatively small. Even if Coralie had lived longer than Delta knew, it was unlikely that she was still alive. Even if she was, the chance of finding her was miniscule if not impossible.

"I said goodbye to her so many times," she said. "The idea that she might not be dead didn't even cross my mind."

I reached across the bed and placed my hand on hers. Tears streamed from my eyes as I wished there was something I could do to take the unimaginable pain from her.

"I'm sorry, Delta," I said, "I didn't know. If I had known..."

My voice trailed off. I didn't know how to finish my sentence. What would I have done if I'd known? It would have been a terrible secret to keep, especially since I really had no idea what had really happened to Coralie. I would have felt it necessary to tell her, but would I have wanted to unleash this pain on her? I had inadvertently given her hope, only to rip it away from her again. I had given her a burst of fresh air and then thrown her again into the dark musty closet of grief, this time with more guilt and sorrow heaped on top.

"It's not your fault," said Delta, barely able to keep her voice from wavering. "There is no sense in you feeling guilty for something you couldn't have changed."

"You can't feel guilty either," I said. "How could you have possibly guessed that the child you were given, if it wasn't Coralie, wasn't your child at all?"

She said nothing, but nodded as the tears streamed down her face.

"You have done so much good, Delta," I said. "Think about your boys. Those boys wouldn't have had a chance if it wasn't for you. You made strong men out of them."

She picked at the tape on her hands, though I could see

they had begun to shake.

We said nothing more after that.

FOR THREE DAYS I cared for Delta. I brought her food that she didn't eat, books that she didn't read. For three days she did nothing but stare at the wall or the ceiling or the curtained divider that circled her space in the clinic. I tried to talk to her, but she didn't respond. I kept administering IV fluids and spent my time off sitting in the chair beside her bed.

Sometimes when she slept, I checked her pulse, or watched her chest for a sign that she was still breathing. Her body was alive, but she was so lost in her grief that even her boys couldn't find her.

"Is she going to die?" asked Harris.

He and Vaughn had come by after their daily chores. I could tell they were exhausted. With both Jude and Finn gone in search of help, and Red dead, the work of five young men had been heaped onto them. They were both gaunt and sickly looking, and their worry for Delta was written clearly on their faces.

"I don't know," I said. I had to be honest. It was surely possible to die of a broken heart, though I hoped from the depths of mine that Delta would find a way out.

I had told the boys earlier what had happened, why she was in the state she was. I didn't want to betray her confidence, but they needed a reason why the only mother they'd ever had was in a catatonic state. There was nothing medically wrong with her, so there was very little I could do for her other than keep her hydrated, adding as many vitamins and nutrients to her fluids as possible.

"I don't want her to die," said Vaughn. His voice was so quiet I barely heard it above the humming sounds of the equipment in the clinic.

I looked at the men standing beside the bed. It was hard not to call them boys, even though they were both in their thirties. They were doing their best to hide their emotions, but it wasn't working. I could see the strain in their eyes that mirrored my own.

"She's not going to die," I said, more confidently than I felt. "Delta is just about the strongest person I know."

They nodded.

"You know how she always talks about riding the current?" I said.

They looked at me.

"When stuff is hard, or impossible, or whatever, sometimes you need to ride the current," I said. "That's what she's doing. Her grief was too hard, she was too sad to do anything about it, but when she's ready, she'll plant her feet and she'll come back."

My words seemed to give peace to their minds, at least for the time being. I sincerely hoped that I hadn't thrown them a rope that wasn't tied to anything.

ON THE FOURTH DAY I sat by her bed, my legs pulled up to my chest and my journal on my knees. I had started journaling early in my medical career, in hopes of keeping track of my patients, my medical research and my someday discoveries. Over the years the journal entries had changed. Short of basic first-aid—I practiced little medicine here—so it seemed silly to journal about it, but the habit had taken root and it was rare that a day went by that I wouldn't scribble something into it. The posts grew more introspective and contemplative. I taught myself about myself as I wrote. Sometimes my thoughts were jumbled in my head, and writing them down gave reason to their madness.

"She's dead."

I hadn't noticed Delta move or change before she spoke. My head snapped up and I could see her still staring at the wall.

"Delta?"

She turned her head to me.

"She's dead," she repeated.

"Who?"

"Coralie. I'm her mother, I would know if she was alive."

I stood beside the bed and looked into her eyes. She seemed lucid.

"Do you know what day it is?"

She raised an eyebrow. "She may be dead but I'm not."

Reaching out, she picked up a glass of water, took a healthy sip and started unwrapping a granola bar that sat on the rolling table beside her bed. I had given up bringing proper food since she wasn't eating it anyway. I figured if she woke up hungry, a stack of packaged foods would be enough to hold her over until I could find some decent food.

"Are you back?"

"I was never gone," she said. "I know you were here. I saw you, I heard you, I just didn't..."

I let her trail off and didn't press her for more. She would tell me if she needed something.

She chewed the granola bar slowly, her wrinkled face thoughtful.

"I needed to ride the current, right?" she said.

I smiled and patted her hand.

"Right."

"It took me a long time," she said. "A long time to realize it. Coralie is gone. She was taken from me then and she's gone. When I heard your story, I wanted a shred of hope so badly it burned inside me. I wanted it to be my story. I wanted it to be true so much that I was overlooking one crucial part."

"Which was?" I asked.

"That I would know."

"Because you're her mother?"

Delta nodded. "Once I let myself believe that, I had to grieve all over again."

She turned again to look at me.

"I'm done grieving now," she said. "We need to get ready. My boys are coming to me and we need to be ready for them."

# EIGHTEEN

## *Meredith*

THE SUN WAS HIGH in the sky as I guided Thor into the clearing I remembered from so long ago. The trees spread their bare branches against the sky, silhouetted in the blinding light, sending criss-crossed shadows to pattern the melting snow below. I stood in my stirrups and twisted my body to pull one leg over the massive horse's back. My legs ached and quivered as they adjusted to being off Thor's back.

Holding his reins, we walked together to the far side of the clearing and into the thick shade of conifers.

"I hope I didn't screw up my directions," I said to Thor, having a moment of panic that we would have come all this way to do nothing but get hopelessly lost.

My heart pounding, I let out an audible gasp when I saw the stone face I had been searching for. It was exactly as I had remembered it, only with snow, and some extra fallen branches littering the ground. I searched the terrain for any sign of activity, any clue that people lived here, but found nothing. The packed and melting snow obscured any trace of footprints and I could find no evidence that made it immediately obvious that this place had ever been populated.

I did my best not to lose hope immediately, though my initial excitement at finding the place was deflating at an alarming rate. I knew the door was here, though having only come to this place with a member of the Secret Service, I suddenly realized I had no idea how they triggered the door. I pulled the thick mittens from my hands and began to run my fingers over the rock, trying to discern the outline of the door or find some hidden switch. It was well hidden. Even having seen it open, I wasn't able to find anything. The rock was cold and rough under my fingers covered in lichen and each cleft was jammed with pine needles.

"I don't know how this works, Thor," I said, my voice starting to waver. Exhaustion and hunger were working together to cloud my thoughts, my emotions were running high and threatening to take over. My body ached from the exertion of the days on the trail and fear was starting to creep in.

"Suck it up, Meredith," I said. "Focus. You have been here before."

I took a few deep breaths and continued. My hands shook as I pulled at bits that stuck out and pushed my palm into anything that looked like it might be some kind of button or heat sensor. Nothing moved.

Thor nickered and I snapped at him, frustrated.

"If I knew how to do this I would have gotten in by now," I said, answering what I assume was his wordless question.

My cursing began quietly, but it wasn't long before I was shouting obscenities at the top of my lungs, pounding on the rock face until my hands were raw and bleeding. The tears were coming fast and hot, streaming down my face and soaking into the scarf I had wrapped around my neck.

Thor stood watching me silently as I pressed my body into the rock and let it hold me up. I let myself sob, unrealistically hoping that the door was charmed by some kind of fairy-tale spell, ready to spring open for the next sincere plea. It wasn't.

The rock didn't care if I cried; it didn't care if I screamed at it or kicked it. It didn't even laugh at me, like I figured it probably should, given my performance. I flipped over, leaning against the hard, immobile surface, and slid my back down until I was sitting in the snow, letting the sobs rack my body and empty my soul.

I had failed.

I'd known finding this place and Leif was a long shot, but I'd had enough hope in the fairy-tale ending that I hadn't let myself think about what I would do if no one was here. It had taken me longer to get here than I had anticipated, so we were out of food. It was possible to make it back without any food, but Thor wouldn't be happy and based on the gnawing emptiness that had already found a home in my stomach, it wouldn't be a fun ride for me either. That was assuming we didn't get lost on the way back, and that we'd be able to find the others.

"I'm sorry Thor," I said, tears still falling from my eyes. I could taste their salty heat in my mouth. I pulled my mittens back on and wiped the snot from my nose, the wool scratching against my face.

I didn't know what else to do, so I cried. I buried my face in my mittens and wept until I had nothing left inside me. Thor pushed his nose into the side of my head a few times, but when I didn't acknowledge him, he wandered off to find something to nibble on.

I leaned my head back on the cold rock and closed my eyes. The shadows of the sun through the three branches above made brilliant moving patterns on the insides of my eyelids.

"Meredith?"

The voice was quiet, barely more than a whisper. It had finally happened. I had officially snapped. Thor was speaking to me.

I opened my eyes slowly, squinting in the bright sunshine.

"Meredith Kroeker?"

There was a figure standing before me, though I couldn't make out much more than the shape of his body. He was silhouetted against the sun and my eyes weren't ready for its harsh light.

I breathed a sigh of relief that it wasn't Thor speaking to me.

"Who are you?" I asked, my voice hoarse from crying.

He ran forward without a word, dropping to my feet and gathering me into his arms.

Leif.

I couldn't stop my body from shaking as relief drenched me like a deluge of rain. I cried in his arms, letting him cradle me like a child. He sat beside me and pulled me onto his lap, enveloping me in his strong arms.

"Leif," I said. It was all I could manage to say.

"I thought I had lost you," he said, and I noticed he too was crying.

I turned my head to look at his face, drinking in the sight of him. He was older, his hair almost entirely white, with only a few speckles of black still visible. His face looked worn and tired and thinner than I remembered, but his eyes were the same. The dazzling blue made me catch my breath. How often I had dreamed of this man, and here he was. I seldom let myself think of him when I was awake. It was too difficult to remember how it felt to be in his arms when I hadn't felt a meaningful touch in years. My body craved it, ached for it, but other than the childlike squeezes from Renny, which were disappearing as he grew up, I was seldom touched.

I lifted my hand—the mitten still damp from my tears—and laid it on the side of his face. His eyes were wet with tears and a healthy layer of stubble covered his chin.

"I couldn't get the door open," I said.

He burst out laughing.

"Almost twenty years and the first thing you say to me is 'I couldn't get the door open'?"

"And I love you," I added.

"I love you too," he said, kissing my lips with a tenderness and gentleness that made me wonder if he thought I was fragile and didn't want to risk breaking me.

I closed my eyes and tasted him, trying to remember every second in case this was little more than a mirage.

"Let's go inside," he said, helping me to my feet.

"But the door," I said.

"That door stopped working almost right after the cold came. I guess the mechanical stuff froze up," he said. "There is a secondary hatch we've been using to get in and out."

He took my hand and led me through the trees, up onto the rocks until we came to a thick patch of lichen and frozen moss. He reached down and grasped a handle I couldn't see, pulling open the door to reveal a dark round hole.

"I'm not sure what we're going to do with your horse," he said. "I have doubts he'll make it down the ladder."

I smiled.

"If you have something to feed him, I'm sure he'd be alright. We ran out of food yesterday."

"There's a ladder there," said Leif. "Are you ok to climb down?"

I faltered, my hands were still quivering and they ached from days holding Thor's reins in the cold.

"I'll go first," he said, "and help you down."

I nodded, still not sure of myself.

He slid through the hole with a practiced ease, and guided me down to the ladder. I felt the rungs beneath my numb feet, and his body against my back. Together we climbed down the ladder, Leif murmuring encouragement as we descended into the dark hole.

"That's it, just one more step and you'll be on the ground," said Leif, his hands holding my waist.

Once I was safely on the ground, he scampered back up

the ladder to close the hatch behind us. It closed with a metallic boom, cutting us off from all natural light.

"It'll take a second for your eyes to adjust," he said. "There is light down here, I promise, just not a lot in this section."

I stood there wrapped in darkness, feeling for a second as though this had all been a terrible dream, and I was now alone again. I gasped when I felt Leif's hand on my back. I nearly crumpled beside him.

"Whoa," he said, grabbing me before I fell. "Let's get you somewhere warm and find you some food."

He scooped me up in his arms and carried me through the dark hallway. My eyes were starting to adjust and I could see that he followed a trail of dim lights that lined the corridor. I rested my head on his shoulder.

He turned around and used his body to push a door open, and we were immediately bathed in light and sound. There were people here, laughing and talking, but their chatter ceased almost as soon as Leif walked through the door.

"We sent you out for a rabbit, Leif," someone said.

"I brought back something better. You'll all be pleased to know I captured a President."

I could feel the oxygen sucked from the room as an entire group of people collectively gasped. I raised my hand to pull my ski cap off my head.

A flurry of activity exploded in the room, as people, unsure of what to do in the moment, racked their brains for whatever proper protocol they had used almost two decades before.

"Stop, everyone," I said as Leif gently lowered me so I could stand. "There will be time for protocol later. Right now, I need some food and water. And maybe a chair."

Leif barked out a few orders, including sending a few people to the surface to feed and water Thor, and figure out what to do with him. I was led to a comfortable chair and in only moments, greeted with a bottle of fresh cold water, a cup of warm tea and bowl of creamy tomato soup.

I inhaled the aromas first. My hands and feet burned with pins and needles as they warmed up. Someone had removed my heavy boots and replaced them with thick cozy slippers with fur inside, and someone else had taken my coat and draped me in a blanket that seemed warm from the dryer. I sipped the water first and then brought a spoonful of the soup to my lips, letting the warm creamy liquid coat my mouth and slide down my throat. It was very likely the best food I had ever eaten. I closed my eyes and sighed.

Most of the people had left the room. Leif had given them all jobs. I could see a few people hovering in the doorways, but they said nothing, just stared.

"Meredith, I dreamed of this day, but I'll tell you one thing," said Leif. "I had pretty much given up thinking it would ever happen."

"I know the feeling," I said, between mouthfuls of soup. "I'm just so glad you were still here."

Leif chuckled. "By the time we realized how catastrophic the cold and snow really were, there wasn't really anywhere else we could go, and then after that, well, let's just say none of us figured we had homes to go back to. We were safe and warm here, and we still have a decent amount food left."

"The benefits of living in a presidential foxhole?"

He smiled.

"It would have been better with you here in it."

I nodded. Tears were never far from spilling over, but now they threatened to pour down my face.

"It's been so hard," I whispered as all the struggles of the last decades flooded into my mind.

"You're safe now," said Leif, reaching his hand out to take mine.

I shook my head.

"No," I said. "Not yet."

"Of course you're safe here."

"Here, yes," I said. "But I can't stay here. I came because I need your help. We need to go back."

Leif narrowed his gaze, trying to understand. His face was unreadable.

"I just got you back, and now you want to leave?"

"I'll take you with me."

"It's safe here, Meredith. We have enough supplies to outlast the weather, it's getting warmer."

"I know, Leif," I said. "I assure you, there is a huge part of me that wants nothing more than to curl up in a bed here with you and pretend that nothing out there exists anymore, but I can't."

Tears were flowing freely now.

"I need to go and you need to help me."

Leif nodded.

"As you wish," he said, standing. "Eat your food and we'll get you cleaned up."

"Why?" I asked, widening my eyes and fluttering my lashes in my best innocent look, "Do I smell?"

Leif leaned forward, kissed me on the forehead and smiled.

"Like a barn full of pigs, darling."

IN ALL THE TIME I had dreamed about finding this place— and Leif—again, I hadn't even thought about the deep bathtub. It stood before me, its gleaming white porcelain filled with steaming water. I peeled off my clothing, letting it fall to the floor in a giant filthy heap. They'd told me to just leave them there and they would wash them for me. Secretly I hoped they'd just burn them instead. Most of my clothing was so worn and threadbare that the grime and dirt were probably the only things holding them together.

I caught a glimpse of my naked body in the giant mirror on the wall and gasped. I knew my body was leaner and less filled out than it used to be, but the image was startling. I hadn't seen myself in a proper mirror in almost fifteen years. My once glossy black curls were dull and streaked with white, and my skin was darker, more like leather. I could see bones jutting out that had once been covered in a generous layer of soft fat and smooth skin.

My breasts seemed deflated and my eyes sunken. I turned away from the mirror and focused on the bath.

I couldn't remember the last time I had taken a bath. It was probably such a non-event at the time that it didn't seem worth remembering. Now, after years of having little more than sponge baths with tepid water, the idea of languishing in the hot water seemed almost too good to be true.

I stepped toward the bathtub, the cold clean tiles smooth under my feet. I dipped my fingers in, letting the warm water swaddle them. I couldn't take it any longer. I lifted my leg over the side and plunged it into the water. It was almost too hot, but I didn't care. Pulling my other leg in, I sat down and let myself be covered in the luxurious warmth. The tub was deep, and once I was in it, the water lapped at the top edge of the basin. Someone had added some kind of soap or oils to the water, it smelled rich and floral.

My body melted into the feeling. Warmth had seemed like such a luxury. Even when we had blazing fires to keep us warm, it was impossible to keep your entire body warm at the same time. Whatever side of you faced the fire stayed warm, but you'd need to turn around regularly to make sure the rest of you got the opportunity.

Everything felt light in the water. Muscles that had grown tight and weary softened and relaxed. I lifted up the smooth bar of sweetly-scented soap. As thankful as I was for Angela's homemade soap, I had longed for the simple indulgence of store-bought soap. Something I had taken for granted so long ago. I lathered it between my hands and began washing myself—slowly and methodically—scrubbing myself with the exfoliating sponges and sweet-smelling bubbles.

There was a bottle of shampoo on the side of the tub too. It was a brand I remembered well, and poured entirely too much into my hands.

"Meredith?" I heard Leif's voice through the door as he knocked lightly.

"Come in," I said out of reflex, though I suddenly regretted it. My body had been a surprise to me; I had no idea what he would think. Thankful for the layer of bubbles that gathered on the surface of the water, I smiled as he peeked his head around the door.

"Do you need any help?"

"Need?" I said, my voice coy. "Probably not."

"Allow me to rephrase," he said with a wink. "Can I come in and watch you?"

"If you're going to come in, I'm going to put you to work," I said. "No one gets a free show around here."

"As you wish, Madam President."

He closed the door behind him and sat on the stool near my head as I smeared the handful of shampoo onto my hair.

I felt his hands massaging it in and closed my eyes. Letting the intoxicating feelings rejuvenate my tired soul. I moaned with pleasure.

Leif laughed behind me as his fingers worked the lather through my hair.

"I don't want to alarm you, but I think you might have some mice living in here," he said.

"Doubtful," I said. "Mice are too delicious to last long nearby."

I had meant it as a joke, but Leif didn't laugh, and truthfully it didn't seem funny to me to hear it out loud either.

"I'm sorry," said Leif. "I should have come to find you."

"Don't apologize," I said, turning in the slippery bathtub to face him. "No one needs to apologize for how this all turned out. I'm here, I'm alive, and that's all we need to think about right now."

"You always were a tough one."

I nodded, sliding back into the hot water. I didn't feel tough. I felt naked and scared, I felt like all the fears and problems and horrifying moments had all built up inside of me, ready to burst out into a torrent of insecurity—but at least for the moment, I wasn't alone.

# Nineteen

MY SKIN STILL TINGLED from the bath and I couldn't stop myself from smelling my hair. It had taken nearly an hour of gentle tugging before I could get the wide-toothed comb through my wet hair. I never used to bother with a comb, preferring my fingers as my only tool, but the state of affairs in my hair left little other option. My fingers proved inadequate after only moments, so I'd needed to go hunting for something better. I'd found an array of tools and products in the cupboards by the sink and spent entirely too much time filing my calloused heels and trimming my fingernails.

There was a bedroom for me, set up almost the same as the one at the White House. I didn't touch the bed. I knew that if I did, I wouldn't be able to tear myself away from it. Wearing a thick terry robe I padded into the walk-in closet and selected a pair of fitted sweat pants and a thick warm sweatshirt. There were more fashionable items in there, but I didn't care.

The fleece was soft and new, a bit musty from years in a closet, but fresher than anything I'd worn in years. I pulled on some of the silky underwear and found a stretchy sports bra to wear. The pants would have probably fit me better years ago, but I pulled the drawstring tight so they wouldn't fall down. The sweatshirt was oversized and comfortable, the sleeves covering my hands unless I rolled them up.

Leif and the others would be waiting for me in the control room, he'd said. I could give them the rundown once, and not have to repeat it over and over again. I was thankful for that. I wasn't entirely sure my emotional state would lend itself to more than one explanation.

It all seemed so far away now—a distant memory. I felt like I had somehow removed myself from the situation, that I was looking in on it from a distance. Yet I felt it pull me. I felt the subtle tug as it gnawed on me. I was tempted to forget, to just stay here, safe and warm. It would be so easy.

But I couldn't.

I slipped into my warm slippers and found my way down the hallway to the control room I remembered from so long ago. Most of the computers were dark and unused, though I could see one station still brightly lit. The display showed what appeared to be meteorological data. There was a long table in the center of the room and people sat around it chatting with each other. When I entered the room, they stood and greeted me. It was such a strange feeling to suddenly be the center of attention again. I had grown used to entering rooms unnoticed, or at least unacknowledged. Here I was President Kroeker—out there I was surviving with everyone else. Out there I was Meredith.

Leif gestured to a swivelling office chair at the lead of the table. It had my seal on it, and I wondered if they had to pull it out from a closet before I came in, or if it had just been sitting here vacant the whole time. I walked to the seat, smiling at each person. I recognized them but could only remember a few names from my visits to the bunker. There were about a dozen of them. Less than the number I knew they kept here, but it had been almost twenty years so it was unlikely that no one met with injury or illness. Perhaps some of them left to find their families when the frozen days began. I sat down in the chair and motioned for everyone else to sit. The action felt foreign to me, unnatural.

"Please sit, everyone. I haven't been around proper procedure for so long, that it seems almost silly to start now."

They chuckled, politely acknowledging my attempt at levity.

I scanned their faces as they waited for me to speak, not knowing what to say or how to say it—where to begin?

In the end, I took a deep breath and started at the beginning. I told them of Nadia's attempt on my life, my time recovering and in a medically-induced coma, my escape from the estate and subsequent years with Jude, Rayne and Angela. I told them about the girls that Nadia had collected, her plans for making a secondary society dedicated to breeding, and of those who had made it their—our—goal to stop her.

I could see the faces around me change, from surprise to concern to anger.

"The frozen days are ending," I said, "which means that the time is coming where we're going to need to rebuild. Nadia and I have very different ideas about what that means, and I fear that if she holds onto the control she currently has, our new world will be a vastly different place."

I was relieved to see they were nodding in affirmation. There were days when Nadia seemed so powerful to me, like I had given her an inch and over the years she had insidiously clawed her way to complete power. The guilt of not stopping her sooner was all-encompassing.

"I think it's agreed that we need to do something," said Leif, to nods from the others. "But we're forgetting something. How are we going to get there?"

My heart sank. I didn't understand.

"You guys had lots of vehicles here."

"We did, and we do," said one of the other men, a soldier wearing fatigues.

"Lieutenant Jamison is in charge of our heavy mechanics," said Leif.

"The problem is how to get them," said Lieutenant Jamison. "As you noticed, the stone door won't open anymore, the cold weather and time has seized the mechanics of it. The same can be said for the helicopter port and the small vehicles garage doors. They haven't been opened in years and I'm not sure what it will take to get them open now."

"And if we do get them open..." said Leif.

"We won't get them closed again. This bunker would need to be decommissioned. If this mission fails we couldn't come back."

I hadn't thought of that. I hadn't even thought of what might happen if we failed. Nadia had high levels of security at the estate, manned with heavy artillery and trained to kill. We had a decent amount of firepower here, if it still existed. If we couldn't get it to the estate it did nothing for us. She had the advantage but she also probably wasn't expecting anyone to show up on her doorstep. It wasn't impossible, but it wouldn't be easy, and no matter what, people would die.

"I can't come back anyway," I said, choosing my words. "I need to make a stand against Nadia and only one of us will come out of it alive. We won't need this place anymore."

Leif chewed on his lip and I could see that no one else was making eye contact. They were all distracted by something on the table, or in their hands.

"Alright then," he said. "We only have one option here. Jamison, make a team and see what you can do about getting those doors moving. I'd prefer to travel by whirly-bird, but get what you can. Everyone else, find some shovels and let's get digging."

THERE WERE DAYS WHEN no matter what position I tried to sleep in, it was impossible to get comfortable. This was not one of those days. I could have slept standing up, so crawling into the sumptuous king-sized bed and letting my body slide between the silky sheets felt like heaven. We had been working much of the evening with everyone pitching in. I saw Jamison with cutting torches and pry-bars, others with shovels. I spent my day shoveling on the surface. Thor wandered around the area, well fed and happy, watching the activity with interest. I had tried to release him in hopes that he would find his way home, but so far he hadn't left. I wanted him to go. He had done his job well and faithfully, but having him around was a reminder that we would be leaving him here. He couldn't come on a helicopter, nor could he ride along with snowmobiles. I felt a pang of guilt thinking of him outside as night fell—alone in the cold as I snuggled into my warm bed.

Leif was already in the bed, dressed only in a pair of flannel pyjama bottoms. I had commandeered the matching shirt. There were plenty of pyjamas in my size in the closet, but wearing something of Leif's seemed more appropriate.

"Man, I missed these sheets," he said.

"Why didn't you just sleep in here?" I asked.

"I couldn't," he said. "My bed is comfortable enough, and I couldn't have slept peacefully in here, knowing that you were missing. It made your absence too obvious. To be honest, I tried to forget this room existed at all."

The thought made me sad, though I too had spent time trying to forget Leif, knowing that it was unlikely I'd ever see him again. So many people died in the frozen days, that I felt almost guilty to have found him again.

"Why are we so lucky?" I mused, more to myself than to Leif.

"I don't know," he said, pulling me toward him so my back was snuggled against him and his face nuzzled into my neck.

"Just promise me you won't leave me again."

I promised, though we both knew my words held as much certainty and weight as the wind.

"Maybe we could just stay here," said Leif as I started to let sleep claim me.

I wished that I could agree, that we could somehow forget everything else and hide here, but I knew we couldn't.

"We need to go."

# TWENTY

## *Athena*

"WE NEED TO GO," said Jude, "With or without the tribe."

The rest of the outsiders nodded, their faces solemn and filled with dread. Nova had still not come out of her hut. Dax came and went occasionally but said nothing to anyone. It had been days and there was still no answer. I didn't know what was taking her so long. Perhaps being under Asari's command had rendered her decision-making capabilities useless. What decisions had she needed to make over the last twenty years? This one certainly seemed cut and dry, but I was more a product of my aunt than one of my parents. She had raised me to be a leader, the rightful leader of this tribe, yet here I was, washing my husband's socks.

A growl escaped me. I was sick of it all. I was more than a sock-washer, more than a knife-sharpener. The frustration made me grind my teeth at night while I slept, and as many times as I rehearsed my words to Torren I couldn't quite make them form in my mouth.

I couldn't say no to him. He had a power over me that I couldn't control, and I was used to controlling everything.

My baby flipped in my belly. It always reacted to my frustrations, as if trying to remind me what it was all for. I ran my fingers over the hummingbird tattoo on my wrist. The wings were high, as they had been since I became pregnant. They would stay that way until the baby was born and then begin to move again as I settled back into a normal cycle.

"I agree," said Orion. "We should leave in the morning."

The other outsiders nodded in affirmation.

*Idiots.*

*They needed us. Without the tribe they were sure to fail.*

*They needed me.*

"Athena, do you know where my other mittens are?" asked Torren, strolling into the area where we sat by the fire.

That was it. I was done.

"NO!" I shouted, everyone nearby stopped in their tracks and Torren's eyes opened wide. "You are a grown-ass man! Find your own damn mittens!"

It felt good. So very very good.

I could see the expressions on the people around me. Orion had started to laugh, though he was doing his best to hide it. Leona and Ember looked shocked and Torren was flushing a deep shade of red.

"I'm done with this, Torren," I said, tossing a wet pair of socks in his general direction. "I'm not your washer-woman and I'm not your mitten-finder. If that's what you want, you're going to need to find someone else. If you want a partner, if you want an equal, come find me. Right now, I'm going to have a talk with my mother."

I stood, knocking over the pail of warm soapy water I had

been using for the laundry, spilling it in a cascade of steaming water across the snow. Mila, who had been sitting silently beside me, jumped up onto the log an instant before her boots would have been drenched.

No one spoke as I walked away, though I could have sworn I heard Finn say "Ni-i-ice" under his breath.

I smiled as I stalked away. It was as if a weight had been lifted from me. I stretched my shoulder and my neck, feeling lighter and free of whatever it was that had been holding my tongue for far too long.

Nova's hut was still silent, and I didn't hesitate as I flipped open the flap and slid inside.

It was dim and smoky like all the huts were. Dax wasn't there, but Nova sat silently on a stool by the fire poking it with a stick. Her wolf stretched out beside her and yawned lazily and me as I entered.

"What's taking so long?" I asked. "They're going to leave without us and if they do, they will all die."

"I know," said Nova, her eyes lifted to mine and she studied me with a careful gaze.

"Have you made a decision?"

"What would you say if I said I thought we shouldn't go?" she asked.

"I would say you need to do some more thinking because that's the stupidest thing I've ever heard."

Nova burst out laughing.

"Oh Athena, I had a feeling you'd break out."

I raised an eyebrow.

"What's that supposed to mean?" I asked.

"The serum they gave you, the hummingbird one. Elias had altered my original recipe to make women fertile and submissive at the same time."

"And you let them give it to me?" I said, incredulous. My mother had intentionally given me mind-altering drugs. What was up with that?

"Oh Athena," she said, smiling. "I knew it wouldn't hold you for long. It might have worked on the women they had at the caves, but that was what those women wanted. For you, my dear, it was only a matter of time."

"I just yelled at Torren," I said.

Nova smiled. "Good, he was being a bit of a putz anyway."

"I told him to find himself another washer-woman," I said. "Do you think he will?"

Nova pursed her lips. "I doubt it. You're a catch and a half, Athena, he would be an idiot not to know that."

I was a bit relieved. I really had grown fond of Torren. I wouldn't mind keeping him around, provided he stopped being an idiot.

"So you don't think we should go?" I asked Nova.

She chuckled. "No, Athena, quite the opposite. I just said that because I suspected you had broken free of the serum and I wanted to make sure."

"Seriously?" I said. "I'm in a very fragile state right now and you go and toy with my emotions?"

"You are far from fragile, but yes."

"So we're going?"

"We have to," said Nova. "I don't want my children and grandchildren living in a society where they aren't free to make their own choices. Nadia needs to be stopped."

"What took you so long?"

Nova frowned. "I was hoping I could think of another way, a way to stop her that wouldn't put us all in danger. I'm not ready to put my daughters in the line of fire."

I shrugged. "I'll be fine. Maybe worry about Leona."

"I think you two are more alike than you are willing to admit," said Nova with a wink. I could see her face was strained beneath her light words.

I doubted it, but didn't bother to argue.

"Would you like to help me tell the others?" she asked as she opened the flap and stepped out into the sun.

We walked out of the hut and were met by a crowd. They had watched me storm into Nova's hut and had gathered outside, perhaps anticipating an announcement.

"I've come to a decision," said Nova, in her best authoritative voice. It probably wasn't necessary, since everyone was so quiet she likely could have whispered it. "We will join the outsiders in their plan to release the government's captives."

Applause rippled through the crowd.

"As a cautionary measure, no one who is fertile will be allowed to come. I will not risk losing any other girls to this heinous plan. You will stay here, and take care of the camp."

There were a few moans of displeasure in the group, but they were all young, and inexperienced anyway. They had never seen battle, nor would they be equipped to handle it.

"We leave at dawn. Get ready," said Nova, and the crowd dispersed.

I started back to my hut, but made a detour when I saw Leona talking to Orion and Jude.

"Leona," I said. Her head snapped up at my voice and her body tensed. "Here," I unwrapped her leather sling from my wrist. "You should have this back."

She seemed startled.

"I shouldn't have taken it, but at the time I thought you had taken something from me, and I wanted to take something of yours."

"Thank you," she said, stammering.

I shrugged. "I don't know how the freaking thing works anyway."

I turned away and walked back to my hut. I could feel them watching me all the way.

Ducking through the flap, I knew I wasn't alone.

"Did you have to embarrass me?" asked Torren.

"Did you have to let them inject me with mind-altering drugs?"

He said nothing.

"I get it," I said. "You were scared of me, used to soft little girls like Leona and Ember. You liked me but wanted to tame me."

Torren muttered something under his breath.

"I won't be tamed," I said. "It didn't work, and I'm happier now. If that works for you, we'll continue on and when we get back from this little mission we'll make and raise some untameable children."

"You're going?" he said, surprised.

"Of course. They need me."

"But, the baby."

I rolled my eyes. "I'm pregnant, not incapacitated."

"But..."

"Torren, the baby is the reason I'm going. They need to be stopped because I won't bring my child into that kind of world. If there's any chance in hell of us getting out of there alive and taking down this ridiculous breeding machine they've got going on, they need me... and you."

Torren nodded slowly.

"Ok, as long as you don't do anything stupid."

I laughed out loud. "I never do anything stupid."

He rolled his eyes.

"I'm not sure what I've gotten myself into, Athena," he said. "But I have a feeling life is going to be a lot more interesting from here on out."

"Damn straight."

# TWENTY-ONE

## *Mila*

I DISPERSED WITH THE others. They all seemed busy and determined to get things ready for the trip. I wouldn't be going, which was a relief to me. I'd much rather wait here and be regaled with stories later once all the shooting and killing was done. It wasn't that I was scared. Oh, who was I kidding? I was terrified. I entered my tent and stopped short as I saw my mother piling items up in the middle of the room and packing them tightly into a backpack.

"What are you doing?" I asked.

"Getting ready to go," she said, not making eye contact.

"But Nova said, no fertile women."

"She did."

"And you're packing?"

"I'm not fertile Mila. I stopped bleeding years ago."

I said nothing, just stared at my mother. She looked up to me, her eyes soft.

"It happens, Mila, don't look so surprised."

"So you're leaving me?"

She sighed. "I'm not leaving you, I'm going to go help make sure you can grow up in a world full of people who won't kidnap you or rape you or decide that you belong to them. That's how it was for me and I'm not letting it happen to you."

"And you want to go with Jude?" I said, feeling a bit petulant.

"Mila, honestly?" she said. "I pour out my heart and the dreams I have for you, and you figure I'm going for a boy?"

I shrugged.

"Maybe."

She said nothing but shook her head.

I slumped onto my bed and watched her pack, but it was too difficult to watch. I had just found my mother and now she was leaving. Biting back a sob I jumped to my feet and ran from the hut. I didn't know where I was going, but realistically, anywhere was better than there.

All around the camp were signs of preparation. Women were packing food and gathering cooking pots and weapons. I could see a cluster of women sharpening knives and spears. The outsiders were gathered together talking strategy. Finn, Jude and Rebekkah were describing the estate, discussing weak spots and possible entry points.

I tightened my jaw and walked past them. I don't know how I ended up in front of Nova's hut, but before I knew what I was doing, I opened the flap and walked inside.

"Mila," she said as I came in.

"The thing they did, in the old days, to make women infertile?"

Nova nodded.

"Can you do that to me?"

Nova's brow furrowed and her eyes narrowed on me.

"Come talk to me," she said.

I blinked back tears as she motioned to her bed and sat down cross-legged. I did the same.

"Child, tell me why?"

"I don't want to have babies."

"Why?"

I hadn't prepared an answer for myself, so I stumbled through one.

"They're smelly, and they cry all the time, and..."

"Mila, does this have anything to do with me telling everyone that no fertile people can come on this journey?"

A tear tickled my eye. I brushed it away with the back of my hand and cursed it for showing my weakness.

"I don't want anything to happen to you," she continued, taking my tear as an affirmative response.

"But my mother is going," I said, choking back a sob.

Nova said nothing for a minute.

"I won't take it from you, not now. Not because you're scared and certainly not because you want to go with your mother. If you feel the same way when this is all over and you're a little bit older, please come back to me, but not yet."

My shoulders slumped.

"I know that these last days have been difficult on you," she continued. "I too have seen the changes in your mother, and I can understand how you must be feeling."

"I can't let her go now," I said, "Not now that I can finally talk to her."

Nova nodded, and stared into the fire.

"Mila," she said. "Go find Athena, and bring her back with you."

I got up to leave.

"Ask her to bring her kit with her."

I quickly wiped my face in a vain hope that no one would notice my red, teary eyes. It was pointless since no one out there was paying attention to me anyway. I made my way through the milling people to Athena's hut just as she walked through the flap.

"What do you want?" she asked.

"Nova asked me to get you and she wants you to bring your kit."

I had no idea what was contained inside Athena's kit, nor did I care, but I said the words anyway. Athena raised an eyebrow and went back into her hut, coming out with a small, leather bound package.

"Let's go," she said.

We entered Nova's hut together.

"You needed me?" said Athena, lifting her kit slightly to show Nova.

"Mila does, actually," aid Nova. "Sit, Mila."

Nova motioned to her bed, and I sat down, Athena knelt next to me and untied the leather thongs that bound her kit, unrolling it to reveal a vast array of pointed tools. They looked like paintbrushes, but with needles gracing the tips, some with single ones, others with a gathered bunch. Small glass bottles of black liquid were tucked into pockets. I had seen Athena tattoo women before. I had seen the looks of discomfort and heard the cries and grunts of pain.

"I'm not sure…" I started.

Athena raised an eyebrow.

"Does she want a tattoo or not?" she asked her mother.

"Mila needs to blend in. She'd like to join us on our journey."

Athena laughed. "Ah, the little fertile flower doesn't want to look ripe for the picking."

"Basically."

"I don't need to use the needles for that," said Athena, "so you can start breathing again."

I hadn't realized I had been holding my breath.

"My ink is permanent enough that I could paint it on. It will stain your skin for a while, but as long as you don't wash your face too vigorously, it'll stay there until we get back."

"But if we're not successful?" asked Nova.

Athena looked at me. "She's always worried that we won't be successful," she said, then turned to her mother. "If we're not successful, Mila's fertile status won't be the first thing I'll be worried about."

She rummaged in her kit, pulling out a bottle of ink and a thin brush made of what appeared to be Athena's own hair.

"Lie down," she said.

I obeyed. She knelt by my head and pushed my hair from

my face.

"Don't move, or you'll end up with a crooked line."

I focused on my breathing, inhaling and exhaling as slowly as possible to keep my muscles still and calm. I could barely feel the brush. It was so fine and my skin so weathered from the cold and sun.

She finished quickly, cleaning her brush with a small rag and some clear solution from another bottle. I reached up to touch my face.

"Hey," she said, swatting my hand. "If you touch it now, you'll smear it and then no one will believe your perfect lie."

I pulled my hand from my face and sat up.

"It's convincing enough," said Nova.

"Now go give your mother a heart attack," said Athena.

I hadn't thought about that. She would understand once I told her.

Maybe.

I rose from the bed, thanked Nova and left the hut. I could hear them talking in low voices, but I didn't stop to listen or strain to hear. I had no desire to hear them laughing at me or making jokes. I had gotten what I needed and I was glad about that. As I walked through the camp watching others sharpening weapons like they were readying for a hunt, my stomach churned. I set my jaw and walked quickly to the hut, sliding inside before I could hear the sounds of people noticing my face.

"I'm coming with you," I said to my mother, who was tying up a small sack of tea leaves, compressing it so it would take up less space.

"Mila, you can't," she said, not looking at me. "Nova said..."

"Nova said I could," I interrupted. "I'm coming."

She stopped what she was doing and raised her eyes to meet mine, and I saw the surprise and understanding on her face.

"It's not real, before you ask," I said.

Her eyes closed and she let her breath out slowly.

"You can't come Mila, it's too dangerous."

"If it's too dangerous for me, it's too dangerous for you," I said. "I'm coming, and you can't stop me."

She said nothing but stared at me for a moment. I straightened my back and stared back.

"Then you'd better get packing."

I sat beside her and as we packed in silence, my mind drifted for a moment thinking about how strange a pair we were; both of our faces marred by this world.

WE LEFT RIGHT AS the sun crossed the horizon. I hadn't slept, and based on the faces of those around me, I wasn't alone. The sky was pink and streaked with golden clouds, gleaming as the first rays of sunlight blazed across the sky. It was a frosty morning, but not so cold that it took your breath away. A thick layer of frost coated the trees and fell in clumps as squirrels leaped above us in their clever acrobatics. A group of crows—a murder of crows, Athena had told me once—squawked from the top of a long-needled pine tree as we passed beneath, the racket a distinct contrast to the silence of our party. It was as if no one had fully woken yet, or perhaps were lost to their thoughts.

I trailed near the back of the group with my mother. Neither of us were trained in combat, and carried no weapons save small knives tied in sheaths around the thighs of our buckskin pants. They'd have barely qualified as weapons, more likely to be used to skin a rabbit or a squirrel or slice through a leather cord that someone had knotted too tightly to untie. There were a few women behind us, I knew, but they were invisible, following us in the trees to give us advance warning of an ambush from behind. There were also scouts ahead of us watching. They were trackers and hunters; they knew how to be silent in the woods, unseen by both predators and prey.

We had taken apart some of the huts before leaving, pulling the white furs from the roof to wrap around our packs and over our heads in an attempt to camouflage ourselves against the snow. In the days before—my mother had told me—animals had used to be different colors, black and brown and grey, but those animals barely existed anymore. They were too easy to see against the snow, too easy to hunt. The ones that survived were the pale ones, and soon they were pretty much the only ones that existed. I had never seen an animal in any color other than white.

Nova, Dax and Athena led the group followed by the outsiders. The other women from the tribe formed a kind of protective circle around them. They carried weapons of all kinds: bows and arrows, spears, knives and guns. Asari had kept a weapons cache, which were relics of the days before. We had mainly been forbidden to use them, opting to use mainly retrievable weapons. While guns were efficient, they were finite. While we had some equipment for making bullets, the stores of gunpowder and empty casings Asari had built so long ago had dwindled. It had been years since I had seen any of the women wear rifles slung across their backs, and handguns in holsters. It was jarring to see the shiny black metal and bandoliers amongst the fur and buckskin and wood we were used to.

As the weather warmed and the sun rose higher in the skies, people began to speak to each other again as we hiked. Rebekkah rode atop her horse, which also carried more than its fair share of tarps and supplies. The men took turns guiding the steed, while Ember and Leona walked beside, chatting with Rebekkah.

We walked and walked.

Dutch and Olly broke from the group now and then, turning up hours later with a rabbit or a pheasant. Not to be outdone, some of our own trackers did the same, ensuring they brought back more game, or larger animals. Jude spent much of his time walking with my mother who brightened every time he was near. At times she grasped his hand and held on to him as though he alone was her lifeline. I rolled my eyes, even though from what I had seen it was probably true.

We didn't stop during the day, opting to eat little more than dry smoked meats and berries as we walked. We would stop once the sun set and make camp. We could cook and rest then.

My shoulders ached under the weight of my pack. Orion had relieved me of the cast-iron pot I carried but my body wasn't used to this kind of travel. My feet were numb, something I was deeply thankful for, since I knew that had they been warm, they would have pained me greatly. I didn't understand how the others, many well past middle age, weren't struggling to keep up as I was. Even my mother seemed less winded than I was.

"Starting to think twice about coming along?" asked Athena. She had circled the group a few times, ensuring that everyone was safe and doing what they were supposed to. She also left a few times to meet with the outlying scouts to get updates on their status.

I said nothing, mainly because I didn't want to her to laugh at my out-of-breath answer.

"You're doing fine, Mila," she said. "It's not an easy walk for any of us even those of us who had been trained for it."

I nodded and continued walking, focusing on the people in front of me, matching their steps and doing my best to catch my breath. I didn't notice when they stopped and nearly careened into the back of someone as they stopped abruptly.

Packs were dropped. Arms were stretched high in the air, working out kinks in shoulders and backs. I was relieved and let my backpack fall from my back without even bothering to slow its descent.

I crumpled like a rag doll into a little heap, like a puddle at my own feet. I wanted to cry, but I bit down on the inside of my lower lip until the feeling passed. Closing my eyes, I waited for someone to come, someone to take care of me and make sure I was ok, but no one came. A dusky grey light hung over the camp as fires were lit and makeshift shelters were constructed. I knew I should join in and be useful, but there was nothing left in me. I wanted nothing more than to just curl up in a ball around my pack and fade away into the dark.

"You need to keep your muscles moving, or else you'll be useless tomorrow."

I knew the voice was speaking to me, but it wasn't familiar. My eyelids fluttered open and I found myself face to face with Dutch.

"You need to get up," he repeated. "Move around."

He held out his hand and I lifted mine to take it. I let him pull me to my feet. He slung my pack over his shoulder and I walked with him, stretching out my aching muscles without the added weight on my back. I stumbled over roots and slipped on snow that had turned to ice during the warmth of the day, but he held fast to my hand.

"My feet hurt," I said. The numbness had worn off and was replaced by searing pain from various places on my feet.

He led me to one of the firesides and helped me sit on a fallen tree that someone had dragged in for that purpose.

"Let me check," he said, sliding his hand under my heel and pulling off my boot.

"You've got some pretty nasty blisters," he said. "The fur in your boots is almost gone, and the seams are probably rubbing." It was no surprise to me. My boots had probably been worn by multiple other women, passed down to me once they made themselves new ones.

He peeled my knit wool sock from my foot slowly, they stuck in places, bloody and wet.

"I'll be right back," he said, standing and leaving me sitting alone on the log, crossing my bare foot over my knee so I wouldn't need to keep it suspended above the snow.

He came back with his pack and a small wooden bowl of warm water. It steamed slightly. He opened his bag and pulled out a small section of cloth, which he dipped into the water and began cleaning the blood and crusty fluid from my feet. When he was done, he pulled out a tanned rabbit hide, cut it into a smaller piece, and wrapped my foot with it, tying it securely with a small strap of leather.

"This will help," he said. "The fur will cushion your foot and help it move freely in your boot. If nothing rubs, it won't blister more. Do you have a spare pair of socks?"

I nodded, reaching for my pack and untying the pocket I knew they were in. I handed them to Dutch and he carefully pulled it over the rabbit fur.

"It might shift if you don't pay attention, so check it now and then to make sure nothing has started rubbing, but this will get you through tomorrow at least."

Carefully and quietly Dutch attended to my other foot. I'd never had anyone take care of me like this—it made me stiff and nervous, as his hands worked so tenderly to ensure I'd feel less pain.

"Thank you," I said as he slid my other boot back on.

"No problem," he said with a smile. "Don't forget to keep stretching and drink enough, we still have a long way to go, and it's not going to get easier."

I nodded, tongue tied.

He walked off into the camp, whistling a tune I didn't recognize. I watched him go until he disappeared into the crowd.

"If you're finished crushing on the boys, your mother could probably use your help with the stew," came Athena's voice. A flush crept up my neck and I was immediately thankful for the settling darkness.

"Leave me alone, Athena," I said, with more boldness than I felt. Standing and testing my new footwear, I reached for my backpack and the bloody socks that lay beside me on the log.

"Wash those tonight and dry them by the fire," said Athena. "It's entirely possible you're going to need them again after tomorrow."

I nodded, and tried not to make it obvious that I had originally planned to just stuff them into a pocket and forget about them. She was right. I didn't have an infinite number of socks.

The stars shone above the empty branches and the sparks from our fires chased them heavenward in dancing showers. I fell asleep on my bedroll alone with my belly full, my body tired and my heart renewed.

# Twenty-Two

## *Meredith*

"THIS IS IMPOSSIBLE," I cried, letting myself dissolve into Leif's arms. We had been working on the doors for days and still they hadn't budged. Each night we spent together in this bed had been both a blessing and a sickening reminder that I was failing. My shoulders ached from shoveling and my fingers were bloody where I had gnawed the edges of my nails down to nubs. I hadn't chewed my fingernails since I was a child, but the stress and frustration of the last days had brought the bad habit back. I didn't bother to stop it; I had no other outlet for my nervous energy. Leif did his best to keep me calm, but every day seemed to end in the same agitated frenzy. Days were disappearing, my ability to help slipping through my fingers.

"We're going to get it," he said, stroking my back as I laid face down on the fluffy down duvet. He comforted me like a child, probably because I was acting like one, but the struggles of the past years had taken their toll on me. I was done. Most of the time it felt like I had nothing left to give.

"Jamison is just about the smartest person I've met when it comes to these types of things," said Leif. "Just give him some time before you give up completely."

If there was any chance of us catching up to the others, and hopefully the tribe with them, we needed to focus on the helicopter. Snowmobiles would have been handy days ago, but we had no time left. Until yesterday we had split our time between the underground hangar, buried beneath the clearing, and the secondary garage that housed the all-terrain vehicles and snowmobiles. It had been time to focus. We gave up on the small vehicles and turned all our energy to the helicopter. Everyone save for Jamison and a few others who helped him spent their time shovelling the layers of snow and from the clearing. It would be easier for the doors to function without the added weight, we'd been told, so while it felt a bit like refilling the grand canyon, we'd been making good progress. Another solid day of digging and it was possible that they'd be clear enough to move—assuming Jamison could get the mechanical parts working.

"I just keep thinking about those girls," I said. "I knew what Nadia was up to, but I had never thought she would take it this far. I feel nothing but guilt for not having tried to stop her earlier."

"What could you have done, Meredith?" Leif asked, "You can't beat yourself up over things you never could have accomplished years ago."

"But that's the thing," I said. "I could have done this same thing years ago. I could have found you, I could have gotten the ball rolling."

"Then why didn't you?" he asked. I had rolled over onto my side, curled in the fetal position.

"I didn't want to believe it, any of it."

"And now you do."

"I do," I whispered. "I was scared, and alone, grateful to be safe and fed for the time being. I had Renny and Jude to think of."

"And now?"

"I have a country to think of."

"We're going to get it working, Meredith. I know we are."

"And the helicopter?" This was the first time I had voiced my concerns about the helicopter. It hadn't been used in twenty years, and the idea that it might not start had been haunting the corners of my mind since we began this project.

"It will start."

Leif's answer assured me that I wasn't the only person to think of the state of the helicopter. Perhaps we should send someone to give it a once-over tomorrow, just in case we managed to get the doors moving.

"Did anyone feed Thor today?" asked Leif, changing the subject.

I shook my head. "He's gone," I said. "I haven't seen him for a few days."

I sincerely hoped that his absence meant that he had gone to find his way back to his warm stall at the caves, or perhaps he was attacked and eaten by wolves. There was no way to know, but I preferred to focus on the former.

"He's a smart horse," said Leif. "He'll find his way home."

"I hope so," I said. At least one of us should make it out of this alive.

"You need to sleep, Meredith."

I knew he spoke the truth, but I wondered if the constant chatter in my mind would allow me that luxury. At the very least, I needed to rest my muscles.

I rolled over as Leif pulled the blanket out from under me and covered me in the voluminous blanket. He tucked me in and stoked my head with his strong hands. The thick layers of blisters and scabs that covered his hands matched my own, and I knew from the lines on his face that he was as weary as I was, but in the moment, I didn't care. I wanted someone to take care of me. If he did that for me tonight, perhaps I would have the strength to take care of them tomorrow.

JAMISON LET OUT A string of curses. If I had been of a more genteel breed, it might have made me clench my teeth, but I wasn't. It was nothing I hadn't heard before and definitely nothing I hadn't said myself once or twice. I didn't condone foul language as a general rule, but I accepted its necessity in desperate times.

If any time could be considered desperate, it was this one.

Daylight was fading quickly and still the doors had not opened. The snow that covered the hidden doors had been cleared, and every hope now sat squarely on Jamison's shoulders. I didn't envy his position, though I too wanted nothing more than to push him to work faster.

He hadn't showered or shaved in a week and his eyes

held a kind of frustrated frenzy that made me think he wasn't sleeping well either. None of us were, and the stores of coffee had taken a sharp decline in the last week. There was no such thing as rationing anymore. We ate what we needed to keep up with the heavy labor and consumed as much of the hot caffeinated beverage as we needed to keep going. Whatever we didn't eat or carry with us would be abandoned anyway.

"If I cut through this latch," he said, coming out of his head for a moment to answer our questioning looks, "we might be able to slide the doors open manually. It would require a hell of a lot of force, but I think if we all worked together it might work."

"Then why the cursing?" asked Leif. "That sounds to me like good news."

Jamison raised an eyebrow. "Because there's also a very distinct chance that cutting that latch might compromise the structural integrity of the entire door, which would cause it to drop directly on top of the helicopter."

*Oh.*

I exhaled slowly and closed my eyes. Why did every ounce of good news always seem to come with a bucket full of bad? I knew from the silence both Leif and Jamison were having the same thoughts. I wanted to bang my head against the wall.

"We have to try," I said, pressing my fingers into my temples. "We have no other choice."

"EVERYONE IS GOING TO need to start pulling when I give the signal," shouted Jamison, loudly enough to be heard in the clearing through the crude hole he had cut just for that purpose. He and some others had welded heavy metal loops to the edge of one of the doors and long chains crossed the clearing where they were held by ten soldiers, including Leif, who were readying themselves for the most difficult tug-of-war they'd likely ever be part of. Another loop had been attached to a long length of thick cable, which was then strung up into one of the nearby trees. Jamison had the thought that if the door did start to fall apart, adding some extra support from above might keep it from crushing the helicopter before the soldiers could pull it clear. I was in the hangar with Jamison, delegated to hand him tools and watch for any signs of buckling on the door so he could get out of the way.

"Cross your fingers, Meredith," he said as he raised the reciprocating saw from its perch at the top of the ladder on which he stood.

I didn't reply, not wanting to betray how hopeless I felt.

The saw started up with a horrible growl that echoed though the hollow space of the hangar. As Jamison touched it to the metal it screeched and sent a shower of sparks to the cold concrete floor.

"Halfway," shouted Jamison, to me, presumably, since it was doubtful anyone on the other side of the door could hear him over the sound of the saw. I held my breath, willing the door to stay together, praying that the soldiers upstairs would have enough strength to get it to move.

"I'm through," shouted Jamison as the screeching sound of the cutting saw waned and stopped.

"Now!" he shouted as loudly as he could though the hole. "Pull!"

We could hear the sounds of the chains pulling taut and the grunts and shouts of the people outside.

Nothing happened.

Jamison jumped down from the ladder, dragging it across the floor to a safe spot.

"It's not working," I said.

"But it's not buckling either. Just wait," he said. "This will work, I know it will."

We held our breath and waited. I was about to turn to Jamison with my panicked thoughts when a smile broke across his face. A tiny creak, and then a scrape—it wasn't much, but light was beginning to stream through a slowly widening gap between the doors.

Jamison hooted and laughed, picking me up by the waist and whirling me around.

"Let's go help," he said, grabbing my hand and dragging me to the ladder that led to the surface.

We climbed through the hatch and ran toward the others, who said nothing as we took hold of the chains and pulled with them. The door was starting to really move now, the grinding sound reverberating through the cold, still air. I wanted to cheer and laugh and cry all at the same time, but I couldn't. Every ounce of energy I had was going into pulling those chains. Tears slipped from my eyes and blurred my vision, but I didn't need to see, I just needed to pull.

It felt like it took hours before we heard Jamison give the all clear, but it was probably only a few minutes. The chains fell in a resounding cacophony that mixed with the jubilation of the soldiers. I had nothing left to join in, but just sat on the ground and cried, listening as they shouted and laughed. Night was falling. Another day was done and we were only halfway there, but the realization that it could be done lifted a weight from my shoulders, freeing me like only this small success could. We were still a long way from joining the others, but we had taken a step forward.

Tomorrow we would do the other door. Tomorrow, we would get in the air.

# TWENTY-THREE

## *Athena*

IT TOOK FOUR DAYS of walking before my father sent me to the forward scouts for an update. The terrain had grown increasingly difficult and it became necessary to stop multiple times a day to rest. It was nearing midday and there were few people left on their feet. Some had even stretched out entirely on the ground in hopes of letting their backs settle and refresh. I could hear the soft groans of pain and the grimaced faces of fatigue. We had been scaling hills for two days and now, on the switchback paths that had likely once been a highway up the side of the mountain, we were fading. While the walk was easier, it was discouraging to be gaining elevation so slowly. It was dangerous to go too quickly, smarter to let our bodies adjust to the elevation changes, but I was impatient. Being sent to the scouts was a welcome diversion. I was able to hike alone, taking a steeper shortcut through the trees rather than following the road. It was more difficult to climb the increased grade, but it was a nice change from the constant gradual uphill.

I let out a low whistle through my hands and hiked as I waited for a return call. If they heard it, they would know I was looking for them and make themselves visible. Even I had a hard time finding my fellow tribe members when they were trying to be invisible.

I heard no return call and continued up the steep incline. My thighs burned from the climb but it was a good feeling. A feeling of accomplishment.

Every few minutes I whistled and listened for the returning one, hearing nothing. The sun was starting to set and I let out one more call before heading back.

"Athena," I heard the voice behind me.

I spun in place, nearly stumbling down the hill I was perched on.

"Sorry to startle you," said Moira, one of the scouts. "I was coming down the hill to the camp and caught a glimpse of you."

"Have you found the estate yet?" I asked.

Moira sat on a rock, stretching her legs.

"Not yet, but we're getting close," she said. "We did find something of interest though; it's not far if you've got enough stamina left. We decided to camp there, and I drew the short straw, so I was on my way back to give your folks a report."

"What is it?" I asked.

Moira's eyes twinkled, "well that would ruin the surprise." Moira was only about six years older than I was, brought to the tribe by her aunt Heidla, one of Asari's closest confidantes. She had no children of her own, but Moira's parents were dead and Heidla had taken her in. There were very few other women close to my age, since I had been one of the first born into the tribe. Most were my mother's age or older. Moira too was fertile, but the heavy tattoos on her face made that almost indiscernible. She was a valued tracker, and really, the other scouts were much older and needed their rest, which was probably the real reason she had been sent back toward the others.

"Come on," she said. Long black hair hung braided down her back and nearly touched the hem of her jacket. She was one of the most beautiful people I'd ever met, I remembered being very nervous to do her tattoos, fearing I would mess up and ruin her face. She had an intricate design of apple blossoms on the left side of her face, which made it look like her deep brown eyes were peeking out from behind the branches.

I walked behind her, following her footsteps until we found the road again. She turned and we walked side by side up the wider path.

"I hear you gave your man a tongue lashing," said Moira, chuckling. "I was hunting, I didn't see it happen, but you were the talk of the camp when I got back."

I flushed. I wasn't ashamed of what I'd said to Torren, but I wasn't interested in being the source of gossip.

"I figured it was only a matter of time. I'm actually surprised we didn't place bets on it. That would have been fun."

"Oh, hush Moira," I said.

"Is he going to bail on you now?"

"I don't think so," I said, "If he was going to, he probably would have by now."

"You going to try to run him off?"

I shook my head. "I like Torren, I think it'll be better now."

Moira nodded. "You two could make a really strong team if you wanted to."

I agreed. There weren't many men I had met that I would have the patience for. Torren was a good man. Steady, but still somewhat malleable.

"We're almost there," said Moira as we came around a bend. "The highway doesn't switch back or go any higher from here. It follows the curve of this mountain and ends about a mile from here where there are some remains of an old suspension bridge."

She motioned toward the woods above us.

"Maybe another hundred yards," she said.

I followed her through the trees, doing my best to keep up and not make it obvious that I was starting to fade. I sincerely hoped the other scouts had made something warm to eat. I was famished and starting to feel a bit lightheaded. My mother had never complained about me doing physical activity while I was pregnant. She had cautioned me to listen to my body, that I'd know if I'd overdone it. I was getting close to that point.

Just as I was about to ask that we stop, I saw the camp. They had built a fire and beside them stood a heap of twisted black metal, sticking out from the snow like some kind of prehistoric carcass.

"What is it?" I asked.

"A helicopter," said Moira, "at least it was. Right now it's not even useful as a backrest. Go take a look through the window."

I stepped forward and found the window Moira spoke of. It was covered in frost but someone had scraped a fist-sized patch, so I pressed my face and hands to the glass to see inside.

I jumped back instantly, shouting something unintelligible. Moira and the others laughed.

"There are people in there!" I said in a loud whisper.

"Yup, three of them, pretty well preserved too it looks like."

"How long have they been there?" I asked.

"Hard to say," said Moira, "They basically just froze and didn't decay any. They could have been here for weeks or years."

It was true. At this elevation it was doubtful that any of the snow had melted at all last summer. Even now the temperatures were colder than they had been at home.

"So weird," I said, peeking back through the glass. There was one figure dressed in a red parka with a hood that covered his or her head, and two figures sat in the cockpit of the craft, still obviously bloodied and injured.

"I know, it's wild. Anyway, we should get going if we're going to make it back to the others by dark."

"I need something to eat first," I said. "I'm famished."

I could smell whatever it was that the other scouts had cooking and headed over to their fire to sit.

"Right. Baby, huh?" asked Moira.

"Yup. I just need a short break and we can go."

Moira sat on the ground beside me.

"I can go on my own if you want to just stay here for the night."

I shook my head and accepted a small bowl of rice and beans, digging in quickly.

"If I don't go back, they'd worry about me, and the last thing I need is Torren and my mother teaming up and telling me I should head back home."

"Do you need to?" asked Moira.

"No," I said. "I need to stop this crazy Nadia person."

"I hear you," she said. "I don't know if I'm going to have babies or anything but if I do, I want them to not get screwed over by the government."

I laughed. "That's a good dream if I've ever heard one."

All the women around the fire laughed.

I finished my food and felt instantly better.

"Let's go, Moira," I said, standing and gathering my things. "Let's go tell the others about this."

"Right behind you," she said, "To be honest, I'd rather not sleep right next to a frozen tomb. Hiking back down the mountain seems like a better option."

I nodded. "Me too."

"I KNOW EXACTLY WHERE that is," said Jude after Moira and I had finished explaining about the helicopter. "Or at least, close enough that we'd be able to get to the estate from there."

"That was the helicopter Rhea and the other girls came on," said Finn.

"Rhea's helicopter crashed?" asked Ember, her mouth dropping open and her coal-like eyes wide.

"It did," said Jude. "That was right when we got there. The weather was awful. It's really a miracle they survived at all."

"Not everyone did," I said, "There are still bodies in there." Jude and Finn nodded. "The only ones to survive were the seven girls. Luckily they were smart enough to find a GPS tracker the pilot had or it's very likely they would have frozen to death out there."

No one spoke. We were getting close and the realities of our mission were starting to sink in. This wasn't a hunt or a game. There were people up there who would stop at nothing to accomplish their plan and would spare no one. We had our work cut out for us.

Nova sighed. "How far do you figure we are?"

"If Jude is right about how to get to the estate from the crash site, we'll find it by noon tomorrow and send word back down."

"Another solid day of walking for the rest of us," said my mother, thinking out loud. "We'll find a place to camp that's near enough, but still well out of sight and camp there. We're going to need a day or so to rest, scout and strategize before we go in."

"You're right," I said, looking around the camp. There was an air of exhaustion that hung like smoke around the inhabitants. I could see it in their road-weary eyes, the grimaces as they rubbed their sore feet or stretched their aching muscles. I too was weary of the walk. What had started as an exciting adventure, full of determination and purpose was losing its luster.

"We should also send a few people on a hunt," said my father, "Tomorrow, perhaps, while the rest of us walk. Having a good meal will help us find our energy again."

"I'll go," said Orion, who was quickly joined by Olly in volunteering. "I could use a diversion."

"Me too," said Dutch with a wink, "And I'll need Orion to carry whatever big game I take down."

Orion grinned and gave Dutch what appeared to be a playful punch to the shoulder until Dutch stumbled sideways with the force.

"I'll be leaving then, I need to get back to the others so I'll be rested enough to get an early start tomorrow."

"Before you go, Moira," said Finn, edging himself to the front of the group, Jude not far behind him. "Whatever you do, don't go too close. They have some pretty serious security systems and if you trip them before we get there, we'll lose any advantage we might have."

She nodded. "I'll let the others know too."

Moira disappeared into the darkness of the trees and we watched her go. No one spoke, weighed down by the heaviness of our task and our own depletion.

"Go rest," said Nova, finally. We dispersed back to our fires and bedrolls.

I watched as one by one everyone closed their eyes and fell asleep. It was silent except for the crackling of wood on the multiple small fires and the deep rumble of snores. I lifted the furs that covered Torren and curled up into his warmth, smiling as he slid his arm around me and pulled me close. I felt the baby flip in my belly, and almost instantly fell asleep.

# TWENTY-FOUR

## *Meredith*

"JUST BECAUSE THE FIRST one worked, doesn't mean we're out of the woods, Meredith," said Leif as we ate a hasty breakfast. I was eager to get going. There was much to do.

Jamison had already left for the hangar. He needed to move all the loops and chains from the first door and weld them to the second one. The heavy-weight cable would also need to be attached and strung into the biggest tree they could find.

"I know," I said, still buzzing from the accomplishments of yesterday. It was the first time in more than a week that I was starting to think this mission wasn't completely doomed. One more huge effort and we should be able to get the second door open and the helicopter out. I shoveled another heaping spoonful of hot oatmeal into my mouth.

"Slow down, Meredith," said Leif, laughing. "Jamison still has a few hours of work to do, and you jittering around beside him isn't going to make him move any faster."

I rolled my eyes, though I knew he was right.

"The rest of us have plenty of work to do," he continued. "If we're going to be ready to fly today, we need to gather supplies and decommission the bunker today."

We hadn't bothered to even pull out the decommissioning protocols until today because there was no point in doing it if we wouldn't be able to leave. Now that it was looking more likely that we'd be taking off soon, it was time to start getting rid of anything classified, sensitive or dangerous.

"Is Emily taking care of the travel supplies?" I asked.

Leif nodded and I was pleased. She seemed to be an exceedingly capable person, and I trusted her completely. My instant devotion for her likely came mainly from her similarities to Delta. She was unflappable, smart, calm and focused. I knew I could rely on her judgement. There were still many supplies in the bunker, but the helicopter couldn't carry much more than personnel and weapons, which were probably the most important things to bring. We'd need some food and first aid supplies, but very little else. It seemed a shame to leave everything else, especially since it wasn't exactly clear how much longer the cold weather would last. Some of it could be secured and retrieved later, but now that the hangar doors were open, the security that had been so carefully constructed was now useless.

It seemed like too perfect a coincidence that the siren began to wail just as I had been thinking about the security system. Leif stood instantly, calling out orders to everyone in the mess hall. Spoons clattered to the table and the sound of boots on the floor became the only thing I heard.

"Go to your room, Meredith," said Leif, his eyes darting around the room. He had pulled out his sidearm and was holding it ready. "Now. I'll cover you."

I was flustered and nearly tripped on my chair as I stood and stepped back. The chair fell backwards onto the floor as Leif's hand pushed me forward.

"Run," he said.

"What's happening?"

"I don't know, but it doesn't matter. We need to get you into your room."

I hurried through the halls. Shouts and gunshots echoed through the cavernous hallways.

"Hurry," said Leif.

I ran faster and he followed me.

We burst through the door to my room, and Leif took the lead, dragging me by the hand to the wardrobe. I had never used it, and hadn't even bothered to look inside. Everything I needed was in the restroom cupboards or the giant walk-in closet.

"Get in," he said, pulling the door open. There were some coats and things hanging in it.

"Get in?"

Leif nodded, but I could see he was confused. "No one briefed you on this?"

I shook my head.

"There's a false back in it," he said, "Feel in the top right corner for a button, it'll open to another small bunker, fully stocked."

He grabbed my arm and pushed me inside.

"There is a lock on the inside, don't open the door for anyone but me," he said. "I'll come back when it's all clear,

Madam President."

It wasn't until I heard him say those words that I felt truly frightened. For Leif to call me 'Madam President' meant that he was thinking of nothing but business. His strict military training had taken over. I was no longer the woman he spent the night with. I was his President, his Commander-in-Chief.

The wardrobe door slammed behind me. I ran my hands over the back wall. They shook as I searched for the switch and I couldn't stop them no matter how much I tried. The button was smaller than I anticipated, and I must have slid my hand over it a few times before realizing it was there.

I pressed it and the back of the wardrobe pushed open into a dark space. I slid through the opening feet first, but the drop was farther than I was prepared for and I fell to the cold hard concrete floor with a painful thud. The wardrobe door closed behind me, plunging me into darkness. My ankle throbbed and tears sprang to my eyes. I must have rolled it when I hit the ground. Muttering under my breath, I spread out my arms, reaching all around me until I brushed the nearest wall with my fingertips. I pushed myself onto my knees and started running my hands over the cinderblock walls searching for a light switch. Steadying myself on the wall, I got up onto my good foot and ran my hands against the higher parts of the wall. I could feel the edge of the door I had come through and cheered silently as my hands slid over a switch. I flipped it on and the room was bathed in light. At the edge of the door was a heavy deadbolt, I turned the knob and it slid into place with a grinding metallic noise.

The room was small and sparse, but I laughed out loud when I saw a twin-sized bed in the corner, complete with sheets that matched the much larger one on the other side of the wardrobe. I glanced around; there was a tiny restroom with a sink, toilet and shower and a table with two chairs.

I hobbled across the room and sat down on the bed. My hands were shaking and my ankle was starting to really hurt. I lifted my leg and inspected it. I knew I shouldn't take off my boot, but I was sure that I'd find whatever splints or bandages in here that I'd need. It had already started to swell, but I was reasonably sure I hadn't broken it. I left my sock on and limped over to a short bank of cabinets against the wall beside the table. I opened and closed cupboards—pocketing a chocolate bar I spied as I went—until I found what I was looking for. The first-aid kit was heavy and jammed full of supplies. I found an elasticized bandage and hopped back to the bed. I wrapped it around my foot and lay back on the bed, propping my foot on top of an extra pillow.

I could hear a commotion and a handful of gunshots above me. I closed my eyes, hoping Leif was safe. A tear slid from my eye and I felt jittery and tense.

"Come back to me, Leif," I said. "I don't care about anything else, just come back to me."

Breathing deeply, I did my best to steady myself. Emergencies had always been a part of my life as the President. I'd never truly been alone through them, even during standard drills I'd had Secret Service members with me. I pulled the chocolate bar from the pocket of my hooded sweatshirt and unwrapped it, breaking off a piece of chocolate and shoving it into my mouth. Leaning back on the headboard, I waited... and waited. I wanted to pace the room; anything to use up the nervous energy, but my ankle objected. Instead I finished the chocolate bar and two others I had seen beside it. They made my stomach churn, but I didn't care.

I didn't know how long I'd been stuck down there alone before I heard a knock on the door.

"Meredith?"

Leif.

I breathed a sigh of relief and stood up and hopped over to the door. Unlocking the deadbolt, the door swung open and I smiled when I saw Leif's face in the opening.

"Is everything ok out there?"

"I'm not sure yet," he said, sliding himself through the hole and onto the floor much more gracefully than I had. "From what we can tell it was a group of hunters. We've noticed them in the area for a while, but I guess having the hangar partially open finally allowed them to notice us."

"What did they want?"

Leif shrugged. "Food probably, shelter maybe? We didn't stop to ask them while they were shooting at us."

"Did you take any captive?"

Leif stared at me with a blank look, as if I had suddenly sprouted a second nose.

"We are ordered to exterminate all threats to your safety."

"Oh," I said, feeling silly. Of course they were.

"Are you alright?" asked Leif.

"Yes," I said, "I mean, no, well, I hurt my ankle, but it's fine."

I was still standing by the door, so he scooped me up in his arms and carried me to the bed.

"Let's take a look."

He unwrapped the bandage with a slow, gentle touch, cradling my foot in his strong hands.

His hands could kill, I mused. Had they? Just now? Had he taken a life and now was calmly inspecting my ankle?

"I don't think it's broken," he said.

I shook my head. "I just rolled it."

"We have some better splints in the infirmary," he said. "You'll be able to walk with them and not worry about rolling it again. We'll get you some ice and some ibuprofen there too."

He wrapped my ankle again and helped me to my feet.

"Don't try to put much weight on it until we get it iced and splinted," he said. "Hang on, I'll just lift you out of here."

He had me in his arms and was halfway to the door when I realized something.

"Wait," I said.

Leif stopped suddenly and glanced around the room, ready for anything.

"Relax," I laughed. "I just don't have my other boot."

Leif smiled and turned back to the bed, leaning over so I could reach the boot. Once it was safely in my hands, he lifted me into the wardrobe. I slid out from behind the coats and onto the soft rug, getting out of the way so Leif could follow me through.

"I'll get you to the infirmary first and then I'll go see what's what."

I nodded as he helped me to my feet.

"You want me to carry you?"

"I'd rather walk, if that's ok," I said. It was a stubborn remnant of being the President. Never let anyone see your weaknesses, never give them a reason to doubt you.

"As you wish," said Leif, "But can I kiss you before you go out there with your tough face on?"

I laughed.

"I'm glad you're ok, Meredith," he said after he had given me a soft, lingering kiss.

"Me too," I said. "About you."

He raised an eyebrow in mock cockiness. "Was there any doubt?"

I rolled my eyes.

"Coming from the man who's been safe and warm and well fed in this foxhole while I fought for my life out there, who knows?" I said. "Maybe you'd gone soft."

"Ouch," said Leif with a twinkle in his eye. "Maybe you should help me to the infirmary. They might be able to do something about my wounded ego."

"I don't know," I said. "Wounded egos are notoriously hard to bandage."

"Then I suppose this is it."

"Suck it up, buttercup," I said, putting my arm over Leif's

shoulder. "And let's get moving, we have a lot to do before we leave."

I COULD TELL BY the look on Leif's face when he came back to the infirmary that the news wasn't good.

"What's wrong?" I asked, pushing my legs off the bed so they dangled from the edge. I had a molded splint on over my sock, and the ice and ibuprofen had helped immensely with the pain and swelling.

"Jamison is dead," Leif said, "And three others with him."

The news hit me like a freight train, knocking the wind out of me. I had heard the scuffle, the gunshots, but I had foolishly assumed all the firepower was coming from us.

"Not Jamison," I said in a whisper, suddenly sure all hope of us getting in the air had flown out the window.

Leif nodded slowly. "I don't know if we're going to be able to get that door open, Meredith. Even if we cut the latch, it took all of us to move it. With four less people..."

He trailed off and I followed him into that bleak darkness.

It was over.

We were done.

I sank back onto the bed and tried not to let the disappointment envelop me. I wanted to say there was another way—that we could figure it out—but I didn't have anything left.

"I'm sorry, Meredith," said Leif. "I know how much this

meant to you."

"Meant to me?" I laughed, the cackle exploding from my mouth as I spit the words out. "This isn't about me. This is so much bigger than me."

"I know," he said. He pulled a chair up and sat on it beside the bed, laying his head on the mattress by my hip. I reached down and ran my fingers through his cropped hair.

"I wish I could fix it for you, but I don't know how," he said, his voice muffled by the mattress.

"I know," I said, suddenly cursing Nadia. I should have stopped her a long time ago when I had the chance, and now it was looking more and more like stopping her would be impossible.

"WE COULD DISMANTLE THE snowmobiles and if we rigged up a pulley, we could hoist them up through the hangar door," suggested one of the soldiers. I remembered Leif refer to him as Estevan.

"That would take days," said Leif, standing in the middle of the mess hall where we had gathered to brainstorm our options. "And does anyone here know how to dismantle a snowmobile, rig up a pulley or put a snowmobile back together?"

"Cutting down the other garage door where the other vehicles are would be a smarter option," said Emily, "But it wouldn't be quick, and we'd still be days away from the estate on sleds. At that rate we'd might as well start walking."

I was dismayed. I had secretly hoped there would be some feasible option presented, but so far, there was nothing that would get us to the estate quickly. For all I knew Jude and the others had already tried to get in. Even if the tribe was with them, there was little chance of their success. Nadia would take no prisoners.

We sat in the room, staring at each other, no one able to offer up another plan.

It really was over.

"Let's eat something," said Leif finally. "Maybe some food will get the brain juices flowing."

Just as we were about to get up from the tables to prepare some food, one of the younger soldiers raced into the room. He wasn't any older than Jude. We had left him in the hangar to give us advance warning if anyone else decided to attack.

"There are people outside," he said, breathless.

"Why didn't you hit the alarm?" asked Leif.

The man's eyes opened wide. "They said they meant no harm, and sir, they asked for Madam President by name. Her first name."

Leif hurried to the door, the young solider fast on his heels. I too dropped the freeze-dried ration packet I had chosen and followed. I could hear the boots of the others behind me, unwilling to miss whatever was happening.

We were up through the hatch within minutes, soldiers popping out one after the other like rabbits from a hole.

I caught my breath as soon as I was outside, partially because the air was cold and I hadn't thought to grab my coat, and partially because of what I saw.

Standing at the edge of the clearing was Thor, flicking his ears and waiting patiently. On his back was Fernie with young Renny seated in front of him. Gibs and Shi were standing beside the horse with Rayne and Angela.

"Hey there, Meredith!" said Rayne in his booming voice. "Fancy meeting you here."

I laughed and hurried forward, Leif reached for my arm, but I shook it off.

"They're fine, Leif."

I hurried to my friends with tears in my eyes.

"You miss us, or what?" asked Rayne as I hugged Angela.

"You have no idea," I said, "How did you find me?"

"I know how to track a horse, Meredith, what do you take me for?" said Rayne. "And then, we found Thor and he kind of brought us back this way."

I could sense that the other soldiers had gathered behind me. Leif was so close I could almost feel him.

"I don't believe we've met," said Rayne to Leif, stretching out his hand in greeting.

"I'm sorry," I said. "Rayne, this is Leif."

I finished the introductions, gently reminding Leif that our guests had been the ones who had kept me safe for the last decade.

"And this is Renny, the boy I told you about." I said, pulling him down from the horse in a giant bear hug. After the day we'd had, I was having trouble controlling my emotions.

"Why did you split off from the others?" asked Rayne.

I shrugged. "I'd hoped to find some back-up," I said. "But my plan hasn't been working so well."

"Does your plan have anything to do with the giant hole in the clearing?"

"It does," I said. "There's a helicopter down there and we were about to get it out when we were attacked. We lost too many people and now we're stuck."

As I spoke, the realization struck me.

"Rayne, I think you guys got here at exactly the right time," I said, smiling at Leif. "Let's get that bird out of there."

# TWENTY-FIVE

## *Shayna*

I CURSED LOUDLY THOUGH no one was there to hear me. I leaned forward and rested my head on the clear glass dome that entombed Kenzie's supine figure. I could tell she was not well just by looking at her, but the tests confirmed it. If I didn't wake her up—and soon—her kidneys would fail and one by one the other organs would follow. I could hook her up to a dialysis machine in hopes of buying some time, but time wasn't the only enemy here. I closed my eyes and let the pale blue light from the eerie sarcophagus filter through my eyelids. The others weren't far behind. We had days, perhaps weeks and they would all follow along behind Kenzie. She was only the first because her body had been taxed so much more than the others. Her strong fertility had resulted in eight live births plus multiple miscarriages in the years she had been under. The constant high levels of medications combined with the detrimental effects of so many pregnancies had racked her tiny body.

"Are you ok?"

I hadn't heard the door open, so engrossed in the thoughts I was having.

"Not really," I said, not lifting my head. I didn't need to; I knew it was Delta that had joined me.

"I can't let her die," I said, my voice hollow.

"Then don't."

I lifted my head and looked at her. She seemed older, somehow, even though I had seen her at breakfast. Perhaps it was the sickening blue light that made her cheeks seem so hollow. Her eyes were darker and tired.

"You think I should just wake them up?"

Delta sighed. "I don't think we have much of a choice. I had hoped someone would come by now, but I don't know what's going on out there."

She was right. I had been hoping too, dreaming that Amos would come for me, hoping that somehow Jude, Finn and Meredith had managed to pull together an army of people that were on their way to rescue us, but we had heard nothing. We couldn't rely on what may or may not be happening out there. I didn't even know how many survivors still lived beyond the walls of the estate, never mind the number who would care about what happened inside it.

"I don't even know how possible that is," I said. "I could wake her up, and we could hide her somewhere for a little bit, but it wouldn't take them long to find us. Plus, I would need some machines from the clinic to assess her health once she's awake..."

I trailed off. As much as I had thought about it, the more difficult it became. Years ago I probably could have woken them up with minimal side-effects, but now? Now I couldn't even predict how their bodies would react. Waking her up could possibly be as sure of a death sentence as staying asleep.

Delta walked to me and laid her hand on mine.

"We're out of options, Shayna," she said.

"Can't we keep riding the current?" I knew the answer but asked anyway.

Delta smiled, her face weak and her eyes brimming with tears.

"This river ends in a waterfall. We have no choice anymore."

I nodded, tears filling my eyes. We had prepared for this, talked about it almost non-stop for the last few weeks. Nadia knew we were no friends of hers and no matter what the situation it was unlikely we would make it out of this alive anyway. She needed me for my medical expertise and Nadia assumed Delta's age had rendered her unable to stand up to her anyway, but we were on borrowed time. All Nadia needed was a plausible excuse, any treasonable offense—real or imagined—and we would be done.

Waking up Kenzie would do it.

"I don't want to die," I said, my hands shaking.

"Neither do I," said Delta. "But if this is the end of me, I want to say I finished strong. I did what needed to be done while I had the chance."

I knew how she felt. If I was honest with myself I knew it was our only option. I couldn't have their blood on my hands either. They had done nothing wrong and if I could do anything at all, I would give them a chance.

Inhaling a strong deep breath to steady myself, I nodded. It was time. It was time to be serious about our plans. Time to plant our feet.

"Let's do this."

LESS THAN AN HOUR later we met back in the small, dim room full of silent sisters. We hadn't needed to plan anything, having run the scenarios so many times that we both knew them in our sleep. We had been collecting some items we thought we might need over the last weeks, things that wouldn't be missed like medical supplies and food. We had amassed a stash in Rebekkah's room. My room or Delta's would be too obvious and Rebekkah's wing was typically ignored. I wasn't even sure Nadia would know how to find her way there. It would only buy us a small amount of time, but a little was better than nothing.

"There's a small chance they won't notice she's missing right away," I said.

"We can only hope," said Delta.

The process of waking Kenzie up enough to move her was complex, and by the time I was done it would be approximately one o'clock in the morning. At that point we could hopefully move her without being detected.

I scrubbed my hands to surgical standards and Delta helped me into a gown. Allowing germs and bacteria into Kenzie's body now would be detrimental. She had been in a sterile environment for so long, I wasn't sure how well her immune system would still be working. Pulling on my gloves I ran over the procedure in my head.

"Hang on," said Delta, coming up behind me as I stood facing Kenzie. She lifted the back of my gown and slid a hard object into the waistband.

"A knife," she said. "I couldn't get any guns, but the boys had hunting knives and said we could use them."

I nodded without speaking. My lips moved as I recited the steps to myself as she dropped my gown back down over the hidden weapon.

Slowly and deliberately I started to work. Pressing a button on the side of the enclosed tube caused a hissing noise as the glass slid back, revealing my patient. I would dialyze Kenzie to remove the toxins from her blood once I had disconnected the steady drip of medicine. Her body would flush it out eventually, but because her kidneys were already on the verge of failure, I figured it would be better to relieve them of that additional strain. Once her blood was flushed, she should start to come around, assuming there were no other issues. That step alone would take hours, though it wouldn't be immediately noticeable to anyone who walked into the room.

"How long do we have?" asked Delta.

"They're checked every four hours," I said. "Assuming the nurse or doctor on duty cares—which is becoming increasingly rare these days. I volunteered for the overnight shifts, but that doesn't mean no one will come in."

At the very least our being here wouldn't alert suspicion,

though the dialysis equipment might. They'd been watching Kenzie's kidneys for a while and I hoped I could convince whoever came that they had finally failed and dialysis was necessary.

I finished what I was doing and slid the glass back over her.

"What do we do now?" Delta asked.

"We wait," I said, pulling off my gloves and tossing them and the gown into a trash can.

Delta sat in the only chair in the room and I sat on the floor beside her leaning against the wall and pulling my knees up to rest my arms on them.

"How long will it be until she wakes up?"

"I don't know," I said. "That's the part that makes me nervous. It could take an hour, maybe three or four before she starts to move, though more than that before she's fully coherent."

Once she was starting to wake up, it was extremely likely that she would start to move, or mumble or moan well before she would understand enough about her situation to lie still. If someone came in and she was moving or speaking we'd be discovered immediately.

"Then we wait," said Delta. Reaching down she took my hand and squeezed it. "You're doing the right thing."

"I know," I said, squeezing hers back. "We wait."

TIME MOVED MORE SLOWLY than I'd ever known it to—there were times that I looked at the clock and could have sworn it must have moved backwards. Only three hours had elapsed and still nothing. I monitored Kenzie's vitals regularly, sometimes doing little more than hovering over the monitors and watching her heart beat. It had sped up in the last hour, which made me think she was coming out of her deep sleep and preparing to wake, but even that was no guarantee it would happen soon.

My muscles ached from the awkward vigil I held on the floor beside Delta. It was nearing midnight and still there had been no sign of awakening. I yawned and stretched my shoulders and shifted to a more comfortable position.

"My butt hurts," I said, moaning as I adjusted myself.

"How much longer do you think it will be?" asked Delta.

It was the same conversation we'd had almost every hour as the time ticked slowly by.

"I didn't know an hour ago, and I sure don't know now," I said. "Her dialyzing should be done soon, but I had hoped she'd be starting to come out of it by now."

Delta nodded and we both fell silent as we watched Kenzie. A twitch, a flinch, any tiny movement would indicate that our waiting was coming to an end, not that Kenzie waking would be anything beyond the very beginning of our coming adventure. Adventure. That's what I'd call it. It sounded better than mutiny or treason. Nadia would surely see it that way, but could it truly be wrong to save a life? I didn't want to think about it, though visions of the consequences we would surely face had perched themselves in the deeper recesses of my mind. They would not sit quiet, nor did I truly expect them to.

"Did you see that?" asked Delta.

I snapped to attention.

"What happened?"

Delta frowned. "Maybe nothing, now I'm not sure if I imagined it. I thought I saw her eyes flutter."

I pushed myself up, bracing my hands on the walls as I stood. Delta was on her feet, still watching Kenzie.

She lay as still as she ever had and nothing noticeable had changed from the last time I checked on her. I approached her slowly, watching carefully.

Then I saw it. It was subtle, almost imperceptible, but it was there. Her eyelashes fluttered and I noticed a distinct twitch in the corner of her mouth.

"She's waking up," I said in a whisper. Delta met my eyes across the tiny girl's sleeping form. I knew that she too understood the gravity of what we were doing, but neither of us could back down now. As scared as we were, it was our only option.

Kenzie gasped slightly, sucking in a quick breath, and let out a quiet sigh. I reached down and took her hand, squeezing it. Delta did the same thing on the other side of the bed. Before long we could see more signs of life. Her hand quivered under mine, and I rubbed it, warming it with my own shaking hands. I wasn't sure which of our hands shook more.

"Kenzie?" said Delta, her voice low and soothing. "Kenzie dear, can you hear me?"

Her dry cracked lips parted and she responded with a moan. Her eyelids fluttered as if her eyes underneath were scanning the room.

"Kenzie?" I said and her eyes opened, not much, but she opened them. "Kenzie, wake up."

I knew she would come around slowly, but anxiety was starting to overcome me. I needed her awake. I needed to get her out of here. I needed... I needed this poor child to live.

"Mom?" she said, her voice hoarse and raspy. Tears sprang to my eyes. I couldn't control them any more than I could control my shaking hands. It was one small word and it shattered my heart. She wasn't waking from a nightmare; she was waking up to a nightmare. It wasn't fair. She was almost thirty years old, and here she was, nothing more than a child looking for her mother. She herself was a mother many times over, and I doubted she had any idea.

Her eyes opened fully at the exact moment a tear spilled from my eye and ran down the side of my nose, pausing on the edge of my lip. She focused on the ceiling first, and then looked from my face to Delta's.

Delta was crying too, and reached out a hand to stroke Kenzie's face. They hadn't shaved her head recently, and she bore about an inch of thick black hair. Her curls were gone but her beautiful blue eyes shone under the dim lights.

"What's happening?" she asked.

"We'll explain later, dear," said Delta. "Right now all you need to do is wake up."

"I'm awake. Help me up."

"Not yet," I said. "You haven't used your muscles in a long

time, Kenzie, we need to take this slow."

I noticed the confusion in her eyes, as her brain tried to reconcile everything she was experiencing. She was groggy and weak. It would take a long time to bring her back to proper health. Her muscles were atrophied from disuse, and though she had been fed well, she'd need a lot of physiotherapy to get back to normal. She had a long road ahead of her if we managed to find her enough time to get better. I choked back a lump that had grown steadily in my throat. This wasn't the time. Kenzie needed us right now.

Her vitals were normal and the dialysis had finished. I disconnected her from the machine, and pressed a square of gauze firmly against the punctures in her slender neck.

"Did Margo come back?" she asked, settling her eyes on Delta. "I told her not to go, but she didn't listen. I told her..."

"Margo didn't make it," said Delta, the tears making tracks down her wrinkled face. "We'll explain everything later, I promise."

"Oh," said Kenzie.

A sudden bang startled me and nearly caused me to release the pressure I was putting on Kenzie's wound.

"What in the hell...?"

It was Doctor Anderson, his fat, sweaty body silhouetted in the doorway. He had gained tremendous amounts of weight in the years we'd been here, which was impressive, since I often found myself hungry even after our strictly rationed meals.

I exchanged a look with Delta and then looked back as Dr. Anderson stormed into the room.

"What do you think you're doing, Dr. Murray?"

I faltered, scrambling for a reply that might seem feasible—that would somehow justify my actions. Kenzie's eyes were terrified, unsure of what was happening and unable to do anything about it.

"Her kidneys were failing..."

"Her kidneys were fine," Dr. Anderson bellowed, grabbing my wrist and turning me around to face him. I stood my ground, holding the gauze on Kenzie's neck as well as I could.

"Get your hands off the patient," he said, bits of spittle flying in my face as he spoke.

"Dr. Anderson," said Delta. She had come around the bed and now stood behind the livid doctor. "There is a perfectly reasonable explanation, if you'll allow me."

The Doctor spun around to face her and before he could say anything I heard his strangled cry. He lurched backwards and stumbled, trying to regain his balance. He failed, hitting his head squarely on the heavy dialysis machine, landing with a giant thud on the ground, unconscious—Delta's hunting knife embedded firmly in his gut.

"What did you do?" I asked, knowing full well.
Delta stood before me, shaking, as blood poured from the wound in Dr. Anderson's side. I dropped to my knees and tried to stop the flow with my hands.

"I need some rags," I shouted, and Delta ran to the clinic to find some. She returned with an armload of clean towels and crouched beside me.

"Check on Kenzie," I said, realizing I had stopped putting pressure on her wound when I moved to help the doctor.

Delta stood and checked, whispering encouragement to Kenzie.

"She's fine, the bleeding has stopped."

"Put a new piece of gauze on her neck and tape it down," I said, throwing out instructions while I worked.

"If you save him, the first thing he'll do is mount our heads on spikes," said Delta. "You know that right?"

I did. Very well.

I pressed the towels into Dr. Anderson's flabby belly.

"I can't just let him die, Delta," I said. "I took an oath..."

An oath I took very seriously, so seriously that I was here now, making sure Kenzie didn't die.

Delta nodded, and left the room, coming back with a pillow.

I knew what she was going to do and did nothing to stop her—though my eyes pleaded with her for some other way.

"It has to be done," said Delta, crumpling to her knees by the head of the unconscious doctor. She lowered the pillow over his face and pressed down, suffocating him.

I watched him as he died there on the floor. His breathing slowed and when I checked for a pulse, I could find none. I nodded to Delta.

"Now what?" I said, pushing myself to my feet and pacing the room.

"He was old, and fat," said Delta. "Would it be all that

suspicious that he died?"

"But what if someone sees the knife?"

"Stitch it up, who is going to look?"

I nodded then stopped, looking down at the body in front of me.

"It could be an appendectomy incision," I said, the words tumbling from my lips before I had fully formed the thoughts. "If I stitch him up, we could say he came to me in pain, and I tried to operate, but his appendix had already burst and he died in surgery."

"Sounds completely plausible to me," said Delta.

"Go find Harris and Vaughn" I said. "We're going to need help getting him into a body bag."

I went to the clinic as Delta left in search of her sons. They would be easy to find at this time of night. They were likely sound asleep in their beds. Finding a suture kit, I walked calmly back to Dr. Anderson.

"Is he dead?" asked Kenzie with a rough voice.

I nodded.

"Good," she said. "I never liked him."

"Me neither."

"When did he get so fat?" she asked. I would have burst out laughing at her candor if the answer wasn't so horrible.

"You've been asleep for almost fifteen years," I said, almost unable to believe my own words.

"Oh," she said and fell silent as I worked.

I had just finished sewing up Dr. Anderson's wound with

practiced stitches when Delta arrived with two men who had obviously dressed in a hurry. Harris' jeans were crooked and he was barefoot, while Vaughn sported the craziest bed-head I had ever seen. They both were yawning and bleary-eyed.

"We need to get him onto a gurney," I said. "There should be a body bag in the back of the closet to the right of the clinic door."

Delta went back to the clinic to find the thick black bag. She returned with it and a gurney before I had finished taping a piece of gauze over the wound. I took my scissors and cut his shirt open as I would have if I'd needed to perform an emergency surgery.

"Kenzie?" said Harris suddenly, as if he'd just woken up to notice that she was awake.

"Hi," she said. "I hear I've been asleep for a while."

She spoke as if she was trying to convince herself. Harris and Vaughn both nodded, their eyes wide, surveying the scene.

"I'll explain later," said Delta.

Harris shook his head. "It's pretty obvious what happened," he said. "You don't have to explain yourselves to us."

Vaughn crossed the room to take Kenzie's shaking hand.

"You look really old," she said.

Vaughn shrugged and ran his other hand through his hair.

"It's what happens," he said.

I moved the gurney until it ran parallel to Dr. Anderson's dead body and lowered it to its lowest setting. Delta spread the thick black body bag across the bed and opened the zipper.

Harris and Vaughn joined us.

"Lift on three," I said.

I counted and together we heaved the massive body onto the gurney.

"I call his food rations," said Harris, who was noticeably thinner than he should be. Vaughn snickered and Delta smiled, though not widely enough for it to touch her eyes.

The bag barely zipped over his belly, and I breathed a sigh of relief as his face was swallowed by the shadows in the bag.

"Are we taking Kenzie out of here?" asked Harris.

"That's the plan," I said. "We'll need to move fast. Security will be making their rounds right away."

"Too late if you planned to get out before that," said Harris, "We saw them moving on our way here. They didn't notice us, but they're out already."

For an instant I panicked. Too much had happened in the last hour and I was no longer thinking clearly. We had Dr. Anderson in a body bag, and a frail girl that would immediately be noticeable to anyone we happened to meet along the way.

"You could put her in there," said Vaughn.

I followed his gaze to the lumpy black bag on the gurney.

We all stood there silently, looking from the bag to Kenzie and back again.

"She's so tiny," said Delta, "It might work."

Kenzie had said nothing, but though there were tears in her eyes, I could see that she had set her jaw.

"I'll do it," she said, a tear sliding down the side of her face.

"I need to get out of here."

"We won't leave you in there a second longer than necessary," said Delta, grasping the girl's hand.

"I know."

Harris stepped forward and slid his arm under Kenzie's arms as Delta lifted her from the table. Sliding his other arm under her knees, he raised the wisp of a girl from the table without any effort at all.

"Sheesh Kenzie," he said with a wink. "You've gotten a little bit heavy."

"Shut up, Harris," she said, a smile tickling her lips. "You're just old and weak."

"Probably," he said, nodding solemnly.

Delta unzipped the bag far enough that Dr. Anderson's legs were visible. It was the most logical place to put her, since there was extra room at the bottom of the bag. Vaughn heaved his legs apart so there was a space for Kenzie, and Harris laid her gently down, her head at the doctor's feet.

"Can you curl yourself up?" I asked.

"Not easily," she said.

I moved forward to help her pull her legs up so she was a tiny ball.

"You'll be able to breathe for a little while, but try not to move, especially if we're stopped."

Kenzie nodded. I kissed her gently on the head before pulling the zipper over her, hiding her in the bag.

"Is it obvious?" I asked, once they were both hidden inside.

"Well, I saw you put her in there," said Harris. "But I doubt I'd figure you were smuggling someone else in the bag if I hadn't."

"Good enough," said Delta, "Let's get moving. Boys, you go first and meet us at Rebekkah's room. If you see any security, just go back to your rooms and find us later, when you can."

"Be safe," said Vaughn, his hand resting for a moment on Kenzie's hidden body.

They left, and suddenly I was terrified.

"What are we doing?" I asked Delta, feeling desperate and anxious.

She rested her hands on my shoulders.

"Take a few deep breaths," she said. "You can't go out there looking terrified."

I nodded and inhaled, sucking as much oxygen into my lungs as possible. I didn't know how she was able to remain so calm. I had noticed a slight tremor in her hands as she had raised the pillow from Dr. Anderson's face, but my own hands still shook more than hers. Straightening my back and running my hands over my hair, I nodded. This was not the time to lose control.

"Let's go," I said.

Together we pushed the gurney into the clinic and then through the second set of doors into the hallway. There was a makeshift morgue on the property though it was little more than a basement workshop with an incinerator at the far end of the estate. It was impossible to bury the dead here and with any chance of disease, cremation was really the only way to dispose of a corpse. The staff wings weren't far from the morgue, but security didn't patrol there. If we made it out of the clinic and main areas, no one would stop us.

The florescent lights flickered and hummed above us as we pushed the gurney. One of the wheels squeaked on the tile floor and I groaned. It felt like a siren, pealing out and alerting everyone of our presence. I clenched my jaw and pushed. It took both of us to keep the gurney moving at a decent pace—not so slow we'd be in the hallways longer than necessary and not so fast that we'd look suspicious. There was only one elevator big enough for the gurney and it wasn't much farther. Once we got Dr. Anderson into it we would be nearly home free. We could carry Kenzie back up through one of the back stairwells and no one would notice. At least, no one who would care. It wouldn't be long before the kitchen staff started waking up to prepare breakfast, but we still had more than enough time.

"Dr. Murray, stop where you are."

I closed my eyes, took a deep breath and followed the command. The voice came from behind me and I took a second to make sure I was properly composed before turning.

"Yes?" I asked.

"Who died?" said the security guard. It was Hank, and for that I was grateful. He was a burly hulk of a man with a heaping helping of authority, but he was a grandfatherly type who had a soft spot for doctors who quietly kept him medicated enough to hide the effect of the early stages of dementia. I smiled at him, relieved. There were others on the security force that weren't as malleable and forgiving as Hank.

240

Setting my face to the appropriate level of sadness and exhaustion for a doctor who had done everything she could for her dying patient, I sighed out loud.

"It was Dr. Anderson," I said, shaking my head. "He came to me in pain and it turned out to be appendicitis. While I was operating, he coded on the table and there was nothing I could do to get him back."

Hank nodded slowly, "He wasn't exactly the healthiest guy around, I guess."

I lowered my voice. "Between you and me, I would think a doctor should know better."

He reached over and squeezed my shoulder.

"It's been a long night for you, you want me to take him down to the morgue so you can go get some sleep?"

"No," I said, almost too quickly, and then fumbled for an explanation, "It's rather cathartic for me to do it, but thank you."

"Alright," said Hank. "Go on and finish up then, I won't hold you up any longer."

I turned back to Delta as Hank strolled away, whistling and gave her a relieved look. That couldn't have gone better.

"Hank, what are they doing?" came another voice down the hallway.

I swore under my breath. I knew that voice. It was Nadia's favorite Secret Service member, Cyrus. He was—plainly—a jerk, which was probably why Nadia kept him close to her. Why he was wandering the halls at this hour was beyond me, since he rarely left her side. I had learned long ago to stay out of his way. He was a small man with a disproportionately-sized ego.

"Dr. Anderson passed away during emergency surgery, appendicitis," said Hank, visibly agitated by the younger man. "Dr. Murray and Ms. Parsons here were taking him down to the morgue."

"And did you open the bag to check?" asked Cyrus, "Or do we just believe what everyone tells us around here?"

"Well, no..."

Cyrus pushed the older man out of the way and stalked to the gurney.

"Open it up."

I nodded, and tugged at the zipper, opening the black bag to reveal Dr. Anderson's face.

"Nice try," he said. "Keep going. I'm going to need to see some proof of Hank's story.

"Yes sir," I said, pulling the zipper farther, until the neatly-stitched wound in his side was visible. I wasn't able to pull it much farther without exposing Kenzie.

I met Cyrus' eyes and steadied my gaze. I needed him to believe I felt I had nothing to hide.

"He died of a heart attack on the table," I said. "There was nothing I could do."

We locked eyes for longer than I wanted to, but I knew what he was doing and held firm, waiting for him to relent and tell us to continue. My muscles were tense under my clothes, but I did my best to appear calm and unconcerned by his presence. I knew Kenzie knew better than to move or speak, but I could hardly breathe knowing that she too was probably holding her breath.

Finally he shrugged. "More food for us, I guess."

He winked at me which made my spine crawl. I forced a smile to my face and pulled the zipper back up, swallowing Dr. Anderson and hiding Kenzie in the shadowed depths.

I nodded to Delta and together we pushed the gurney toward the elevator, silently waiting for something else to happen, for the other shoe to drop. It didn't. When the elevator door closed, I pressed my back against the wall and slid down to the floor.

"We're almost there," said Delta. I didn't know if she was speaking to me or Kenzie, but it didn't matter.

The elevator dropped slowly, making my stomach turn as we descended into the belly of the estate. I had only been down here once or twice in the decades we'd been here, and I had little desire to return, but I would do what needed to be done to save Kenzie's life.

"Do you think you can manage Kenzie on your own?" asked Delta as the elevator stopped on the basement floor and the door opened to the silent dingy halls. "We'll get everything done faster if we split up."

"I think so," I said, peeking out the door before unzipping the bag. "Kenzie, do you think you could get onto my back?"

She wasn't very heavy, but she also didn't have much muscle mass left. Giving her a piggyback was likely the best bet and would allow me to move more easily than carrying her in my arms.

Kenzie nodded, she was white as a sheet and obviously

relieved to be getting out of the bag. I helped her sit up on Dr. Anderson's legs and turned my back to her. Tears came to my eyes as I felt Delta arrange her frail arms around my neck.

"I'll lean forward as much as possible, but hold on as well as you can," I said, lifting her fragile body from the gurney and setting out into the hall.

Delta quickly zipped up the gurney and I could hear her grunting as she wrestled with the squeaking metal contraption, disappearing into the shadows alone.

"It's not far, Kenzie," I said quietly. She had rested her head on her arm and I could feel her warm breath on my neck.

This was all so very wrong.

"Thank you," she whispered. My tears spilled over, and even if I could have reached my face, I wouldn't have wiped them away. These girls deserved each one that fell.

It was strange that I still thought of them as girls. They hadn't been girls for many years, yet still they seemed somehow unchanged—frozen in time in their glass bubbles, their bodies changing and growing. Hunched over I found myself out of breath before I reached the first landing. Kenzie wasn't very big, but I had grown much older too. I wasn't accustomed to carrying much weight. Biting my lip I pushed forward.

"We're almost there, Kenzie," I said, willing myself to believe it. No matter how quickly we reached Rebekkah's room, we were far from safe and this was far from over.

# TWENTY-SIX

## *Mila*

I PULLED THE RABBIT furs from my feet and cringed.
They were caked with blood and clear fluids from the multitude of
blisters that covered my feet from toe to ankle.

"That doesn't look good," said Jude, who had joined us at
our fire every day since we left.

"It doesn't feel good either," I said, dipping a rag into the
small can of water I had boiled. Laying the cloth over the open
sores, I sucked air through my teeth as pain shot through my feet.

Why had I even come? I had been given a pass—a gift—the
ability to stay at the camp, safe and warm and blister-free. Why
had I been so stupid? Now instead of a warm hut I was out in the
woods less than a mile from an estate where horrible things were
happening.

We had arrived here the day before and Nova had insisted
we take this day to rest and recuperate from the hike, gain our
strength before we... what? I didn't even know what we were
planning on doing.

I gently wiped the caked blood from my feet, soaking
the rag again and again until the water in the can was a murky
brown. They felt better in the cold air, but I knew that once I put

them back into my boots it would be more of the same.

"What size are your feet?" asked Jude.

I raised my eyebrow and nodded at my exposed foot.

"About that size, I reckon," I said. What a ridiculous question.

He started to laugh at what must have been a bewildered look on my face.

"I suppose that's right," he said. "Back in the olden days, when I was your age, we all knew the size of our feet. That's how we'd know what shoes to buy."

"I've never bought shoes," I said, a flush creeping up my neck.

"Hang on... I might be able to help you."

He stood and walked off into the crowd, returning a few minutes later with Rebekkah on his back.

Crouching, he let her slide off his back and onto the hard packed snow beside me before running off to join someone who had called him.

"Jude tells me you're having shoe issues?" she said and glanced at my feet. "Ouch. He wasn't exaggerating."

I shook my head. "Do you know something that might help?"

She smiled and reached over to squeeze my shoulder. "I do, mine." She pointed to her own boots. They were black and shiny and had thick tread on the bottom.

My mouth dropped open and I stared at her while she smiled at me.

"It looks like our feet are a similar size, though you'll need to try them on to be sure." She reached down to grab a handful of her thick pants and pull her foot onto her lap. She quickly undid the latches and fasteners and slid the boot off. "Do you have decent socks?"

I didn't see anything wrong with the ones I had, though they were rather worn and stained.

She didn't wait for me to answer before putting her fingers in her mouth and whistling.

"Finn doesn't pay attention if I call him by name," she said, winking at me. "He's the one who taught me to whistle like that, but I bet it grates on his nerves."

I smiled.

Sure enough, Finn appeared seconds later, his shaggy locks bouncing as he sauntered toward us.

"Need something babe?"

"Can you get one of the spare sets of socks from my pack?"

He nodded and headed off, not even bothering to ask why. He returned with a pair of thick wool socks that matched the ones Rebekkah was wearing. She waved him in my direction and he passed them to me. I had never felt socks like these. They were almost as soft as well-worn leather, and knit with the tiniest stitches. They were thick, but not coarse, and even softer on the inside than they were on the outside.

"Did you make these?" I asked, amazed at the workmanship.

"I'm pretty sure those were made by a machine," Rebekkah

said, laughing.

"They have machines that make socks?"

She nodded, still chuckling. "At least they did before everything froze over. They had whole factories that made nothing but socks I bet."

My mind sufficiently boggled, I slid one of the socks onto my foot. It was warm and soft, hugging my feet but not so tight that they were constricting in any way.

"Just wait until you feel the boots," she said. "I remember how they used to feel. There was nothing better than a good pair of shoes."

I took the boot she handed me, while she pulled my sad worn moccasin over her beautiful sock. It looked out of place on her. Everything she wore looked new and clean and perfect. Her pants and jacket coordinated and had so many zippers and pockets that I wondered if she knew what was in them all.

I pushed my foot into the boot, pulling it up with both hands until it popped into place. The fit was as close to perfect as I could have hoped for. Perhaps these new shoes were like that for everyone, the thick foam in the sole cradled my foot the way one would carry an egg, supporting and cushioning in all the right places. I sank my other foot into the second boot and rose to my feet. I couldn't control the look of wonder that must have spread across my face, and I could see the joy on Rebekkah's face as she watched my reaction.

"It's so soft," I whispered, knowing full well that I hadn't properly conveyed the depth of the new sensation. Rabbit fur was soft, this was entirely different.

"I'm so glad they feel good," said Rebekkah. "They were kind of wasted on me."

I took a few steps, marvelling at how the thick sole protected my foot, such a marked difference from the thin leather that did nothing to disguise the jagged ice and rocks beneath my feet. For the first time in my life I felt invincible. The pain from the sores on my feet had all but disappeared, and with these feather-light boots, I felt renewed.

"Thank you," I said to Rebekkah, meaning the words but knowing they were insufficient.

"Enjoy them," she said, before nodding to Finn who came to carry her back to their fire.

I don't know how long I tested the boots before I realized the people around my fire were gone, and it wasn't the only fire that had emptied. A few stragglers remained but most of my tribe and the others who had joined us were gone.

"Where did they all go?" I asked one of the older women who was still resting in the warmth of her fire. She nodded her head up the mountain. I thanked her before heading in the direction she indicated.

They weren't far from camp, and though there were many of them they scarcely made a sound. It wasn't until I had joined them that I realized anyone was speaking at all.

Finn and Jude stood near the front of the cluster of bodies, talking quickly, but low enough that I had to strain to hear them.

"The sensors will go off if anyone crosses them," Jude said, pointing into what appeared to be nothing but air. "And we will lose any advantage we had."

"They run from tree to tree in a perimeter around the estate, starting at six inches above the ground and every six inches from there up to nearly eight feet," added Finn. "Nearly invisible to anyone who doesn't know what to look for."

I had no idea what they were talking about until I glanced at the tree behind them. Camouflaged into the bark were a series of nodes, perfectly in line and exactly six inches apart. Finn was right, I wouldn't have noticed them otherwise, but now that I saw them I had no doubt they were man-made. Nothing in nature followed that kind of pattern.

"How are we planning on bypassing them?" asked Leona.

"Jude and I have been scouting to find a place that might work for crossing," said Finn, "But it's completely impractical for a group our size."

"And we haven't found a good spot yet either," added Jude, "At least not one that doesn't offer a significant risk of injury." I could feel the energy leaking from the group like a water skin with a hole in it, emptying to the ground in a flood of silent frustration and anxiety.

"It's not hopeless," said Jude, apparently sensing the same mood I had. "If either Finn or I get across without setting them off, we have friends inside who can shut the system down long enough for us to get to the estate."

"If they don't catch you first," said Nova.

"That shouldn't be a problem," said Finn.

Nova sighed, "I'm glad you are confident, but forgive me if I continue to be cautious with my optimism."

"Caution is a good thing," said Rebekkah, from where she sat on a small rocky ledge. "Caution will keep us alive, but if there are any people who can get into that estate without being seen, it's Finn and Jude."


"WE FOUND A SPOT that might work," said Jude, "Though it's impossible to tell if there's anything under the snow."

They had been searching for the remainder of the day, analyzing trees they could climb and low branches that spanned over the invisible fence, but so much came down to that one simple problem. How does one safely drop from a tree into the snow without worrying what was beneath?

"It could be a thick, soft drift, or it could be solid rock with no more than a dusting of snow," said Finn. "Or a crop of jagged rocks just waiting to break your leg. You just never know."

The skies were beginning to darken, the tendrils of night reaching toward the still bright horizon, threatening to overtake it. There was little daylight left and though Jude and Finn were anxious to cross the perimeter, it was looking less likely as the minutes seeped by.

"Take me there," said Athena. "I have more experience in the woods than you two, you're probably missing something."

Torren stood silently behind her, equally intent, though

saying nothing.

"We'll all go," said Orion, standing and reaching for his bow.

I doubted his intent was to include me in his assertion, but I stood with everyone anyway. There was nothing more interesting to do than follow along.

It wasn't far, perhaps a mile or two from camp, but the terrain was difficult and as a large group we were slow. The twilight crept in on us and as the night air cooled, a wispy fog settled between the trees. No one spoke. I marvelled at how silently we moved, considering the size of our group. I could hear little but the gentle whispers of rubbing cloth and the occasional crunch of the snow beneath our boots.

I nearly walked into Orion when he halted in front of me, stopping just before my face plowed into the middle of his back. Everyone had gathered in a clump, and I struggled to see around the cluster of bodies.

"C'mere kid," said Orion, reaching for my arm.

I reached back to him, and before I could figure out what his intention was, he pulled me toward him, planted his other hand under my arm and swung me up and onto his shoulders as easily as a mother would lift her child. I muffled a squeak that slipped from my lips.

Orion was taller than almost everyone there, and from his shoulders I had a completely unobstructed view of everything in front of us. His hands held my knees and I wrapped my hands under his soft, bearded chin.

In the fog it was actually possible to see the thin red streaks cutting through the settling night. As strange as it had been to try to imagine this invisible barrier, it was almost stranger to see it—bands of light, perfectly aligned in rows, ominous and fierce in their silence.

Finn spoke in a low, deep voice, and I had to strain to hear him. I did my best not to move and rustle on my perch so Orion wouldn't have trouble hearing either. It was impossible to catch every word, but I managed to hear enough to make sense of it.

There was a tall tree with a good thick branch, sturdy enough to support the weight of a few people at least, but I could see their concern. It was high, too high to easily drop from.

"Can you drop a rope from the limb?" asked Leona.

Jude shook his head. "We thought of that, but we wouldn't be able to get far enough from the fence that we wouldn't risk swinging into it as we climbed down."

"The only logical way to do it is to jump, and propel ourselves away from the fence as we do."

I could almost hear the sounds of brains working around me, calculating the height of the branch, the unknown surfaces underneath and the possible risks.

"We don't have many people," said Nova, quietly. Dax nodded beside her, understanding her words. "We can't risk injuring someone we'd need to fight."

Her words sent a sombre weight across the silent group.

"You can risk me."

The words seemed to float through the cloud of

uncertainty, cutting through the fog and though they were quiet, no one seemed to miss them.

"Don't even start, Rebekkah," said Finn, hissing at his wife.

"It's the smartest option," she said. "If you got me up there, I could drop and tie the end of a rope to something so you could slide down."

"Rebekkah, you're pregnant," said Nova under her breath.

She nodded. "I know, but not one of us standing here is immune from risk right now, and there's no telling if we're getting out of this alive anyway. I don't want to risk my child any more than I want to risk my husband, or my friends, but I told myself early on that if there was anything I could do, I would do it."

Her eyes pleaded with Finn in the fading light.

"Let me get you in there."

Finn's clenched jaw relaxed almost imperceptibly, but his eyes betrayed him. It was our best shot and he knew it.

"You're going to break a leg," he said.

"Maybe both of them," said Rebekkah, her eyes shining, knowing he was giving her his blessing.

"I don't want to have to carry you all over the place just because you feel like being a hero."

"You'll carry me and you'll like it," said Rebekkah, raising her eyebrow, a smile playing on her lips.

"You're right," he said, leaning forward to kiss her. "I will."

"Your body should protect the baby well enough," said Nova, "but try not to land on your stomach."

"I wasn't planning on it," said Rebekkah. "That would hurt.

I'd prefer to land on the useless parts if I can manage it."

Nova smiled, but it didn't reach her eyes.

Archer reached his hand out to Jude. In it was a thick coil of sturdy rope.

Jude took the rope and nodded, pulling himself up into the lowest branches of the tree and starting to climb. It was hard to see his dark clothing amid the branches, but a few moments later he landed with a gentle thud.

"I tied up one end of the rope and wrapped it around the branch," he said, then turned to Rebekkah. "The rest of it is bundled and ready to drop to you once you're on the ground. If you can take it and tie it to something a little ways away, we could slide down after you."

Rebekkah nodded. "I can do that."

"Finn, I think you'll be able to manage her up the tree, but you'll need a boost to get you up into the branches."

"I can help with that," said Orion, pushing forward through the crowd. "Sorry kid, you're losing your seat."

I let him lower me down from his shoulders and he moved to the tree, Torren silently following his older brother.

With practiced ease, Finn and Rebekkah arranged themselves so Rebekkah was hanging on to Finn's back. I hadn't noticed before but Finn's jacket had something like stirrups attached to them on both sides. Jude pulled the straps from his friend's hips and secured them around Rebekkah's thighs. It was ingenious. Rebekkah could hold on and Finn had his hands free for climbing.

Together they moved toward the men at the tree, and Orion held out his hands to balance Finn as he lifted a foot to Torren and slid it in the step he made with his hands. Orion braced his arms and let Finn use them to climb, putting his other foot into Jude's hands. Once he was fully extended, he reached up a hand and grasped the lowest branch that was sturdy enough to bear their combined weight.

"I'm not high enough," he said, "I can't curl us both up there."

Orion crouched and put his hands on his thighs.

"Use my shoulders," he said.

Finn lifted his legs and set his boot onto Orion's shoulder pulling himself up from the branch until he was standing on the straining man.

I could hear the grumble from Orion as his mighty body slowly straightened to a standing position, braced by Jude and Torren.

"Got it," said Finn as he crawled onto the branch, Rebekkah still securely hanging from his back.

Orion groaned as he was freed from the weight. I hadn't noticed that I'd been holding my breath as I slowly let it out, watching as Finn and Rebekkah disappeared into the branches.

"You need a boost too?" Orion asked Jude.

"I don't need one," he said, "But if you're offering..."

"After those two I could probably just toss you up there."

Jude chuckled and stepped into Orion's waiting hands and placed his hands on the bigger man's shoulders.

It seemed like such an easy movement, and before I knew it Jude was gone too.

We stood in silence, counting our breaths as we waited. I wasn't sure if there would be some kind of signal before she jumped, so I listened carefully. If there was a signal, I didn't hear it, but I did hear the heavy thud of her body hitting the ground. I sucked in a breath and waited, watching the black spot that had appeared in the snow on the other side of the fence, willing it to move.

It didn't. My heart began to pound in my chest, and in a singular motion we all moved closer to the barely visible fence, straining our eyes in the disappearing light.

"Rebekkah?" someone whispered.

"Rebekkah!" I could hear Finn's voice from up in the tree. He hadn't even attempted to be quiet.

"Oh, I'm fine," she said with a giggle. "But I think I sprained my ankle."

Finn's exasperated growl bellowed from the tree before Jude shushed him.

Rebekkah continued to chuckle quietly as she rolled herself over. Using her hands, she pulled and slid herself away from the fence to the base of another tree. I couldn't see the rope anymore, but I knew she was securing it.

Before long I could see the shadowed figures of Finn and Jude sliding down the rope.

Finn went to help Rebekkah while Jude approached the fence with caution.

"We're going to try to find our friends inside," he said. "And I'm hoping that they will be able to shut down the fence, but if you don't hear from us or if the fence doesn't shut off within the hour, feel free to climb the tree and come after us."

"If we don't hear from you, I'd assume they found you," said Orion, "and in that case we can just run through the fence."

Jude nodded. "Very true, we'd have lost the element of surprise. Though, Orion, I don't think you'll be here."

Orion snorted in surprise.

"We need you to come with us. Finn and I were discussing it and we could use someone of your size and strength."

"Alrighty," he said, moving toward the tree.

"And," Jude said, causing Orion to pause, "We need someone small."

I held my breath as one by one, I felt every eye fall on me.

"No," said my mother. I didn't know where she was standing but I knew her voice. "Jude, you're not taking her."

"I'm sorry Phoebe," he said, "We should have talked about this earlier, but we only now realized how much easier she would make it."

My mother stepped forward to the fence and I could see her face in the moonlight.

Orion moved to her and placed his hands under her chin lifting her face to look at his.

"I won't let anything happen to her," he said, his voice low and comforting. They stood like that for what seemed like a long time, my mother seemingly drawing the strength she needed from him.

It did not escape my notice that no one had asked me.

# TWENTY-SEVEN

## *Shayna*

IT WAS QUIET IN Rebekkah's room.

She had only been gone for a few weeks, but the air seemed stale and unused. Kenzie's weight on my back had grown heavier as I hurried through the halls. It was a relief to bring her inside, close the door behind me and lay her gently on the bed. I could feel her relief too as she melted into the soft mattress. She was shivering, though I didn't know if that was from cold or shock. Her fingers trembled like leaves on a dainty branch. She had been holding on as tightly as she could, and I knew she would be exhausted.

"Let me find you some more blankets," I said, running my hand over her forehead. No fever, that was good.

I opened the closet where I knew the heavier wool blankets would be. It was the same in every room. They were neatly folded on the shelf. I took both of them, unfolded them and draped them over Kenzie's body. I sat down on the other bed and leaned forward, resting my elbows on my knees. It felt good to stretch out my back and shoulders and for a moment I let myself believe that we were safe. Here in this dark room we were free of all the terrible things that existed beyond its walls. I knew the feeling wouldn't last, and soon the dam would break and let it all in again. But for the moment, I let myself believe the lie.

I could hear Kenzie sniffle and pushed myself across the space between our beds to my knees on the floor beside her. Tears were flowing from her eyes as she cried without making a sound.

"Everything feels wrong," she whispered.

"Everything is wrong," I said. "But you leave that to me. All you need to do is rest."

"What did they do to me?"

I knew she wanted answers, I knew she needed answers, but I hesitated all the same. I didn't want to be the one to tell her. I didn't feel up to breaking her heart.

"I'll tell you," I said, my voice cracking, "Soon, I promise."

She nodded, and as her eyes closed I felt the shame envelop me. I hadn't done this to her, it wasn't my idea, nor my actions that put her into this place, but I had done nothing to stop it. All these years I knew what was happening, all these years I had pretended my hands were tied, but I was no less capable then. I watched her in silence until I heard the quiet click of the door. Harris and Vaughn slipped into the small room, Delta right behind them. She closed the door behind her and the four of us looked at each other with wide eyes. I could tell they were all thinking the same thing I was: a combination between "Why didn't we do this sooner?" and "What on earth were we going to do next?"

Delta went to the closet and pulled out one of Rebekkah's emergency candles, a thick, heavy thing in a jar. She lit the wick and the glow of candlelight danced on the walls around us. I waited for her to say something wise, some sage tidbit of wisdom that could cause us all to breathe a little easier and offer a tiny bit of hope.

She said nothing.

Perhaps even Delta was all out of hope.

We sat in silence in Rebekkah's room, watching Kenzie sleep. They would notice she was gone soon enough if they hadn't already, and come looking for her. This wouldn't be the first place they'd check, but the estate wasn't that big. We couldn't hide here forever. We needed a plan, but so far I was coming up empty.

Lost in my thoughts, it wasn't until Harris stood from the bed and crossed the room to the window that I understood the sound I'd been hearing, a barely noticeable clicking.

"It's Finn!" he said in an excited whisper. Delta, Vaughn and I scrambled to our feet and pressed our faces against the cold, frosted window.

It was true. There on the ground beneath the window stood Finn, and on his back, a smiling Rebekkah. He motioned for someone to meet him at the back door.

"I'll go," said Harris.

"Take Vaughn with you."

Harris shook his head. "I'll attract less attention on my own."

He was right.

"Take them to the clinic," I said. "It's close to the garages and they can hide their outdoor gear in one of the closets there. I'm pretty sure Rebekkah's wheelchair is still in there too."

It was entirely likely that no one had really missed her. No one paid much attention to her as it was. Finn, on the other hand, had been the subject of much debate over the last weeks. Everyone was used to seeing him around and his sudden disappearance had not gone unnoticed.

Harris left quietly, and we waited. Every breath seemed like an eternity and my heart pounded in my chest like the bass at the rock concerts I attended so long ago.

Finally the door opened and I held my breath as Rebekkah wheeled herself into the room, Harris right behind her, holding the door.

Delta hurried to the girl and leaned in to hug her. I could see her shoulders shaking as she held the girl. When they parted, Rebekkah looked at me.

"I'll need you to check me out later," she said "I have a hunch I broke something, but it's not causing me pain, so it can wait for now."

I nodded. Not for long, but it could.

"Did you find any help?" asked Delta.

"We did," said Rebekkah, "We found Jude soon after we left. He and Meredith were with Rayne, just like you thought they'd be."

"Did you go to Amos?"

Rebekkah nodded, "We did, but he refused to help us."

Delta cursed under her breath and my eyes went misty.

"Did you give him my letter?" I asked.

"We did."

I set my jaw and nodded, disappointed in myself for carrying even that tiny bit of hope that he would come for me.

"It's not all hopeless," said Rebekkah. "We found Rhea's family in our travels. They were with Amos and his community. Her father and sister came with us, and we met a tribe of female warriors in the woods on the way here. They are just outside the perimeter fence."

"Can we turn it off?" Delta asked Harris.

"Not easily. The security office always has someone in it and we don't have a key."

"Finn has that covered... but he's going to need a bit of help from you two."

"C'mon Vaughn," he said, "He told me he'd fill us in when we got back to the clinic."

They left.

"Is that Kenzie?" Rebekkah asked suddenly, apparently just noticing the sleeping figure on the bed. "How did you get her here?"

"It is," said Delta, "But that is a story for a different day. Right now we need to know what your plan is and how we can help."

# Twenty-eight

## *Mila*

I COULDN'T HEAR JUDE anymore. I had to rely on the directions he had given me. His voice had carried through the air shafts for a while, but as I moved farther from the main vertical shaft that he and Orion had lowered me through, he became more difficult to hear.

"Four rights and then the third left," I reminded myself. That's what was left in this tedious journey.

"It's not going to be fun, Mila," Jude had said as they looped the rope under my arms. "I'd go myself, since I've been in there many times, but I'm too big to do it quietly."

It seemed so long ago, that conversation on the roof. I felt like I'd been in these shafts for so long, inching my way, sliding and pushing with my hands and bare feet. I had left my boots up on the roof, knowing their hard rubber would bang against the shiny tunnel. The socks Rebekkah had given me were too soft to have any traction, so bare feet it was. I actually longed for my old buckskin boots as my bare feet pushed against the cold metal, but I would be there soon enough.

I could hear people talking on the other side of the metal, voices and laughter echoing through the tunnels. I tried not to breathe for fear they would hear me. Surely if I could hear them, they could hear the little sounds I made, amplified through the vents.

I pushed myself slowly, trying to move as quickly as I could. We didn't have much longer to get this done before the others at the fence came after us, destroying any advantage we may have had.

My toes ached as I pushed myself around the last corner and found myself at a closed vent. There were no screws holding it to the wall, Jude had told me that, a simple push and I'd be free to crawl out.

Through the slats of metal I could see a tiny room, filled with bright lights and strange beeping noises. There were so many buttons, so many... I didn't even know what to call the things I saw in there. I'd never seen anything like it. I held my breath, waiting for the fear to subside, running through the instructions Jude had given me. He'd drawn a simple diagram on the snow of the roof, explaining what I'd see and what to look for.

"It will all be labelled," he said. "The switch for the fence is marked 'perimeter'."

I didn't want to tell him that I didn't know how to read, but I didn't see any way around it. I think he realised the problem when I had started to cry.

He had watched me in silence for a moment and then took his stick and wrote out the series of symbols I had seen before but never understood.

"This is what it will look like," he'd said.

I analyzed the letters, memorizing their shapes and patterns as much as I could, counting them and making sure I knew the first and last ones.

I closed my eyes as I lay beside the vent. Getting this right made me more nervous than the two men inside the room. Finn and Jude would take care of them.

Breathing slowly through my open mouth, I waited.

The knock on the door was crisp and loud, a happy staccato echoing through the little room.

"Who's that?" asked one of the men before swivelling around, his chair squeaking beneath him. He groaned as he stood. I heard the sharp scrape as the door opened.

"Hey Fellas," said Finn, in the smooth way he spoke that made my knees tingle. "We just wanted to say hi, and let you know we're back... and TAG."

I heard them laugh and the clatter of two sets of feet running in opposite directions.

The man shouted something, some string of words that made no sense and the other was on his feet too. Within seconds the room was empty and the door clicked into place. It was silent except for the beeping and whirring of the machine on the wall.

I laced my fingers between the metal slats of the vent and pushed. I needed more strength than I thought before it gave way. Setting it gently on the floor I tumbled from the hole in the wall with about as much grace as the baby fawn I'd watched enter the world only weeks ago. How had so much changed since then?

My muscles ached as I stood and I quickly stretched

them out as I scanned the noisy bank of lights. Jude had said the switch I was looking for was on the right side of the table, so I turned there, doing my best to ignore the rest of it. Even being able to ignore half of the strange machine, I felt overwhelmed. There were so many markings and letters and things I didn't understand, and I knew I didn't have much time. I scanned the switches and buttons, mentally ignoring the ones that were the wrong shape and size until I came across one. I counted the letters that marked it. It was the same pattern as the one Jude had written.

My fingers trembled as I touched the cold metal switch and I closed my eyes and flipped it.

Nothing happened.

There was no noise, no lights, nothing. I hadn't asked Jude what would happen when I actually flipped the switch, but it seemed strange that nothing did.

I stood there for a moment, staring.

I had to get out of here.

They were going to come back.

I dropped to the floor again and slid myself back into the hole, feet first. I'd have to wiggle through the vent backwards this time, which wasn't ideal, but I had no choice. The cover needed to be put back and there wasn't enough room to turn around.

My heart raced in my chest, and a rushing sound filled my ears as I lifted the vent and pulled it back into the wall. The door opened with a bang and even the walls rattled. I flinched and yanked my fingers back from where they were sticking out of the vent.

I couldn't move. I couldn't breathe.

The man growled and made more noise than was actually necessary for what he was doing. He pounded at something and his angry voice filled the room.

"We got one of them, but I lost the other one. Get everyone looking for him."

Got one.

I pressed my lips between my teeth and willed myself not to cry out. I didn't know who they had, and even though I wasn't the biggest fan of Jude, I didn't think either of them deserved whatever horrors lived in this place.

The man left the room again, and I flattened my hands against the metal duct and pushed myself backwards, retreating into the maze of tunnels. I moved for a while until I felt the urge to scream dissipate, then stopped, silent and unmoving in the dark. My hands trembled and I clenched them into fists to stop them. I felt suddenly trapped, as if the tunnels were slowly crushing me.

Jude hadn't told me where to go.

# TWENTY-NINE

## *Athena*

"WE NEED TO GO," I said, my voice as firm as possible without sounding angry. I was angry, but no one needed to know that. I was sure Torren and my mother could tell, but I didn't really care.

"Have patience, Athena," said Nova, exactly what I knew she'd say.

"It's been long enough," I said. "If they haven't gotten the fence turned off by now, they're not going to."

Her eyebrow raised.

"You know how long it will take them?" she asked. "You've been in there and know what needs to be done?"

I rolled my eyes. It was a childish move, I knew, but she brought that out in me sometimes.

"We wait," said Dax.

I could see Torren pacing by the fence, watching it as if he'd be able to see something. The fog had dissipated, so the only way you could know if the fence had turned off was to touch the metal plates that were attached to the trees. They vibrated slightly, almost imperceptibly. Phoebe had her fingers on the one nearest us. She had taken her post the moment Jude was out of sight and hadn't moved since. I knew she would alert us the moment they turned off, but I was done waiting. Dutch and Olly hovered near her, probably ordered by Jude to keep an eye on her.

Even Leona stared into the blackness beyond the fence, Ember beside her, both sitting on a rocky ledge. Rowan leaned against a tree behind them, staring into space with the same bored look that the rest of us had.

I wanted to say more, convince them all that I knew best, but it was pointless. They would wait, and there was nothing I could do about it, short of running through the fence myself and forcing their hand.

I could do that. I would. But not yet.

I could feel Torren behind me. He had this strange way of calming me which angered me as much as my mother's patience. I didn't want to be calm. I wanted to fight.

"You wanna back off?" I said without looking at him.

"Not really."

I turned to face him and raised an eyebrow in an identical copy of my mother's face.

He snickered.

"You insist you're so different from her," he said, "and yet..."

I rolled my eyes again. What did he know? I found myself a rock to sit on and pulled my knife from its sheath on my thigh and my stone from the pocket of my coat.

"You think your knife might be dull?" asked Torren.

"I know it's not," I said. "It gives me something to do. I'm sick of waiting."

He sat on the ground beside me, leaning his back against my rock.

"I don't want you to die."

I snorted.

"I'm serious Athena."

"You think I can't defend myself?"

Torren shook his head.

"I know you can," he said. "But I also know you don't think. I don't want you to do something stupid in there."

In some ways he was right. I knew how to fight, and kill, though I knew very little about battle. That alone was probably the reason I was so riled up.

Leave it to Torren to tell me why I felt the way I did.

"I don't want you to die," he repeated.

I shrugged in some self-conscious show of bravado.

"What difference would it make?"

He turned to me on the ground and reached up to take my face in his hands. I didn't want to look at him. I didn't want to let those eyes see inside me to the places I didn't let anyone.

"It would make a difference to me."

I took a deep breath, feeling like I should answer, but something happened. I could feel the energy in the group shift as people all around me rose to their feet and pulled out their weapons. Torren and I stood at the same time and looked into the darkness. I was disoriented. They were all looking the wrong way. The fence was behind us.

I shoved my stone into my pocket and held my blade—loose, but ready.

To my left I could see Leona on her feet, knives in her hands too, and Ember beside her with Leona's bow drawn. I'd never seen her with a weapon and almost laughed, but there was nothing wrong with a show of force even if it was imagined.

Together we stood, looking into the forest in silence, until I heard it. A horse snorted. It wasn't one of ours.

"Archer?" came a deep voice from the woods.

Ember's father lowered his bow.

"I'm here," he said. "Lower your weapons everyone."

I lowered my arm, but kept my knife at the ready. I could tell most of my companions were doing the same, though it didn't escape my notice that Leona sheathed her knives.

They began to move. From out of the shadows I could hear the sounds of horses and as they moved into the moonlight I saw them. They had huge horses, much like the ones Leona and the others had brought with them. There were probably twenty or thirty men, dressed in furs and dark clothing. The horses snorted, sending clouds of foggy breath from their noses.

One of the men rode closer to us and slid down from his saddle as he neared my mother. I tightened my grip on my knife, unsure of this man with the rifle slung across his back.

"Hello Nova," he said. "I didn't think I'd see you again."

My mother took a deep breath and exhaled slowly.

"Hello Amos."

They stood, facing each other for longer than I would

have expected.

"I understand you might need some help."

Nova nodded. "We do."

Amos nodded.

"We will help you then."

I could see Leona and Ember whispering to each other as Archer moved forward to greet Amos.

"Is Rayne with you?" Archer asked, scanning the tree line.

Amos shook his head. "I was going to ask the same of you. I thought he left with you."

Archer shook his head.

Amos seemed confused by this. I didn't know who Rayne was, but somehow he was important.

"Do you know who Rayne is?" I asked Torren in a whisper.

He nodded. "Orion told me about him. I think he's the Shepherd's brother."

I had heard them all talk of the Shepherd—Orion, Leona, Torren, even my mother. The way they had spoken he seemed almost larger than life to me. This man, however, was not the giant leader I expected to see.

"Where is he?" I asked, as if Torren might know better than the people who had actually met the man.

He shrugged and slid his arrow back into his quiver.

"Let's go find out what's going on."

I followed him to where Amos and the others stood, talking in hushed voices. I could hear Archer and my mother explaining the situation, describing the estate as Jude and Finn had described it to her.

"We will follow your lead," said Amos. "Just tell us where you need us."

Nova nodded.

There was little more to say.

"It's off."

I heard the voice, as soft as a breeze, then stronger.

"It's off!"

The entire group took a collective breath and turned toward Phoebe who still stood with her fingers on the plate.

I looked from her to the darkness beyond the fence and stared into what lay beyond. It was a place I had never seen, held an enemy I had never fought.

Torren slid his hand into mine and together we looked forward. We moved as one.

It was time.

# THIRTY

## *Shayna*

"LET ME LOOK AT your leg," I said.

Rebekkah turned her chair toward me and began unzipping the snow pants she was wearing. They had a zipper that went all the way down the side which was convenient, and probably the entire reason she chose that pair.

"We should probably hide these anyway," she said. From the waist up she was dressed like anyone else in the estate, but the insulated pants were a dead giveaway that she had been outside. "I didn't have time to take them off at the clinic, and I figured if my leg was bleeding it might be more noticeable."

I nodded. That was smart.

I inhaled through my teeth when I saw the blood on her jeans.

"That doesn't look good."

With one hand under her heel, I gently lifted her foot and pulled off the tattered buckskin boot she was wearing. It seemed strangely out of place, but I didn't mention it.

"Feels fine," said Rebekkah. "One of the few benefits, I suppose."

"Do you have scissors or anything in here?" I asked.

She shook her head.

"Here," said Delta.

I turned to see her handing me the hunting knife I'd last seen plunged into the belly of Dr. Anderson. She had cleaned it nicely, but it still caught me off guard.

"That'll do," I said. I slid the knife under the hem of Rebekkah's jeans, blade out and pulled the fabric tight on either side. Doing my best not to brace the blade on Rebekkah's already swollen ankle I pulled toward me, cutting the fabric with ease. It didn't surprise me that Delta knew how to keep her blade sharp.

It was as I had suspected. Her tibia had a compound fracture, low on her shin. Blood was seeping steadily from the puncture.

"I'll need to patch you up," I said. "We can't risk infection."

"You could cut it right off," said Rebekkah. "It's not like I need it."

"I could," I said. "But let's get out of here alive before I do that."

Standing, I brushed my hands on the bedspread. Bloody handprints on my clothes—even as a doctor—would be suspicious.

"I'll run to the clinic and get what I need to patch you up," I said. "Delta, could you cut her out of those jeans and a towel or something pressed on there to slow the bleeding?"

Delta nodded and helped move Rebekkah over to the bed while I took a breath and opened the door.

"Good luck," said Delta as I slipped into the hallway.

I did my best not to move too quickly or seem suspicious,

consciously slowing my steps and avoiding the urge to glance around.

The clinic was dark and mostly empty. We usually just kept a nurse on rotation in case someone came in with an issue, but those were few and far between, usually little more than a headache or a cold. I waved at the nurse on duty as I strode through the room to the storage closet at the back. There were far less supplies than there had been when we arrived, but we still had some of almost everything. Whoever had stocked the estate sure knew what she was doing, or at the very least was very lucky.

I pulled some supplies from the shelves, stuffing what I could into the pockets of my lab coat. I put the suture kit into the waistband of my jeans, right at the small of my back. I'd need to set the bone, disinfect everything, and stitch her up. A splint would be helpful too, but we'd have to improvise. Rebekkah wouldn't be moving her leg much anyway, so a heavy layer of cloth could do the job.

Passing a mirror on the way out, I was satisfied with how well I had hidden the supplies. At a quick glance, no one would notice.

The nurse had gone back to her magazine, so I didn't bother to say goodbye. Pushing open the clinic door I found myself face to face with Nadia.

"Dr. Murray," she said "Have you seen Dr. Anderson?"

Was this a test?

"He's... um..." I said, stammering. "He's dead."

Nadia's eyes narrowed. "Well, that would explain why I

couldn't find him, what happened?"

How was it possible she didn't know? Did that mean she also didn't know that Kenzie was gone?

"Appendicitis," I said. "I did an emergency surgery, but it had burst already. He had a heart attack on the table."

I was amazed at how easily the lie flowed from my lips.

"Well then," she said, her voice short and terse. "Who is checking on the girls?"

"I was just there. Everything is fine," I said, hoping my voice sounded light enough to keep her from being suspicious and asking any more questions.

A shout caused her to glance over her shoulder just as someone crossed the hallway. We looked too late to see who was running, but a security guard ran by, after him.

"Good grief," said Nadia, muttering under her breath. "What's going on now?"

She walked in the direction of the commotion and I took the opportunity to slip away. More guards raced past me, presumably to join in the chase. It had to be Finn or Jude. I hurried back to Rebekkah's room, this time less worried about being seen. Half the people in the hallways were running anyway.

"Did you get what you needed?" asked Delta as I closed the door behind me.

I nodded.

"I think the boys might be in trouble," I said.

Delta exhaled so it made the wispy hair around her face flutter upwards.

"I think we're all in trouble," she said.

"It was time," said Rebekkah, though I could see the lines of worry on her forehead.

"The baby," I said suddenly. In all the excitement I had nearly forgotten Rebekkah was pregnant.

"The baby is fine," she said, in a firm way that made me wonder if she knew that for sure, or was just saying it to help herself believe it too.

"Any bleeding?"

"No."

I nodded and left it at that. "We'll check it out tomorrow."

If we made it to tomorrow.

Delta was holding a folded towel on Rebekkah's leg.

"The good part about this is that you're not going to feel it," I said. "I need to set the bone, stitch you up and wrap it."

I handed Delta a cotton sheet I'd found in the closet. "Could you tear this into long strips?"

She took the fabric and pulled out her knife to cut through the seams, and as she tore, I sat on the bed next to Rebekkah.

"Hang on to the headboard and brace yourself as best as you can," I said, getting a firm grip on her foot. I wasn't sure there weren't other fractures in her ankle, but for now this one was the most pressing.

I set the bone quickly and went to work stitching up the puncture. There were so very many things that could go wrong, complications I'd need to watch for, but for now I just had to hope she would be fine.

"I have to admit," I said as my needle threaded through her skin. "It's nice to work on someone in an emergency situation who isn't screaming."

Rebekkah laughed. "You're preaching to the choir here. I'm glad I'm not screaming too."

"So, how did you do this, exactly?"

"Jumped out of a tree."

Delta snorted as my mouth dropped open.

"Why on earth were you jumping out of a tree?"

She winked. "Because if you were patching up Finn or Jude here right now, he would be screaming."

I nodded and left it at that.

Within minutes her leg was bandaged and wrapped and she was back in her chair with a pair of sweatpants and some slippers that covered the bandages.

"What can I do?" asked Rebekkah.

"Recover?" I suggested.

She rolled her eyes. "My leg will do that for me, whether I sit in here or not. I want to help."

I glanced at Delta who shrugged.

"She could probably get around more easily than you or I," she said. "Attract less attention."

I nodded.

"Someone needs to go check on the children," I said. "Once Nadia realizes what's going on, if she hasn't already, they will be her final move. She's not going to want to give them up."

Rebekkah nodded.

"I'll go," she said, turning her chair to the door. Delta opened it for her.

"Hide them if you need to," she said as Rebekkah ventured alone into the hall.

Delta stared at the door once she was gone.

"I don't like this," she said, her voice barely above a whisper. "I knew we'd have to plant our feet eventually, but I was hoping that it wouldn't get this bad."

She turned and sat down beside me on the bed.

"Nadia is a terrible person," she said. "We all know that. Someone needs to stop her, but I wish someone else would come and do it for us."

I patted her knee.

"I've already lost Simeon, and Red. I don't know where Rayne, Elias, and Amos are, and now Jude and Finn are doing... I don't know... something that's going to get them in trouble. Just being here is putting them in danger." She looked at me with tears in her eyes as she spoke. "I can't lose anyone else."

I wanted to tell her everyone was going to be ok—that we were all going to get out of this—but I knew she'd see through my attempt at bravado. Instead I said nothing.

She inhaled in a long drawn-out breath and exhaled slowly, as if pushing some hidden reset button. I watched as she transformed back from scared, lost Delta to the strong, invincible one I was more used to seeing.

"What the...?" she said, looking over my shoulder, and starting to laugh.

I turned to see Jude's face pressed against the window from the outside. I hurried to the latch and pushed it open so he could crawl inside. There was a rope around his chest, but I could tell he'd climbed much of the way on the brick ledges on the outside of the building.

"What are you doing?" I asked as he crawled through the window. "Your hands must be frozen."

He pulled the rope from around himself, dropped it through the open window and gave it a tug. It disappeared up like a slurped spaghetti noodle.

"Who's up there?" Delta asked. "Finn?"

Jude shook his head, blowing on his hands to warm them. He wasn't wearing any boots either, presumably for better footing while he climbed.

"You don't know him," he said. "He's one of the people we brought back with us, and let me tell you, it's handy to have a giant on the roof."

Neither of us asked what he meant. For now it didn't seem important.

"Where's Finn?"

Jude frowned. "The guards caught him. I barely got away. Found one of those old dumbwaiter shafts. Got in without anyone seeing and shimmied my way back up to the roof."

"Back up?"

He shook his head. "Long story. We got the perimeter fence turned off so the others are coming. I saw some movement in the woods from the roof before I climbed here."

"What's going to happen?"

Jude shrugged. "I'm not exactly sure. The plan was to draw as much of the security team outside, and engage them there. How they'll do that is kind of up to them."

I peeked outside, though I could see nothing in the dark.

"Once most of the guards are distracted, we can find Nadia. Hopefully then she'll be more vulnerable."

"And cornered," I said. "So, desperate and unpredictable."

Jude nodded. "Is she ever predictable?"

"Touché."

"How'd you guys get Kenzie in here?" Jude asked, suddenly realizing she was sleeping on the bed.

"That's a long story too," Delta said. "She wasn't doing well; we needed to get her out before her organs started shutting down." His eyes filled with tears and I knew the question he was having trouble asking.

"She's alive," I said. touching his elbow, "She's fine for now."

He bit his lip and pushed back any fears that had started to creep in.

"Rebekkah?"

"She went to go find the children, and hide them if necessary."

"Good plan."

"What are you going to do?" Delta asked Jude.

"I need to find Mila."

"Mila?"

"We brought her with us. She's the one who turned off the perimeter fence, and I realized I didn't tell her where to go after that. She's a kid, and probably stuck in an air vent somewhere. If I don't find her, her mom might kill me."

"Then go," said Delta.

He gave her a quick kiss on the cheek, and hurried from the room, turning toward the back steps that would take him to the basement, presumably to find an entrance to one of the air shafts.

"I want to go check on the girls," I said. They were probably fine, but staying here was making me itch. I felt helpless and trapped. "Can you stay here with Kenzie?"

"It's probably best," said Delta. "Nadia doesn't trust me, so if anything is happening out there, she'd probably assume I had something to do with it."

"She is a smart woman," I said, with a wry smile.

"Hopefully not smart enough."

# THIRTY-ONE

## *Mila*

THERE WAS SO MUCH commotion in the halls, and a siren had begun to peal throughout the estate. It was shrill and hurt my ears, even from inside the air ducts. It made moving easier, since I didn't need to worry as much about being quiet. People weren't paying attention anyway. I had tried to get out of the ducts a few times, but many of the vents were screwed to the walls from the outside. Either that or the rooms were full of angry-looking people. I pushed my way down the next duct, hoping to find a way out. My feet were starting to ache and I was tired of crawling around.

I made it to the vent and peered through the metal slats. It was a room—a bedroom—bigger than any I had ever seen. There had to be a dozen beds. I could hear someone crying—more than one person—but I couldn't see anyone. Whoever was in there had to be sitting against the wall that the vent came through.

There was a knock at the door. Someone moved to open it, a woman, perhaps the same age as my mother, maybe older. I could hear them talking, but I couldn't quite make out the words. The woman left, and someone else came in. My breath caught in my throat when a woman in a wheelchair rolled into the room.

"Where did Annie go?" asked a small voice.

"She wanted to go see what was happening," said Rebekkah.

"What is happening?"

Rebekkah rolled forward until she was almost in front of the vent.

"There's a problem," she said. "But don't worry, I'm here to make sure you are all ok."

Other small voices asked questions I couldn't make out, but Rebekkah answered them as calmly as she could. I listened to her and felt more at ease.

"Rebekkah," I whispered. She didn't hear me.

I coughed slightly to clear my throat and called again, poking my fingers through the holes in the vent. "Rebekkah."

She heard me this time.

"Who's calling me? Everyone, be quiet."

I wiggled my fingers. "Over here, in the vent."

She turned and I saw her eyes.

"Who's in there?"

"It's me, Mila."

"Mila? What are you still doing in there? Didn't Jude get you out? Hold tight for a second while I find something to unscrew the vent."

She rolled away and looked through the closet.

"I have a spoon," said one of the girls in the room. She moved to where I could see her, crossing the room. She wasn't much younger than me, dressed in a white nightgown that fell to the floor. Her skin was dark and her black hair was tightly braided against her head.

"Thanks Aster," Rebekkah said, and came back to the vent.

The spoon was clumsy, but it worked well enough. Within minutes she had the screws out and together we pushed out the vent.

I tumbled into the room no more gracefully than I had the first time, and was immediately surrounded by a flock of giggling girls in nightgowns. They were all different ages, some barely older than babies, others like Aster, close to my age.

"Girls, give her some room."

They obediently stepped back.

"Who is she?" asked one of the little girls, her bright eyes watching me from behind her plump fingers.

"This is Mila," said Rebekkah, "and she's a friend of mine."

The girls giggled.

My muscles ached and I stretched them a bit before trying to get up. My feet tingled with pins and needles and my hands were stiff.

The girls talked all around me, and as Rebekkah reached out to help me to my feet. I caught a movement in the vent from the corner of my eye. I was about to scream when Jude's head popped through the vent.

"Jude!" said Rebekkah.

"I see you found Mila before I did," he said, laughing. "Is the door locked?"

Rebekkah shook her head and went to the door, locking it

quickly as Jude extracted himself from the vent. I could see why it made sense to send me, he barely fit through the small space.

"Hello ladies," he said to the nightgown girls. "My name is Jude, and I don't know any of you, but I know your mothers."

"We don't have mothers," said one girl.

"You do," said Rebekkah, "And we're here to make sure you get to meet them."

I watched as they looked at each other with wide, confused eyes. Some of them looked like sisters, and I felt like I needed to line them up and put them in groups. A few of them had dark skin like Aster. Others had pale blue eyes and dark curls, a few were blonde.

"For now, I think you guys should stay here," said Jude. "Now that I know where Mila is, I'll climb back to the roof and see if I can't figure out a way to get you all out of here."

Rebekkah nodded. "We're fine here. Stay safe."

Jude smiled at her then looked at the rest of us. "Mila almost blends right in," he said.

"I was thinking the same thing," said Rebekkah with a smile. "Aster, could you go find one of your extra nightgowns?"

Aster ran off to a chest of drawers, and Jude got onto his knees to crawl back into the vent.

"Jude," said Rebekkah, moving toward him. "Finn?"

Jude frowned and shook his head. "They caught him, but I'll find him."

Rebekkah bit her lip and nodded.

"I'll be back in a bit," he said.

And with that, he was gone, slithering into the duct like a rat into a hole.

I pushed the vent in after him, kicking the screws under the nearest bed.

"Alright Mila, time to get you some camouflage," said Rebekkah, holding out a crisp white nightgown.

# THIRTY-TWO

## *Athena*

THE FIRE BLAZED WITH a heat that licked at my face and singed the tips of my hair, even from where I stood at the edge of the clearing. It hadn't taken us long to pile up enough wood to make a statement. They had seen us. That was obvious. Their alarms had begun to ring shortly after we lit the giant bonfire. I stood, watching the giant estate through the flames and billowing smoke. I knew that in the trees around me were warriors, perched and ready. The rest of us stood around the clearing, blending in to the trees around us.

Waiting.

The men on their horses stood silently behind us, their rifles ready.

I scanned the building, waiting for a sign that they were coming, but I saw nothing. I'd seen faces peering from behind curtains, curious and afraid.

They should be afraid.

The doors hadn't opened yet, but as I watched the building, I noticed movement on the roof. There was a man, dressed in black from head to toe carrying a sniper's rifle. I lifted my bow, the arrow already notched and took aim. It would be a difficult shot, not the farthest I'd taken, but tricky nonetheless. I'd need to get him before he settled down low on the roof and would be impossible to reach.

As I steadied my hands, I saw another figure approach the first, and even though he was little more than a shadow, I knew him immediately.

Orion moved quickly and quietly until he was right behind the man, reached for him and in one swift motion snapped the man's neck. The dead man fell like a rag doll from the roof and landed with a thud directly in front of what appeared to be the main door. Orion stood at the edge of the roof and scanned the trees. I smiled and let out a battle cry, joined by the men and women who surrounded me.

"How did he get onto the roof?" Moira asked from behind me.

"I don't know," I said, "But I'm wondering if he could use some extra help up there."

"It's an ideal spot," said Torren. "We'd have them completely surrounded."

I agreed.

I whistled, shrill and loudly enough that Orion looked at me. Pointing to myself, and then to him, I asked him without words how we might get up to him. He motioned around the right side of the building. I nodded and ran to my mother.

"I'm going to take some more of us onto the roof," I said. "Are you ok down here?"

Nova nodded, Dax beside her, a spear at the ready. "We

can hold the woods."

Hurrying back to Torren and Moira I slung my bow over my shoulder.

"Get Leona, Ember and Rowan. We're going to the roof."

Together we wove through the edge of the forest, the tiny branches breaking as we plunged headfirst through the shadows to where Orion had gestured. He was following us from the roof, walking on the edge as we ran through the woods. It was quiet back here, and away from the fire and the others it seemed empty and cold.

"Climb the snow," called Orion from the roof. Behind the building, where the forest rose before us up the mountainside, was a giant hill of snow that reached the roof.

"Whoa," said Moira, "That's convenient."

"Must be from the avalanche Jude was talking about," said Leona, starting up the hill.

It was steep, but far from difficult, almost like climbing a ladder or a tree with lots of branches. We reached the roof with little effort and found not only Orion, but Jude, who was pulling on a pair of boots.

Another battle cry rose from the woods and we ran to the edge. Men had started to assemble in the clearing, weapons drawn and calling orders to each other.

"There's not enough," Jude said.

"Enough what?" I asked.

"Guards," he said. "Nadia didn't send very many out, which means she's worried. She kept a lot of them inside, presumably with her."

"Is that a problem?" I asked.

"Yes, and no," said Orion. "We have the advantage in the woods, but they had the advantage inside."

"They could be setting traps for us inside, which would be more dangerous for us than fighting in the open."

"Then we should go in now," I said and glanced around at the concerned faces. "They'll expect the others to come in through the front door once they've taken out those guards, if we come in another way, there's a chance we could take back the advantage."

Jude nodded. "She's right."

We turned from the edge of the roof and found ourselves face to face with Phoebe.

"What are you doing here?" asked Jude, obviously upset.

"I followed Athena," she said. "Mila is inside, and I want to come with you."

"You were supposed to stay with the others," said Jude, "Dutch said..."

"Don't be angry with him," said Phoebe, "They were taking good care of me, but so much was happening. I need to come with you."

"It's too dangerous," I said, pushing past her. She grabbed my arm.

"I'm going to come with you whether you agree or not."
I raised an eyebrow.

"Fine," I said. "But if you get yourself into trouble, don't expect me to come rescue you."

She let go of my arm and followed.

"The easiest way in is the stairs, but they'll be monitoring those for sure. I've been going in and out through either the fresh air shaft or the dumbwaiter shaft," said Jude. "I think our best bet is the dumbwaiter. There's more to hold onto in there, and we wouldn't need ropes."

He showed us the opening. It was a small hatch beneath a large square machine which likely held the mechanisms for whatever a dumbwaiter was.

"Once you get through that hatch, it's basically just a straight drop, so don't be hasty," said Jude. "There are lots of places to step and grab, but it's also really dark and going down is a whole lot harder than going up."

"Are you going to be ok in there?" I heard Orion whisper to Leona.

"I'll be fine," she said, waving her hand. "I can climb with six-and-a-half fingers better than you can with ten."

One by one people disappeared through the hatch—first Jude, then Torren, Leona, Ember, Rowan, Orion, Moira and Phoebe until I stood on the roof alone. I took a deep breath and climbed down into the dark.

# THIRTY-THREE

## *Shayna*

SHE WAS MOVING THEM.

I stood in the tiny observation room that looked into the clinic where Rhea, Hazel, Shalisa and Willow had been. Kenzie's molded plastic bed was still there, its eerie blue light permeating the room. I was too late. There were guards moving the last of the machines as Nadia watched them, strangely silent. I had expected her to be barking orders, shouting insults and generally behaving like the tyrant she was, but she just stood there, watching. As the last machine was wheeled from the room, she moved from where she stood at the door and looked around, as if saying goodbye to her old home as the movers came and carried away her things. Walking to the window that separated us, she stood, facing me. I knew she couldn't see me, the view from her side of the mirror was only her own reflection. She reached up a hand and tucked a stray strand of hair behind her ear and for what seemed like the first time, I really looked at Nadia. She looked older than I remembered, though I supposed we all were. We were so young when we came to this place, and at the time she seemed so powerful, unstoppable. Now, watching her, she looked tired, and sad. As angry as I was for the things she had done, the people she had used and abused and destroyed, I couldn't help but add a measure of pity.

She was pathetic, and if there was anything I could do about it, she would be dead by morning.

"DO YOU KNOW WHERE they have Finn? The girls?" I asked Harris. He and Vaughn had joined me in the observation room just before Nadia stalked out of the other room. I could tell they shared similar feelings toward her.

"They're barricading themselves in the old dining room," said Harris, "We saw them bring the sisters in there, and Vaughn heard one of the guards say he was taking Finn there too."

So they were assembling themselves for their final stand. It made things easier for us, though I doubted that Nadia and her followers weren't well protected.

The sirens were still blaring, and my head pounded. If Nadia was trying to make it difficult for us to think, she was succeeding.

"We need to get rid of that siren," I said. "And maybe the electricity too, take out any advantage Nadia has over us."

"Won't that be dangerous for the sisters?"

I shook my head. "Each of their beds has enough back-up power for about eight hours. They'd be fine. Plus, Dr. Harris is probably in there with them. I'm sure they'd be closely monitored."

"We know where the main power shut-off is," said Harris,

"Let's go, Vaughn.

They hurried out into the hallways, off to the stairwell. They were headed to the basement, most likely. I didn't know exactly where the electricity panel was, but the basement was full of mechanical rooms, water treatment systems, furnaces, and the huge array of batteries from the solar power system.

I left the observation room and headed for the clinic. I needed to get as many supplies as possible before the lights went out. I had a feeling I was going to need them.

# THIRTY-FOUR

## *Mila*

"THEY'RE COMING," I SAID in a whisper. I could hear the feet running across the hard tiled hallways. I exchanged a look with Rebekkah and I knew.

"Into the vent," I said quickly. Rebekkah turned and helped me herd the girls into the unsecured duct. Aster and Bellis first, then the little ones who would need more help. One by one they disappeared through the dark opening until only Rebekkah and I were left.

"You next," I said. "I can close the vent behind us."

She shook her head, "No."

"We need to get out of here."

"If I leave my chair here they'll know, and they'll follow. Get in there Mila. Get the girls to safety."

I knew she was right, but I didn't want her to be. I was a child myself. I wasn't ready to do something like this by myself. Someone rattled the handle then banged on the door.

"Open up!"

"Just a second," said Rebekkah, shoving me toward the hole in the wall. I hurried inside and quickly pulled the vent closed behind me.

"Go into the first duct on your right," I whispered as loudly as I dared. I could hear the girls quietly sending word to the others down the line.

I didn't have to tell them to be quiet as Rebekkah opened the door to two burly guards.

"Where are they?" one of the guards asked Rebekkah.

"I don't know," she said in an obvious attempt at light-heartedness. "When I got here the room was empty and their nurse was gone too."

"Then why was the door locked?"

"Oh, you know," said Rebekkah. "Just looking for some peace and quiet, these alarms have just about done me in."

As if responding to her voice the sirens immediately stopped. They had been going for so long that the silence felt strange and hollow. Darkness joined the silence as only seconds after the alarms stopped the lights went out, plunging us into a silent night. I could hear muffled gasps behind me, but little more. I was proud of the girls for not screaming.

The flames from the fire outside painted the walls with moving art that would have been beautiful if not for the terror I felt.

"Take her with us," said one guard to the other, "I'm not going back to Nadia without those kids and no one to take the blame for it."

I watched as the guard took the handles of Rebekkah's wheelchair and pushed her through the door into the dark hallway. I pushed myself backwards with my fingers, following the others like mice into the walls.

# THIRTY-FIVE

## *Athena*

I DIDN'T KNOW WHAT I was expecting inside the estate, but it was unlike anything I had ever seen. I had gone with Asari to the old city a few times, but everything there had nearly been destroyed, stripped of anything of value. I stood in the middle of the hallway, surrounded by painted white walls and shining tiled floors. I felt lost inside this strange box, unsure of myself.

We'd climbed down through the dumbwaiter shaft and found ourselves in an empty hallway.

Sirens were shrieking but nothing moved here.

Without warning the sirens stopped and seconds later we found ourselves in the dark again. I smiled. This felt better. I was used to hunting in the dark.

Jude motioned for us to follow him, and we did, twisting and turning until we found ourselves at a door. He knocked quietly and the door opened to reveal an old woman with a long braid of grey hair. She held a candle and she smiled when she saw Jude. Her eyes widened as she noticed the rest of us. We were an intimidating group, I knew, and for someone who wasn't used to our clothing and tattoos, we probably seemed strange and unnerving, but her face softened in the candlelight almost as quickly as her eyes had widened.

"Welcome here," she said, "Come inside."

She held open the door and we crammed into the tiny space, finding anywhere we could to stand. There was a woman on the bed, her eyes darting around the room in nervousness as we invaded her space. She wasn't much bigger than Mila, but much older.

"What do you know?" Jude asked the woman.

"Not much more, I'm afraid," she said. "Dr. Murray went to check on the sisters and hasn't come back yet."

The door opened and someone gasped, probably surprised to be looking directly into Orion's broad shoulders.

"Shayna?" asked the woman.

"It's me," the other voice said, "Excuse me."

Everyone by the door moved aside as she pushed through to where Jude was standing.

"They're all in the old dining hall," the new woman said to Jude. She had long red hair and a white coat. In her arms was a bag filled with something, which she plunked on the floor unceremoniously.

"I cleaned out the clinic," she said of the bag. It seemed like a strange time for cleaning.

"Nadia took the sisters with her and they've holed themselves up in there. Harris and Vaughn got the sirens and the electricity."

"Rhea is in the dining hall?" asked Jude, reaching for Ember's hand. "Is she alright?"

"As far as I know," said the woman. "Finn is in there too, that's what Harris said."

"I guess we're going there, then."

"Here," the woman said, digging through the bag she'd brought. "There were a few headlamps in the clinic. I guess they had them in case we needed to stitch someone up in the dark. Take them."

Jude took one and passed the others to Torren and Orion. "Let's go."

We piled back out into the hallway following Jude. There were times we passed close enough that we could hear the commotion outside. Gunfire popped and I could hear the shouts of our warriors. As we passed a window, I could see the clearing. The fire was still blazing and there were bodies on the ground, but from inside I couldn't tell whose side they belonged to.

Along the way we picked up a few more men. They carried knives and flashlights.

"Have you seen Mila or Rebekkah?" asked Jude.

They shook their heads.

One of them ran a bit further ahead, and as he stepped into the intersection of two hallways a series of gunshots rang out. He crumpled to the ground and the rest of us stopped, doing our best not to run into each other.

Jude looked like he wanted to shout, but he shoved his fist in his mouth quickly motioning for us to go back. We hurried around another corner, and flattened ourselves against the wall, every single one of us readying a weapon.

Jude moaned, stifling a scream, and with his back to the wall, slid down until he was sitting on the floor.

"We should have been more careful." He said. "Of course they'd be there, and now Harris..."

He trailed off, trying to get a hold of himself. The other man spoke to him in a voice so quiet I couldn't hear his words. Jude nodded and after a moment he stood.

"There's only one way we're getting past these guards" he said. "And I don't think any of you are going to like it."

# THIRTY-SIX

## *Mila*

WAS THAT JUDE?

I could hear his voice through the vent not far from where I huddled with the other girls. We hadn't moved since we heard the running footsteps stop just on the other side of the wall.

"Let me get near that vent," I whispered, pushing one of the girls and straining to hear.

"We can get someone in behind those guards to distract them while the rest of us make a run for it," said Jude. "There's a room at the end of that hall that has another door that opens into the hallway. It's our only chance."

No one spoke. The reality of Jude's words hung over all of us. Someone was going to have to sacrifice themselves for the rest of them to make it through.

"Who is going to go?"

Athena. That was Athena's voice.

"I will," said Jude.

Again it was silent.

I could just make him out through the metal slats, as he silently turned to go.

"Jude, wait."

I gasped. It was my mother.

"I need to say something before you go," she said, moving toward him.

I wanted to shout for her, cry out to my mother, but I didn't want to put the girls at risk. It was best that no one knew where we were.

My mother took Jude's hand and looked into his eyes.

"I love you Jude," she said. "And I know you don't love me in the same way, and that's ok. I understand that."

Her voice wavered, and I knew she was crying. A lump swelled in my throat.

"So I want you to go get Rhea, and tell Mila I love her."

With that, she broke into a run. Jude grabbed for her but didn't reach her quickly enough.

"Phoebe, NO!" he shouted.

I couldn't help it. I screamed.

Suddenly a face was at the vent. "Who's in here?"

Athena.

"It's me..." I sobbed. "Mila."

"Stay where you are, and stay quiet, I'll come back for you," she said.

With that, they were gone.

I could hear them all running through the halls and moments later, I heard my mother's scream and the gunshots that stopped it.

Pressing my face into my hands I crumbled. It felt like someone had thrust his hand down my throat and had gripped my heart in his cold fingers. I couldn't breathe, I couldn't cry. I couldn't move. My hands began to shake and I was unable to control them. I lay on my belly in the dark air duct and hoped it would swallow me.

I had nothing left.

Tears began to flow down my cheeks, and I felt a tiny hand touch mine. I didn't know who it was—nor did I care—but I held on for dear life.

# THIRTY-SEVEN

## *Athena*

WE MADE IT PAST the hallway, thanks to Phoebe.

Orion was the only one who suffered an injury, catching a bullet in his thigh as we flew past the hallway. The guards had no choice but to follow us and one of them ended up with my knife in his throat while two others met the pointy ends of Rowan and Moira's arrows. The fourth, seeing the demise of his partners, tried to run, but even with a bullet wound, Orion easily caught him and finished him the same way he did the guard on the roof.

"The bullet is too deep," said Ember, gently touching Orion's wound as he sat on the floor with his back against the wall.

"Just wrap it and we can deal with it later," he said, wincing as she probed the hole in his buckskin pants.

"Someone could go back for Dr. Murray," suggested Jude. "I doubt she's far behind us."

"It's fine," said Orion with a warning tone. "Just wrap it and let's go."

Leona took her knife, cut into the hem of her skirt and tore a strip from the bottom of it.

"It's not the cleanest, but it'll do for now," she said. Orion lifted his leg and she wrapped it with practiced hands and tied a tight knot.

"Let's go," he said, pushing himself up with a groan.

The hallways were empty now, and the silence was eerie. I couldn't tell if the fighting outside had waned, or if we were just too far from the clearing now to hear it.

Jude peeked through a small round window in one of the doors and put his finger to his lips.

"This is the kitchen," he said. "On the other side of it is the room where Nadia has Finn and the sisters."

He pushed the door open with his shoulder, and from his hunched position, he scanned the room.

"Follow me, and stay low," he said.

We followed him into the room. It was unlike any kitchen I had ever seen. There was so much metal and glass, stacks of pots that you could cook an entire bear inside, and more white dishes than I even knew existed. It was hard to follow Jude and not stare at the racks of tools that seemed so foreign to someone who had spent her whole life eating from a hollowed-out wooden bowl. It seemed so extravagant and even unnecessary.

"Get down," I heard Jude hiss and following the others we crowded behind a huge table-like thing that stood in the center of the room. It seemed impossible that we weren't heard as we scrambled behind it like a herd of buffalo. I could hear Orion groan as he crouched and then fell to his knees.

The door to the kitchen opened as we held our collective breath. My fingers tightened around the knife I held. I locked eyes with Jude, begging him silently to let me kill them, but he clenched his jaw and shook his head in a slow, determined motion.

There were at least two of them that walked through the kitchen, based on the number of voices I could hear, chatting easily as if there was no battle happening outside. If they went into the hallway, our cover would be blown. The dead guards were within sight of the door we'd come through. I peeked around the corner to watch them. Hunt them. My heart was racing, much like it did when I would hunt the prey that could just as easily be hunting me. Wolves were a tricky one, since you couldn't be completely sure there wasn't another one sneaking up on you from behind.

They didn't go through the door. One of them opened a different door and walked inside, returning soon after with a tray of food. These lumbering fools seemed less like wolves and more like bears—dangerous, but inherently thick, prioritizing food over almost anything else. Together they went back through the door they came from and I could feel the air lighten around me.

"There are three doors into the dining room from the kitchen," said Jude, in a whisper that I could barely hear. "If we enter through all three at the same time, hopefully we can confuse them just enough to better our odds."

"How many do you think are in there?" asked Torren.

Jude frowned.

"There are more of them than there are of us, that's for sure."

"Then it's a good thing we're such good fighters."

Leona smiled at me in a strange display of sisterly affection that I preferred to ignore.

"I've fought you before, Athena," she said, "And I wouldn't want to do it again."

Jude motioned with his hands, dividing us up quickly into three groups.

"The doors are all swinging doors," he said, "All you have to do is push through them, and you'll be in there. Take your positions and wait for my signal."

I nodded and stood, hurrying to the door. It wasn't the first time I was thankful for my soft leather moccasins and furs that made no sound as I moved. Jude's clothing rustled with every step, and he had to step lightly so his boots wouldn't squeak on the floor.

Moira followed Jude and Vaughn. Vaughn looked completely out of his element with a hunting knife in his hand. He held it too tight. His knuckles were white from the force, I could tell from across the room, but there was no time to give him a lesson. At least he was holding the pointy end in the right direction. It was the best I could hope for at this point.

Ember and Rowan were behind me. I would have preferred to have Leona. Even without half her fingers, she was a competent shot. I'd yet to see Ember use a weapon, much less use one proficiently.

Worst case I could use her as a shield.

Rowan was useful, at least. I'd seen him best the others—

and even me—in tests of force and accuracy. I watched Torren as we waited for Jude's signal, and he winked at me. I smiled, and then pushed the silly, girlish thoughts from my head. There was an excellent chance that we wouldn't both make it out of this. There was no sense allowing any foolish affection now. It could only end badly.

I inhaled slowly, steadying my hands and embracing my racing heartbeat. I let the adrenaline leech into my blood and my muscles and my brain.

I was ready.

On Jude's signal we pushed through the door, I dropped to the floor and rolled to allow Rowan a clear shot as I moved into the room.

There were shouts and the clatters of chairs as people stood and knocked them over behind them. Some scurried for cover, crouching under tables as bullets and arrows began to fly. The sound of gunfire in the relatively small space was deafening, mingled with cries of fear and pain.

Once clear of the door I stood to meet my closest foe. He stood at least a head taller than me, but he raised his gun and aimed at me. I stretched and flung, feeling the blade of my knife slip through the tips of my fingers at precisely the correct moment. I ducked, knowing he had aimed high, and heard the bullet fly by and land with a crack into the wall behind me. The man screamed, my knife embedded deep into his shoulder. His gun dropped from his hand and his eyes widened as I rushed to him, pulling out my knife and stabbing him with it again under the rib cage. He dropped like a stone and I picked up his gun. I'd never used a handgun, but I tossed it to Jude, who seemed woefully short of weapons.

He was managing well enough with a knife and his fists, but I could tell he was grateful for the pistol.

"To your left," he shouted and I spun, raising my elbow in case someone was that close. It connected with a woman's face. She howled as blood poured from her nose, but to her credit, she didn't stop until my knife was buried in her throat.

There was fighting everywhere I looked. I yanked my knife from my last, however incompetent adversary, and wiped it on my thigh, instinctively cleaning the blade.

"STOP," The shout was loud—loud enough to be heard over the sounds of fighting and screaming.

Everyone froze, but no one dropped weapons.

For the first time I really took stock of the room. There were four odd covered coffin-like things near the tall, expansive windows. I could hear them humming now that the room was silent. The woman I assumed to be Nadia was standing beside one of them. In one hand, she held a syringe, and in the other, one of the tubes that went into this strange machine.

"I will kill her," she said, "If any of you even think of moving."

I heard a strangled sob behind me. Ember, probably. Whether or not the woman stood beside her sister didn't seem to matter, since there were three other people holding syringes at the other beds.

Finn and Rebekkah were there too. Finn was sitting in one of the ornate armchairs, his hands taped to the armrests and his feet to the legs. Rebekkah was in her chair, arms taped down as well. An ugly looking man with an unnecessarily smug sneer stood behind them, his handgun trained on the back of Finn's head.

No one moved.

I watched them, analyzing the situation.

If somehow we could manage to fire at the same time, we could take out the key players before they could do anything, but that would be next to impossible.

"Put your weapons down," said Nadia.

"Let them go," said Leona. "Let them go and we will leave."

Nadia smiled, then turned to the guard standing behind Finn and nodded in Leona's direction.

The man raised his gun, and fired.

Orion moved with what seemed to be impossible speed, tackling Leona and tumbling to the ground with her in his arms.

I didn't even have time to look back at Nadia before the room rattled with a deafening bang. As I turned, the enormous windows seemed to shatter in a waterfall of glass before my eyes. I noticed a few of the people standing beside the beds scurry for cover. Cold air wafted into the room, and the air was immediately foggy as the cold and warmth mixed together.

It was our moment.

I flung my knife across the room, where it landed squarely in the throat of the man with the gun. His eyes widened and rolled up into his head as he choked and sputtered. I saw arrows fly from behind me as ropes dropped through the now open ceiling and people dressed in black slid down them like spiders.

I slid my bow from my shoulder and had readied an arrow before I noticed there were people beyond the window. My parents sat together astride one of the giant horses. They were smiling and cheering.

One of the people who came down through the window pulled off her goggles and ski mask, revealing a mop of black curls.

"Meredith!" shouted Jude.

I had heard them speak of Meredith, and though I didn't know who she was, I knew she was no threat. I lowered my bow.

"Where's Nadia," she asked, pulling her gun from the holster on her thigh.

"She was over there, beside Rhea," said Jude.

She moved in the direction Nadia had been, weapon ready, and stopped and smiled.

"She's dead."

Even I couldn't resist cheering at that. Listening to the jubilant sound through the windows as the warriors outside took up the cheer made my heart soar.

"Orion!" I heard Leona's scream through the shouts of glory and turned in her direction.

They hadn't gotten up from the floor yet, and Leona was terrified.

Orion was on the ground, unmoving.

I glanced at my mother, and in an instant, she turned

the massive horse toward the building and all three of them flew through the window, landing hard on the wood floor. The horse sat back in fear as soon as it landed, tossing its head with nostrils flared, unsure of where to go. My mother slid off the horse, leaving my father to reassure the terrified steed.

She ran to Leona and Orion, as Jude hurried to the front of the room, and dragged one of the women from where she was huddling under a table. He pointed his weapon at her and shouted.

"Help him. Now!"

The terrified woman ran toward my mother, who was kneeling beside Orion, searching for a pulse.

"He's alive, but his pulse is weak," said Nova.

"We need to get him to the clinic, right away," the woman said.

One of the big men dressed in black ran over to one of the long curtains and ripped it down from the ceiling in a fluttering mess. Within seconds, he and the others with him had a rudimentary stretcher fashioned from the cloth. They brought it to where Orion was, and the rest of us crowded around, each taking a handful of cloth.

"Lead the way," said one of the masked men.

"Rayne?" asked Jude as we hoisted the heavy, limp man.

"Shut up and get us to the clinic, Jude," said the man, not bothering to answer.

We walked as quickly as we were able, back through the dark hallways, Leona sobbing behind us.

# THIRTY-EIGHT

## *Shayna*

I HEARD THEM IN the hallway, the grunts of exertion and the moans of someone fearing the worst.

I broke into a run and found them, a large group of people carrying the huge, fur-clad man I'd met earlier.

"I'll get a gurney," I said, racing ahead to the clinic. I didn't bother to prop open the doors, as I could hear others coming. I rolled the gurney into the hall just as they arrived, heaving the heavy man onto the clean white sheets.

Dr. Harris was there, and together we hurried to the supply closet as Jude and Vaughn pushed the man into the room.

"Everyone needs to get out of here," I shouted. "Give us room to work."

Most of the people obeyed quickly, filing from the room as quickly as they'd come.

"I can help you," said one woman. "I'm a doctor."

She was dressed in furs, with a long grey braid hanging down her back. An intricate tattoo covered half of her face—wolves, it looked like.

I didn't know if she really was a doctor, but at this point I didn't care. I tossed her a gown and a package of sterile gloves and we went to work.

In minutes we had cut off his clothing and could properly assess.

"This isn't going to be easy," I said.

Neither Dr. Harris nor the other woman disagreed; they said nothing, focused only on saving this young man's life.

We were going to need a miracle.

# THIRTY-NINE

## *Mila*

ATHENA WAS TRUE TO her word. She pried the vent from the wall and pulled me through the opening until we were huddled together on the floor. Her arms wrapped around me as I shook with sobs. She made gentle shushing noises, her fingers running through my hair as she cradled me like a child.

"Mila," she said.

I sniffled.

"Yes?"

"You weren't alone in there, were you?"

I had almost forgotten about the others. My head snapped up and I looked at the hole. Almost hidden in the dark was a tiny face, watching Athena with fearful eyes.

"I'm sorry," I said. "It's safe to come out."

One by one, they crawled from the vent, all dressed the same in matching white nightgowns.

"Let's go find the others," said Athena, standing and taking my hand.

The other girls followed me in silence. The lights flickered to life above us as we walked, bare feet on the cold floor.

"Mila," shouted Rebekkah as we came into the room, she

rushed to the door and quickly pulled us inside. The room was full of people I didn't know. They sat at tables, or stood around talking and waiting.

Leona was at a table, and I could tell she'd been crying.

"Where's Buck?" I asked, instantly terrified.

"He was shot," said Rebekkah in a hushed voice. "They're working on him now."

I nodded, unsure what to do with this added information.

"Excuse me," said a woman, walking up to us. I didn't recognize her. "Did you just call this girl 'Mila'?"

Rebekkah nodded and I took a step backwards.

"It's her, Angela."

I heard Jude's voice from my right. I looked at him, standing beside a sleeping woman in an eerie blue bed. The woman's eyes filled with tears.

"Oh child, I'm so sorry about your mom."

I still didn't know who she was, but she pulled me into an embrace and I let myself be held.

It seemed like everyone was hugging and talking and laughing. We had won, that much I knew. The bad people were dead, and we weren't—at least, not all of us.

# FORTY

## *Shayna*

I YANKED THE BLOODY gloves from my hands and let them fall on the floor, shrugging off my gown like a snake shedding its skin.

I was exhausted, drained, empty of emotion. Walking into the hallway I leaned my forehead against the wall and breathed, slowly and deliberately in an attempt to settle my racing heart.

Tears fell from my eyes, and I did nothing to stop them.

"You did good in there," said the tattooed woman. She had followed me into the hall, and was now leaning her back against the same wall. "Not everyone could have saved him, and I thank you for that."

I nodded.

It was true. He was going to live.

I inhaled, filling my lungs, and stood up to face her.

"Thank you for your help," I said. "I'm sorry, I don't even know your name."

She smiled. "Nova," she said.

I furrowed my brow. Nova wasn't a common name, though I'd heard it before.

"Did you used to work at MedTech?" I asked. She would be about the right age.

"I did," she said, her eyes narrowed, questioning.

I laughed. "My boyfriend..." It seemed strange to call him that, since so many years had passed and I was so much older now, "kept trying to convince me to work there. His brother Elias was a researcher there, before everything froze solid."

"Elias?"

"You knew him?"

"Very well," she said. "Elias' brother? Do you mean Amos?"

I felt a wrench in my heart at the sound of his name. I nodded, unable to trust my voice.

"Are you aware that he's here?" Nova asked.

Blood rushed through my head, and I felt dizzy.

"He's here?"

"Yes, he found us in the woods a few hours ago."

I didn't know how to respond. Jude had come to us to tell us they were all waiting in the smaller dining room. They had moved the sisters there, and assembled everyone. I turned and broke into a run, my shoes squeaking on the floor, and my lab coat flying behind me.

The doors to the dining room were open and I skidded to a stop in the doorway, scanning the room. I saw him in the corner and whispered his name. There was no possible way he could have heard me, but he turned anyway. We locked eyes and for an instant, nothing else mattered. He ran to me and I to him, meeting in the center of the room.

"Amos," I said, tears in my eyes.

"Shayna," he murmured into my hair as his arms wrapped

themselves around me in an embrace I had only dreamed about for nearly two decades.

I melted into his arms, wanting to laugh and cry at the same time.

We parted and suddenly remembered why everyone was staring at me.

"He's going to be fine," I said, loud enough to be heard.

The room burst into shouts of joy and relief, and I planted a kiss on Amos' lips and lost myself in joy.

"OK, I NEED TO know," said Athena. "Who killed the wicked witch?"

We were sitting around tables, laughing and eating. Someone had found some food in the kitchen and considering it was breakfast time, we were all ravenous. I was sitting at a table beside Amos. I couldn't seem to let go of his hand, and it seemed the feeling was mutual.

Dr. Harris and I had started to wake up the girls, but for now they still slept.

"It was Rowan," said Jude, lifting a bottled water in salute.

Everyone cheered and congratulated him, those closest to him thumping him on the back.

He shook his head, laughing at all the attention.

"It wasn't me," he said.

"Oh, don't be modest," said Jude. "It was a beautiful shot,

right through the eye, and I'd know that arrow anywhere. I made it, you remember."

"I didn't have your arrow," said Rowan.

"But you won it from me," said Dutch, taking a large bite of bread.

"I did," said Rowan. "And I gave it to my wife."

The silence was deafening as in one motion, everyone's eyes turned to Ember. She was blushing.

"Ember?" said Leona.

Ember rolled her eyes. "Oh Leona," she said, laughing. "You think your father was the only one who taught you how to shoot in secret?"

The room exploded with laughter, and I found myself sucked into it. The relief was palpable, delicious and full.

"Come with me," said Amos, taking my hand.

"I DIDN'T KNOW YOU survived," he said as we walked outside.

"We don't need to talk about this," I said, shaking my head. "What's done is done."

"I'm sorry, Shayna," he said, "For so much."

I nodded. The sun had risen, but stayed hidden today behind dull, grey clouds. We walked into the woods, the smell of the fire they had lit still lingering among the fresh pine scent. It was almost warm today, the snow was melting beneath our feet.

"Where do we go from here?" I asked. So much had changed in such a short time, and although we all knew Nadia needed to be stopped, I doubt anyone put much thought into what would happen afterwards. I looked up to the sky as the heavens opened and rain began to pour down my face, seeping through my coat and drenching my hair.

"We start again," said Amos, pulling me close.

"Do you think we can?"

He smiled.

"We can always start again."

# EPILOGUE

## *Delta*

"YOU SHOULD HAVE SEEN it Delta," said Jude as I followed him into the dining room. "Nadia didn't stand a chance." Kenzie was nestled comfortably in his arms, still far too weak to walk, or even sit upright for very long. Jude had come to Rebekkah's room to bring us to see the others. He said Shayna had already started waking up the other sisters, and if there were any people I knew who were going to need each other's support, it was them. I couldn't even imagine what it would be like for them once the full realization of their time here came into focus.

Someone had brought a gurney for Kenzie, waiting for her beside the other still figures, and Jude laid her down gently on it.

"Thank you," she whispered, her eyes on her friends. "Have any of them woken up yet?"

Shayna shook her head. "Not yet, but it shouldn't be much longer."

Jude pulled up a chair beside Rhea's bed and sat on it backwards, leaning his chin on the backrest. He slid his hand into hers and watched her sleep.

"Are you hungry, Delta?" Shayna asked. "They've put out some breakfast."

I was. Famished in fact. The stress of the night had taken a toll on me, and my stomach growled at the thought of food.

"It's nothing magical," she continued, "but it's food."

I was starving, but there was something I needed to do first. I scanned the room, looking for the men I carried so long ago as babes. I saw Amos first. His shock of black hair had turned grey, but his eyes were exactly the same as when he was a child. Rayne was beside him, laughing with a familiar hoot. Seeing them filled a hunger I didn't even know I had. It did my heart good to see them.

"Delta," Rayne said as he saw me approach. He reached out and swept me off my feet into a hug only a man like Rayne could give.

"Put me down, you big galoot," I said, though secretly I didn't mind if he held me a bit longer. It was good to feel him. He was really here.

Rayne put me down and gave Amos a chance to hug me.

"I never thought I'd see you two again," I said, tears in my eyes.

I looked away to blink them back, and as they cleared, I gasped.

A woman stood by the table of food, handing out granola bars and steaming bowls of oatmeal.

I couldn't breathe.

I knew that face almost as well as I knew my own. It haunted me in my dreams and plagued me when I was awake. It was his face. She carried it differently, and there were marked variations, but it seemed almost impossible that she would look so much like him not be related in some way.

It couldn't be. It was impossible.

But was it really? Shayna had told me how nurses would steal baby girls from the hospital, sell them to other families.

I chided myself for even thinking it, even getting my hopes up.

But how could it be? How could she look so much like him?

"Delta, are you ok?" asked Amos. "Do you need to sit?"

I shook my head.

"Who is that woman?" I asked, "The one by the table."

"Meredith's military friend?" asked Rayne, "I think her name was Emily."

I shook my head.

"Not her, the other one," I said, my voice cracking as I watched her. "The one with the braid."

"Well, that's Angela," said Rayne, smiling "My wife. Come, Delta, she needs to meet you."

"Wait," I said, gripping his hand with a ferocity I didn't know existed in me. I needed to know. "When is her birthday?"

"June," he said, "June third."

It was as if he stabbed my heart with a knife, I nearly crumpled under the weight of the burden I didn't know I still carried.

"Are you ok?" Rayne asked, leading me to a chair.

"Where was she born?" I asked, sitting down.

"She doesn't know," he said. "She was adopted."

I couldn't help it, I burst into tears.

"Hang on," he said, "Let me get her."

"What's going on, Delta?" Shayna asked. "I saw you start to cry, what's wrong."

I could only manage one word.

"Coralie."

Shayna's eyes widened and her mouth dropped open.

"Where?"

I pointed to the woman Rayne was dragging back to me.

"Delta, this is Angela."

It only made me sob harder, which made the lines of worry on his face deepen.

I looked at Shayna, pleading with her silently.

*Tell them. Tell them.*

Shayna began to recount my story, as best as she remembered it. She talked about the nurses who would trick young mothers into believing their daughters were dead, only to steal them and sell them to families.

Angela's eyes were as wide as they possibly could be, and she held her hand over her mouth, probably realizing why I was unable to form words of my own.

"I think Delta is your mother," Shayna said finally, and I nodded, still unable to speak.

Angela's eyes filled with tears.

"I was born with a different name," she said. "I know because after my mother died I saw my birth certificate."

"Coralie," I said in a whisper.

She dropped to her knees at my feet, taking my hands in

hers and together we wept.

WE TALKED FOR A good hour, once I'd managed to get a hold of myself. My hands still shook, and no matter how tightly I pressed them into each other, I couldn't control them. I felt like I was shaking on the inside, every inch of me vibrated as I looked into her face and knew. For so long I had thought she was dead, yet here she was, and married to my son, no less.

The others had gathered around to listen as I told my story, the one I had only ever believed to have a tragic ending. Strangers wiped tears from their eyes. Meredith just shook her head in disbelief.

"They're waking up," called Jude from the other side of the room, and I got to my feet. He had come to hear the story and he too had marvelled over the coincidence, but it hadn't taken long before he had reinstated his vigil at Rhea's bedside.

I broke through the crowd and wove my way between the tables to where Jude was sitting. Finn and Rebekkah followed me, and I knew the others were not far behind.

Rhea was stirring, they all were.

I would greet them all, in time. I would take their hands and guide them through this, but right now I needed to be here, beside Jude.

"Rhea," he whispered and her eyes fluttered open at his voice.

He stood beside her, brushed back her hair and kissed her on the forehead.

"Oh Rhea," he said, a tear sliding down his face. "I missed you so much."

Her lips parted and I could tell she wanted to speak.

"Take your time, darling," I said.

She took a deep breath and licked her dry lips.

"I love you," she said.

Another tear fell, even though it had felt like I had already cried myself dry. Jude began to laugh and cry all at once.

I looked at Angela and knew exactly how he felt.

# ACKNOWLEDGEMENTS

To be honest, I don't think I even know where to start. So many people have encouraged and helped me in so many different ways that it's almost overwhelming. Finishing this series has been a wild ride, and having you all along for the ride has made the journey so much more pleasant.

Firstly, to every single person who has bought/borrowed/read my books: THANK YOU. Just being able to drain my brain onto a page is a gift, and the idea that people read them and enjoy them, take the time to write reviews and send me encouraging messages is completely indescribable.

To my amazing beta readers, (Heidi Gollub, Sarah Hood, Marissa Knight, Jen Kroeker, Anna McCarthy, Shayna Murray, Laura Pauls, Nancy Paschke, Audrey Plew, Bonnie Reimer, Karen Scott, Jordan Treder, and Ashlea Zirk ) thank you all again for taking the time to read and send me feedback. It never ceases to amaze me how few of your comments overlap each other. I need all of you. Never leave me.

Brian, thank you for crossing out all my superfluous commas and pointing out my egregious errors. You are the only person I can trust to tell me tell me all of them. (See what I did there?) Melissa, thanks for not ripping it out of his hands to read before it released (even though I'm pretty sure you really wanted to).

Again, and I can never really say this enough, thanks to Shayna Murray @mommyoutside and Sarah De Diego @zoojourneys for taking every opportunity to throw my books out there. If I manage to succeed at all, it will be because of you. Also special props to Amanda, Jen, Catherine and Shannon for helping me remember there are people in that big, wide internet-land.

John, thank you for sharing me with the made-up people in my head, and for not laughing when I complained that they weren't behaving. I love you the most out of all my husbands.

Mom, none of my books would have ever been completed if you didn't give me the gift of writing days, Thank you... and you can continue to do so. I don't mind giving you the gift of your grandkids.

Now that this series is complete, I look forward to whatever is coming next. I already can't wait to share it with you (you know, after I write it and everything). Thanks for coming along for the ride!

www.ingramcontent.com/pod-product-compliance
Lightning Source LLC
Chambersburg PA
CBHW030555180626
46816CB00005B/1548